The Incorrigible Miss Pomeroy

by

Dorothy A. Bell

The Incorrigible Miss Pomeroy

Cover Art by *Teddi Black*

The Wild Rose Press, Inc.
PO Box 708
Adams Basin, NY 14410-0708
Visit us at www.thewildrosepress.com

Publishing History
First Edition, 2025
Trade Paperback ISBN 978-1-5092-6197-0
Digital ISBN 978-1-5092-6198-7

Published in the United States of America

Chapter One

England
January 1816

At the old Tudor-styled Copeland Manor, in the stone-block dairy barn, Simon Lawrence jabbed his pitchfork into the stack of hay in the cart. For warmth, he'd dressed in layers: wool trousers over long johns, wool jumper beneath his coat. The stocking cap he'd pulled down over his ears did little to keep his black, curly hair from escaping over the collar of his coat. As he worked, he whistled a tune of his own invention. His breath, an opaque cloud, puffed out before his face.

The smell of rain-soaked earth and the crowded barnyard suited Simon Lawrence. The worries and horrors of the past were behind him. Copeland Manor was home. At last, he was where he belonged. The Manor's peaked roofs and chimneys, at the end of a poplar-lined, rock-walled lane, were barely visible to the coaches, farm carts, and horse traffic on the main artery that connected London to Edinburgh. Simon felt safe here, hopeful.

The country garden at the front of the house was overgrown. He'd take care of that come spring. He'd unearthed the walkway of white stone that weaved a path around to the back of the manor. Here, behind the house, down a slight slope, is where he spent most of his time.

There were several barns and outbuildings containing all manner of farm animals. Slowly, he and Milo Dorsey, the remaining retainer who had been his grandfather's, Sir Simon-Loyd Copeland's, steward, had been making repairs to the cribs, laying down fresh beds of straw, breathing new life into the old place.

"Master Simon."

The questioning, uncertain call from outside in the barnyard put a halt to Simon's whistling.

A short, spry, middle-aged man stepped up the ramp to the wide-open barn door. "Master Simon? You in here?" The sharp-featured little man squinted his black-button eyes, peered into the darkness, and came forward. "I been lookin' for you everywhere. Heard your whistlin' but couldn't figure out where it were comin' from. Had to find you. It's Peg. She's taken off again. Busted clean out of her crib, she has. I looked for her in the corn crib where she likes to lie about. She weren't there, and it didn't look like she'd been." He waved his arms, then wiped his nose with a rumpled handkerchief he'd pulled out of his back trouser pocket.

Amused, Simon leaned on his pitchfork. Lips parted in a grin, and he nodded. "Peg. A more flighty, stubborn, and whimsical female I have yet to meet." He stood the pitchfork up against a center post. "I'll go after her. There's only one other place she'd take out for, and that's across the road to that grove of oaks and the fen. Lots of mushrooms under those trees. Might even be a truffle or two. Can't blame her, I s'pose. A female in her condition is bound to get cravings, but I do wish she'd control her urges. This is becoming a habit."

"Aye, tis that," Milo said. "This is the third time this week she's gone a'rovin'. We'll have to find another way to keep her in, I reckon, or she'll be out and about again on the morrow. Don't understand why she's always galavantin' about. She's got everythin' she could possibly want, a warm stall, plenty of food, you givin' her rubs, and my missus givin' her scraps from the table. Can't have her rovin' about in her condition. Sure hope she settles afore she gets her family."

"I'll get a bucket of her favorite mash and pour a little molasses on it. Perhaps I can persuade her she doesn't need to leave home for a treat, eh? After she has her family, she won't have time to be out and in trouble. She'll have a full-time job feeding the little ones.

"Peg's problem, as I see it, she thinks of herself as a carefree piglet. She needs a job. Once she has her family, I'll wager she'll become a regular homebody. We'll have to do something about her crib, though. We need to take a look and see if we can enlarge it. She's gotten bigger, and it's not just because she's in a family way."

Simon laughed at himself. Amazed at his optimism, he shook his head and thought himself a fool for believing Peg would stay in her pen or her own yard. He and his sister Audry, Milo, and Milo's wife, Ellen, had made a lot of changes to the Manor since he and Audry arrived almost a year ago. In a slight, halting stride, he adjusted his gait to accommodate a stiff right leg and made for the open door of the barn. At the entrance, he removed an empty pail off the hook and slid the fingers of his mutilated left hand around the bail.

He considered stopping at the house to see if Audry wanted to go for a walk with him. She did enjoy the brook, and she might be grateful for a break from her household duties. However, she wasn't overly fond of Peg. The pig's size was intimidating, he supposed.

Simon worried about Audry. The quiet country air had been good for her. She'd recovered from the shock of their parents' brutal death. Her nightmares were fewer and farther apart. She was a good, hard worker. She was young, a mere slip of a thing, dainty and fine at eighteen. He hoped, someday, to see her have more than a life of hard work.

With nothing left of their plantation in the colonies, Simon, recovering from wounds he'd sustained during the skirmish, and Audry, who'd witnessed the carnage, walking but barely cognizant of her surroundings, they'd made their way back to England.

Peg, the small piglet, had made the crossing with them. She, too, had survived the slaughter of her home and family. Bringing her along was the least they could do. Somehow, Simon promised, he'd make her a good home.

Upon their return, they'd sought employment and accepted temporary refuge with a cousin of the captain upon whose ship they'd sailed. The Murphys had four small children, who instantly fell in love with Peg. But the four children and the four adults were cramped all together in the Murphys' small tenement down near the London docks. Simon knew their welcome there was temporary at best.

He had gone to an employment office in London hoping to become a law clerk. Audry, it was hoped, could possibly find employment as a companion or perhaps a lady's maid. Between the two of them, Simon thought they might be able to afford an accommodation of their own. It was because of his application to the law firm of Ledbetter and Tatom that Simon's name was brought to Mr. Ledbetter's notice. Within a month after his application, Simon received a message to report to the employment office as soon as possible. Perceiving he was about to become employed, he didn't waste time to report.

Instead of employment, he'd been informed that Sir Simon-Loyd Copeland, his maternal grandfather, who had passed away, had been seeking his daughter's whereabouts for nearly three years prior to his demise. The lawyer left in charge of the Copeland estate, using Sir Simon-Loyd's daughter's married name, Mary Lawrence, had all but given up hope of finding any heirs. Before his death, Simon's grandfather had informed the solicitor he thought Mary had given her son his name, and he thought his granddaughter's name was Audry, named after his deceased wife. As far as the lawyer knew, Simon was the last male alive on either side of the family and the only member of the Copeland family who could inherit the Copeland family estate. This miracle had saved Simon and Audry from certain penury. Hence, Peg, the little pig, had found the luxurious accommodations she deserved.

Simon assumed his grandfather was desperate to have remembered, let alone put out a search for his one and only grandson. He'd disowned his only child, their mother, Mary, when she'd married Wyatt Lawrence, a man in trade as a tobacco broker, a man of obscure and dubious lineage. And not only had Wyatt Lawrence stolen his daughter, he'd taken the heir to the Copeland name to the ends of the Earth, to the godforsaken wilds of the new colonies. The old gentleman, as Simon understood it, had been ill for many years.

When Simon and Audry arrived, it was obvious Copeland Manor was suffering from neglect. But they were grateful to have a home, more than a home: a beautiful farm, food, a roof, beds, welcoming, friendly people, and to have nothing more to worry about than the care and feeding of the animals.

Simon had wounds, but he was alive. He'd almost lost his arm, and the shrapnel he'd taken in the hip had severed nerves, but he could still walk, and the pain was manageable. And he had Ellen Dorsey's cure-all tonic and rub. He didn't know if either were doing any good, but they weren't doing any harm, so he took his medicine faithfully to keep the dear soul happy.

His mind on Audry, and her future, Simon set off down the lane, whistling, swinging the bucket of mash and molasses in his good hand and his other hand thrust deep in the pocket of his warm trousers. He took the lane in long strides, deliberately working his bad hip, imagining he could bend his knee today.

At the end of the lane, he came to a stop. In utter amazement, black brows knit together. Taking in the sight, he stood for a moment. Peg, his huge, pink, orange, and white pregnant sow, was in the middle of the road wallowing in a very deep, wide, muddy puddle. She was lying on her side, pink, plump titties exposed, grunting and reveling in her mud bath. He had to laugh at her.

As suddenly as Peg's antics struck his funny bone from around the bend in the road, the oncoming carriage sent him into shock and panic. The carriage was headed right for his sow. He couldn't possibly get her out of the way in time to avoid the impending disaster and certain death not only of his hedonistic, prized pig but the passengers of the runaway carriage.

The woman holding the reins of the team, one foot braced against the dash, body bent slightly forward, chestnut mane flying, green cape waving, called to her team in a surprisingly strong and confident tone. She was pulling back on the reins in an alternating rhythm that had begun to slow the team of wild-eyed horses. But Simon doubted she could stop their pace in time to avoid Peg.

Chapter Two

"I'll be very careful. I'll keep them at the same easy gait as you're doing. Please, let me have the ribbons." Pamela's gaze turned toward the road ahead. "There's no traffic."

They'd barely left the home gate. Paul Pomeroy was not altogether immune to his sister's manipulative tactics. Her large, pleading brown eyes were hard to resist. But squaring his shoulders, he hardened his resolve. In truth, he had his hands full controlling these very fresh and valuable cattle he'd recently purchased at Tattersalls. His horses needed schooling, and he needed to become more relaxed and comfortable handling the flashy, well-sprung curricle.

Since they'd arrived home, his sister had set forth upon a relentless campaign to convince him he should allow her to take the ribbons—drive his fancy new conveyance. True, Pamela was an accomplished horsewoman. She did have soft yet confident hands when holding the reins, but so far, he'd remained unmoved from his defensive position.

To himself he reasoned no female, no matter how expert, could possibly handle such a headstrong, unschooled pair of thoroughbreds, nor his unwieldy, pricey curricle. But she was right. Today, the Great North Road was unusually devoid of traffic. It was overcast, mild, a quiet day, and he found himself considering surrender. And besides, his right shoulder ached. Taking down the Christmas decorations in the hall, he'd missed a rung and tumbled off the ladder. He feared his frisky cattle might sense his weakness.

"I managed Father's cattle and phaeton while in London, and he said I maneuvered very nicely among heavy traffic," Pamela said. "Lyle Ferris let me handle his wild-eyed team of blacks, and I must say I believe they behaved better under my hand than they did his."

Patrician nose in the air, she said, "If you don't let me drive today, I'll keep pecking at you until you give over. You know I will. I love horses. There is no need to think I would want them to become harmed in any way." She lay a light hand on his arm in hopes the affectionate gesture would soften him. He was familiar with his sister's maneuver.

****

For Pamela Pomeroy, it was dreadfully dull times this holiday season. The socials were slow, positively flat with only homestyle entertainments. She longed for the pace, the distraction London offered: the busy streets, the assembly rooms bright and stuffy, full of color, and people everywhere laughing and gay, the theaters, the gardens, and riding her favorite mount around the Row in the company of a different admirer each day of the week.

She'd had two seasons. But far from finding one particular young man to whom she could give her heart, she'd made a game of it all. She loved to pit her wits against their silly sallies, teasing and taunting them while giving none of the fawning young bucks the added encouragement to pop the question.

There had been three lotharios who wanted to marry

her in her first season, but she insisted she was much too young at seventeen to settle down and had persuaded her father she needed more time before making up her mind. During her second season, she had used a bit more caution, careful not to encourage any one young gallant in particular.

Come spring, she would have another season, her third, serving more or less as a guide to her younger sister Penelope, who was now seventeen and ready to merge into the stream of society of the Haut Ton of London. Pamela looked forward to her role simply because it would relieve her ennui, but she had begun to think it time to settle. She did hope something or someone would inspire her to accept a life partner. But please, she begged the fates, please let him be interesting and kind. Funny, she would add to her list of requirements. And genuine, not a foppish bone in his body. The hunt was sure to be an interesting challenge, but for now, things had come to a grinding halt. After Christmas, their social life had fallen off, the company had departed, and Pamela had little to occupy her busy, restless mind except for her determination that her best and only brother in all the world, allow her to drive his team of showy whites.

"Pamela, my dear sister, for the last time, I will not give you leave to hold the reins. My cattle are very sensitive and unused to this carriage. Even I have to be careful and stay focused to be sure I won't unintentionally give them an excuse to lose concentration. I brought this pair to the country in particular, so I might give them time to become accustomed to my hands before taking them into London come March with all the traffic and noise. They need calm. This morning is clear enough, but it's far too cold to run them or get them excited. So I'm merely taking them for a slow, easy trot to Stilton and back. Nothing more. I only agreed to take you along because your pacing and fidgets were giving Mother a migraine, and Penny was taking up your mood. Mother needs Penny to concentrate on dresses and fripperies. If you will be patient, after a couple of weeks, I might allow you to take up the reins, but not now."

Pamela gave her exasperating, stodgy brother a hard, penetrating look and then managed a sweet, gentle, calculating smile and changed tactics. Her brother, besides being practical and at all times responsible, was handsome: Chestnut hair, naturally thick and wavy like her own, dark, gold-flecked brown eyes. He was a very manly young man with a high forehead, strong jaw, and a square chin.

Not for the first time did Pamela wish she'd been born a boy. If she'd been a boy, she'd breed racehorses. Race them herself. She'd not waste a moment of her time indoors while in the country; she'd go hunting. Her sister Penny and Paul were the biddable ones. She considered herself a bluestocking. There was nothing a man could do that a woman couldn't do, learn how to do, maybe even do it better if given the chance.

Her sister, stunningly beautiful Penny, fair of face and hair, with the dominant brown eyes, had softer, more delicate features. Pamela dismissed claims she was beautiful, too. At the beginning of her first season, because of her comely appearance and enthusiasm, many assumed her to be silly, innocent.

At the end of her second season, her mother declared her strong personality, along with her beauty, put would-be suitors off. Her mother advised her that most men preferred biddable, docile, domesticated females who would welcome a gentleman's protection as their due. Pamela shunned such nonsense, outriding, outshooting, continuing to out-wit her beaus.

Penny was the quiet one, biddable and willing to be cosseted, caressed, and wrapped in cotton wool. Whereas Pamela couldn't sit still long enough to be held or petted. She fantasized about going into battle with a foe. She looked forward to plotting how to get an invitation to so and so's party so she could capture another unsuspecting heart. The word cunning had been tossed at her head by her contemporaries more than once. She dismissed the criticism. She wasn't cruel. She longed for purpose, a goal, and she hadn't found it yet. She hoped she would know it when it came her way. She really did want to have a purpose, a channel in which to throw her energy.

Paul gave her a side glance. He missed, only by a few seconds, the gleam that came to her eye and the warm sparkle that replaced it. Pamela, eyes wide, beseeching, attempted a woebegone expression she hoped would melt her brother's heart. She even conjured up a small little tear to seep out of the corner of her big eyes. "You said of me, on more than one occasion, that you know of no other girl so naturally born to handle horses or any animal for that matter."

Head to one side, she dipped her chin and tugged on the fingers of her kid gloves. "Oh, I admit I'm not a very dutiful daughter. I'm ashamed I'm not very useful to Mother. I know I should be home helping with the sewing and helping Father catalog his library. And I will, I promised Mother I would tomorrow, I will. But today, today, I want to drive your lovely team of horses and this well-sprung carriage down this quiet road, just for a little way. Say, down to that oak grove. There's a curve there. I won't take them around the curve. I'll give the reins back to you. Please, please, I need a diversion right now. You would be the kindest brother ever if you would allow me this one small favor."

****

Looking over his shoulder, his gaze traveled beyond the hedgerows to the fallow fields dotted with grazing dairy cattle. Paul shrugged his broad shoulders and muttered to himself. "You, my dear sister, are incorrigible."

He pulled the team up, and the carriage rolled to a slow stop. "Damn and blast, here," he said and turned the reins over to her. "Do be gentle. And for heaven's sake, don't bounce around or make silly female noises. I don't want these animals coming up lame before I can take Lucin…uh…can…uh, get them to London for the season," he said, chin pulled in, eyes focused on the horse's rumps.

He was seriously contemplating marriage with Miss Lucinda Abernathy. He'd not meant to give any hint of this to his parents, and especially not to his nosy, managing sister. It would be too much to hope she'd let his slip of the tongue pass. Therefore, with a proviso that she keep his news a secret for the time being, he prepared himself to give over all the details rather than suffer Pamela's badgering interrogation. After all, she could be useful to his cause. Lucinda's uncle, Lord Dwight Abernathy, was one of Pamela's ardent admirers.

****

Pamela, reins now secure and expertly laced between her nimble, kid-gloved encased fingers, a knowing smile on her pretty lips said, "You have no need to dissemble." She expertly flicked the reins, clicked her tongue on the roof of her mouth, and the team moved into a nice, steady trot. "All of London knows you're pursuing the insipid, prissy, voluptuous Miss Abernathy. I've said nothing because I had hoped you'd give her up. Her weeping ways and watery blue eyes give me the pip. As does her foppish uncle." She shuddered.

"That whiny voice of hers…" Mimicking the sickening sweet Lucinda, Pamela said, "Pauly, fetch me a ratafia. Pauly, fetch me a softer chair. Pauly, I feel faint. Where's my vinaigrette? My fan, Pauly, fan me Pauly. Oh, yes, yes, you're such a dear, Pauly." She took a breath and shook her head. "Fetch boy, fetch—you behave more as her puppy than a man when you're around her."

Frankly, not heeding what she was saying, believing her brother now enlightened by her plain speaking, Pamela continued. "At Vauxhall last June, I was tempted to expose her for what she is: a liar and a terrible flirt. She pretended to faint right in front of Lieutenant Preston and some of the other officers. They all caught her, of course. Their hands all over her…her person. I saw her lips twitch. She almost giggled—I know it. She likes to play the demure, delicate flower routine when you're around, but beneath her pretty petals, there lurks thorns, sharp, pointy, poisonous thorns. You can do so much better, Paul. You're not only handsome, kind, and intelligent, but you are rather wealthy and a catch. Don't let Lucinda trap you with her practiced helpless-little-me performance."

Beside her, Paul bristled and rounded on her. "You will not speak of the woman I love in that fashion. I heard about her faint. And it was very fortuitous Preston was there to catch her. I admit I was jealous. She'd declared she was feeling a bit overheated, and I'd left her to get her some punch and a scone. I only wish I'd been there to help."

Sorry she'd hit a nerve, but not sorry to have sounded a warning, Pamela said, "Can't you see, she sent you on a false errand on purpose. No. No, I cannot stand by and watch my brother, my only brother, a brother I admire and look up to, make a terrible mistake. I'm sorry, but I had to speak. And today was as good a time as any. I've said my piece; I'll say no more." She gave her brother a sideways glance and met his thunderous scowl. His expression caused her to squirm in her seat, and she considered that perhaps she had been a tad too blunt.

In that instant, a cart stacked with hay pulled onto the main road, appearing from behind a high hedge. The cart was a large, rattling, two-wheeled vehicle with a squat, red-faced farmer seated behind a team of lumbering oxen. The delicate sensibilities of the team of thoroughbreds took exception to the undignified, offensive, noisy, lumbering wagon and the slow, plodding beasts pulling it. The farmer shouted out a colorful warning curse and cracked his whip over the head of the oxen.

Upon reflex, Pamela's hands jerked on the reins, giving the already flighty team the signal they'd been waiting for. Before she or Paul could brace themselves for the inevitable, the team reared and took off at a run, tails flying, out of control, going down the Great North Road pell-mell with Pamela holding fast to the reins, struggling to bring the team back to their senses.

About to tumble out head first, Paul, taken by

surprise, thrown off balance, tilted over the side of the curricle. Cursing, he grabbed Pamela by her cape and tried to pull himself back up on the seat. It was all Pamela could do to stay firmly seated, concentrating on slowing the silly horses.

Paul, mouth open, eyes wide, managed to get upright and pointed to the road ahead. Pamela saw it, too. Before them, by only a few yards, there lay a pig of such enormous size that, at first, she thought it must be a boulder. Paul tried to grab the reins out of her hands. Although the horses were still running, Pamela could tell by the way they were responding to her alternating release and restrain technique they were no longer in a blind panic.

She called to the horses in what she hoped to be an authoritative tone to whoa and applied a bit more resistance on the lines, giving the team the cue they needed to veer to the side. The team responded to her direction and moved to the left side of the road as she wanted.

The left side of the road, she hoped, would provide more room for them to pass by the mud puddle and the animal wallowing in it. As they passed, the pig rolled over to her other side, giving the carriage even more room to pass but not enough to keep all the wheels on the road.

The carriage tipped to one side and slid sideways.

Paul cursed.

Pamela anticipated and kept her head, concentrating on the horses, not the carriage. The team slowed to a sedate trot, dragging the skidding curricle for a few yards. Congratulating herself, she brought the team to a gradual, controlled standstill, but with one wheel of the curricle sunk down over the side of the road in the ditch. The horses stood quiet, necks bowed, heads down, puffing great billows of white clouds from their flared nostrils.

"There," she said on a deep intake of cool morning air. Lightheaded and giddy with fright, pleased with herself, Pamela lowered her hands to her lap, reins cutting between her cramped fingers. Trembling, she took a moment to recover from her shock and giggled with relief.

"There! There? My God!" Paul shouted and jumped down from the seat. Landing up to his ankles in cold ditch water, he waded through the bracken and sludge of the ditch and scrambled up the bank to get to his cattle. "You've ruined them. Ruined, I say, that's what you've done. Never should have listened to you. Never will again, and that's for sure."

Startled by the tone of his voice, the horses sidled and reared their heads. Pamela held tight the reins, and Paul ran a gloved hand down the neck of one of his lathered team.

"You better lower your voice, or you'll have them taking off again," she said. "I saved your life. These horses weren't ready to be out on a common highway harnessed to an unfamiliar conveyance. You should've been desensitizing them in their paddock. They aren't ruined, not by a long chalk. They're a bit winded, I grant you, but they are far from ruined. You can't blame me for their behavior. I had nothing to do with them taking it into their heads to take exception to that farmer and his oxen."

Managing on her own, she awkwardly slid off the tilting seat to the ground and tied the reins off, then lowered the anchor stone and slid it behind the wheel to keep the carriage from moving. Legs trembling, she stamped her foot. "You cannot stand there and tell me I did not handle them admirably, because I did." Hands on hips, close to tears, she pressed her lips tightly together.

Paul had the pair of thoroughbreds held tight by their bridles, checking their mouths, inspecting the traces. Knees still shaking, one hand on the frame of the carriage to steady herself, Pamela said, bending forward a little to get in her brother's face, "I got them back under control. You have to give me that at least. If it hadn't been for that…that…lump of lard…," she said. Without looking, she waved her arm back toward the mud puddle where the swine had been. "I would have been able to slow them down gradually to a more reasonable gait. And I wouldn't have had to go to the side of the road in order to miss the animal in the middle of the road. And I wouldn't have gotten the wheel of your precious carriage in the ditch. But as it was, I feel I used a great deal of skill. You could be a little more grateful if you please," she said, even though she was sure her brother did not care a fig for her feelings at this moment.

Never mind she had been scared half out of her wits. Never mind she'd never had a runaway team on her hands before. No, Paul was only concerned with his addlebrained team. "I'm overheated too, you know. I need some assurance, or at least allow me the luxury of having a fit of the vapors."

"Shouldn't have let you have the reins in the first place. Never will again. You were out of control. And my curricle—if you haven't broken an axle with your misguided maneuvering, it will be a miracle."

His precious team, taking exception to his tone,

arched their necks and pawed the ground.

Pamela stamped her foot again and considered socking him in the arm at the very least or maybe box him soundly about the head and shoulders. She was stopped by a calm, soothing voice from behind her.

“Can’t see that standing around bickering is going to help these animals.”

Chapter Three

Both Pamela and Paul spun around to see who had spoken. Their gaze met a warm grin and a pair of laughing blue eyes that mocked them and their present predicament. The man had a pail of something in his hand, and the great mound of pig that had been in the middle of the road was munching and grunting, emitting disgusting, vulgar noises of pleasure as she delved into the bucket for another mouthful.

Without thinking, finger-pointing accusingly, and finding a new target upon whom she could direct her frustration, Pamela said, "And, who might you be? Is this animal yours? It doesn't belong on the road. Well, answer me. Does it belong to you? She almost caused us serious harm."

****

"She could say the same of you, Madame. You barely avoided causing her serious harm," Simon said. Grinning, he made a mocking bow and tipped his hat. As he was about to introduce himself and lay claim to the pig, as requested, the team of horses lurched and created a distraction that waylaid his intent. Eyes wide, skittish, they threatened to get out of hand once again, apparently disturbed by the presence of his overly enthusiastic pig.

Simon put his good hand on the nose of the nearest steed and soothed the beast with a slow, gentle stroke. "Fine pair of animals, but they'll soon take a chill standing about. After a good run like that, I'd get them into their stalls and give them a good rub down."

The young lady bristled and opened her mouth to give him a retort, but the young gentleman diverted whatever she was about to say. "Quite right," he said.

Ignoring the flushed and fuming young lady, the young gentleman came around to the side of the curricle to stand next to Simon. "I would be greatly obliged to you if you would help me get the carriage back on the road so I can turn them around."

"Certainly," Simon said. The young man indicated the young woman should take the bridles. Simon handed her the pail of mash. He followed the young man around to the rear of the carriage to assess the damage.

****

Pamela was about to follow Paul and the impudent farmer around to the rear of the curricle when she noticed the handsome, arrogant farmer had a bad leg; he had a slight limp. He ordered her with a wave of his arm, as he retreated, to take the head of the horses and lead them forward while he and Paul pushed from behind. She thought to refuse his presumptive, arrogant order, then the farmer, by peeping around the side of the vehicle, an impertinent grin on his face, said, "Please." The urge to throw the bucket at his head nearly overwhelmed her.

She was left with little to do but obey and smolder ineffectually at the injustice. To add to her humiliation and frustration, Pamela found herself being nudged and pushed backward by the giant pig who had one objective, and that was to get the mash in the bottom of the pail. All while the horses snuffled and shook their manes in objection to the nearness of the pig.

The depth of Pamela's unreasonable outrage

puzzled her. She found it confusing. Normally, she would dismiss the antics of the working class, but this man's grin inspired an unusual degree of ire. She put it down to her recent fright. Her emotions were exposed—on the surface. Considering his disability, the stranger was all things kind and helpful. She straightened her spine, tamped down her unusual reaction to his grin and those blue eyes, and did as requested.

There was no difficulty maneuvering the curricle out of the ditch. Pamela led the team around, the big sow at her side, so the team and the curricle were facing back in the direction toward home. This left them all standing in front of a stone wall and a tree-lined entrance to Copeland Manor, the roof of the Tudor structure barely visible beyond the overgrown vegetation.

The pig persisted in following Pamela and the bucket of feed, like a bee to honey. The pregnant sow had taken quite a fancy to her, snuffling her cape and gloved hands. Pamela couldn't resist scratching the ridiculous creature behind her warm, soft, velvety, floppy, pink ears.

"It seems, dear lady, you have a way with animals. The way you handled the horses and now Peg. She doesn't take to everyone." The farmer's soft voice caught Pamela off guard. He came to stand beside her, looking at her with his steady, penetrating gaze. The smile on his lips and the twinkle in his eyes hinted that he might be laughing at her.

It took her a moment to decide if there was a compliment in his words or if he was being sarcastic. Lips pulled to the side, eyes narrowed, she stared at him, trying to see past his smile into his head. She came to the conclusion it was foolish to allow this bumpkin to cause her one moment of discomfort. She made a little noise that was supposed to be a snort of dismissal and quickly looked away. Pointing her nose upward, she searched for the right words to give him the set down his impudent manner deserved.

"I am not a dear lady," she said. The moment the words were out of her mouth, she realized she'd insulted herself and shook her head to bring herself back to good sense.

She waved her hand in front of her face to wave aside her silly comment. "I know…I know enough about horses to know this pair of pig-headed equines have no business harnessed to this type of carriage. Not today, anyway. They are still green. My brother thought otherwise, not me. And… your horse of a hog had no business being in the middle of the road. That's what I know." Lips pressed tightly together. She hated that she'd broken out in a cold sweat and that she was about to cry. She also was aware the farmer was entertained rather than chagrined by her attempt to give him a set down.

****

Simon choked back his amusement and forced himself to make a serious, albeit a tad provoking, comment. "May I remind you this team of horses was out of control. You would never have been in danger at all if you had been going at a proper rate of speed, which you were not."

Voice cracking, on the verge of blubbering, she said, "*I* was not out of control. Yes, the *horses* were out of control. *I* was applying control." She paused and took a deep breath, obviously gathering her composure. "This…this team of chuckle-headed beasts took exception to a farm cart, of all things. It was only because of my skill there was no serious damage to your precious pig or my brother's silly, frivolous, impractical carriage."

Simon couldn't help himself. He burst into laughter. "As I said, you have a way with animals," he said, pointing at Peg, who had abandoned her bucket and was nuzzling the young lady's hand with her muddy snout. And the young lady, apparently without thinking, was giving Peg the rubs she craved.

****

Pamela, breath coming in short, halting bursts, once again found herself the object of the pig's affection. Backing up, she tugged her cape and skirts aside, but the pig wouldn't be discouraged. The animal rubbed her ample, muddy shoulder against Pamela's side, coming up to her waist, nearly knocking her over. She, naturally, massaged the sow's ears in self-defense.

The farmer, laughing, reached out for her elbow, but it was Paul who saved her, his arm around her waist. "Cut line. Stop playing with the pig. I need to get my horses home, and I should think this man would like to get his pig back where she belongs. Thank you for your timely assistance. Excuse my sister. You know, female, a bit testy right now. On the defensive, you know. I daresay she's a little hysterical after her clumsy escapade."

Pamela spun around, intending to slap her brother across his unprepossessing face. She'd had enough of his highhanded, pompous, arrogant insults.

"It was nothing," the farmer said. Stepping forward, he put himself in the way, making it impossible for Pamela to follow through with her assault. She suspected he'd done it on purpose. Ignoring her, the farmer held out his right hand for a handshake with Paul, keeping his left hand in his coat pocket. "Glad we all came about no worse for wear. I hope your team will be all right."

Pamela bit her lip, squeezed her eyes tightly shut, and mumbled her thank you. She moved around to the side of the curricle to climb aboard. From behind her, a pair of strong hands fastened around her waist. She looked down, expecting to see her brother's hands. The mutilated four fingers on the man's left hand took her by surprise. She became flustered, absent-minded, and slipped on the foot-board of the curricle, which caused her to fall back into the farmer's body. She emitted a small whimper of dismay and heard him chuckle but was too embarrassed to look into his face. He had his arms locked around her now, balancing them both so they would not go all the way down into the ditch.

Between clenched teeth, she said, "I can manage very well on my own, thank you."

"I have no doubt of that, dear lady. But in this instance, you don't have to. I am pleased to offer my assistance." He stepped back out of her way and swept her a slight bow. "Allow me."

Gathering her composure and her skirts, she approached the step of the curricle once more. He put his hand, his mutilated hand, beneath her elbow. His other hand was pressed against her spine. She steadied herself and found her seat.

****

Simon observed, with a good deal of interest, the young lady adjust her dark green skirts and cape about her black stocking-encased ankles and dainty, black, soft kid, booted feet. He also caught sight of a trim calf. Her brother did nothing to help the young lady into the conveyance, he hadn't even offered her a hand up. He sat with a petulant scowl on his face.

Once upon the seat, the lady did not give Simon another glance but looked straight ahead, sitting very primly in the fancy vehicle.

He watched the curricle pull away and stared hard at the young lady's proud profile as it passed him. The girl's nose was straight, her complexion flawless, her eyes warm and full of fiery lights that declared her high spirit.

Her body was firm, and she was heavier than she looked. This he could testify to, for he had held her in his arms even though for only a brief second. Her waist was small, but her hips were full, and her breasts were round and soft. If he closed his eyes, he could smell the fragrance of her hair—maybe roses? No, lilies? Tiger lilies. She'd left behind her scent when her head had fallen back against his shoulder. He tipped his head to the side to inhale and closed his eyes, yes, lilies.

"Well, Peg, it seems our little adventure is over," he said, looking after the retreating conveyance. "I feel as if I've just had a near miss with a snarling termagant, don't you?

"No? Well, you did all you could to win her over. Mighty comely termagant, I admit," he said as they headed back up the lane toward home. "You took to her right off, I noticed. Birds of a feather perhaps," he said, laughing and could only imagine what the lady's acid response would have been to hear his analogy. He prophesied the lady would not appreciate his comparison. Peg merely grunted obligingly, and Simon took this as an affirmative. He continued to converse with her all the way home, discussing with her the day's events so far, asking her advice on what they could do to please her, and convince her to stay in her home yard.

Chapter Four

Paul, reins in hand, set his high-strung, precious team of white Arabians at a sedate pace back down the road, headed toward Pomeroy Chase and the home gate. Pamela, beside him, sat in stoney silence, and wished she could keep her mouth shut. She knew she talked too much, especially when she was nervous or felt guilty for some ridiculous act of misbehavior. It was a fault of hers to go headlong on the defensive. She knew her flaws.

A pair of laughing, taunting blue eyes would haunt her dreams—those eyes and the feeling of strong arms banded around her waist. Why this should be, she blushed to think and reminded herself the man was a farmer, nothing else, probably less than a farmer, probably a migrant worker. Yes, the man might be a farmer, but he'd been everything kind and considerate. Her bigoted thoughts sickened her, which intensified her mortification.

He certainly appeared to be a peddler in his old, smelly coat. But his voice was smooth and cultured. Now that she recalled, yes, there was definitely something aristocratic about his voice and manner. But his hand, whatever had happened to him? Perhaps it was a birth defect, or he'd had a terrible accident. He could have been in the military, perhaps injured in battle. The hand certainly didn't stop him from doing his work. He was strong, very strong.

She looked to Paul, who was quiet, behaving as if he were the injured party, which fanned her ire anew. "Why did you not at least give me a hand up into this ridiculous conveyance? You could have helped me. You should have helped me," she said, near tears.

"You looked to be enjoying yourself," he said, his gaze straight ahead. "Why you must throw yourself at everything in trousers, I shall never understand."

"Oh, oh, oh, you, you are a despicable, horrid, conceited beast today. Why? Why are you being so nasty? I did not throw myself at that man, and you know it. You left me to fend for myself, and he, very rightly, tried to assist me as a true gentleman should."

****

Paul gave her a quick glance and looked away. He'd deliberately wounded her, and he knew why. She was right about Lucinda. He hated that Lucinda addressed him as "Pauly."

To taunt him, a few of his closest chums had begun to use the handle as well. He feared the title would stick. And he knew Lucinda sent him on far too many missions. And he knew she was an outrageous flirt, but she was so, so beguiling, so adorable, soft, intoxicating.

He had deliberately ignored Pamela to punish her for being right and a damn fine hand with the reins. Yes, his rude, dismissive, insulting behavior in front of a complete stranger made him a despicable, horrid beast. She'd been right to say he couldn't have done better to avoid that pig and the ditch. And the horses and his carriage had taken no harm. She'd kept her head and managed very well indeed. Which irked him, wounded his male pride, and in general, because it made him appear an incompetent, ungrateful fool in front of a man close to his own age, who seemed vaguely familiar.

To Pamela, he said, "Sorry. I'm a pathetic cad. I behaved badly. You managed admirably to avoid that pig and you brought us to a safe halt, no damage to cattle or carriage. Well done."

Pamela sat very still, very quiet for a long moment. He feared she might not be so easily brought around. At last, she spoke. "Oh, never mind. I do understand. You had to defend your bruised male ego, never mind that you did it at my expense in front of a stranger, a neighbor perhaps."

"Did you see?" Paul asked her.

"See what?"

"The poor chap's hand. Must have been a soldier. Didn't ask him, of course, but that must be it. His voice and manner didn't seem to be the common type. Could swear I know him from somewhere. He looked familiar to me, the smile, the open face."

Pamela nodded. "I thought his speech sounded rather educated, and his deference to me was gentlemanly, at once odious and impertinent, as imperious gentlemen are wont to be. It has been my experience that some people often behave in such a manner when caught out in the wrong. His pig was in the middle of the road, after all. Looked to be an expensive animal. Seems a bit irresponsible to me. He was unapologetic, a bit bold, perhaps, for a laborer, but all in all gentlemanly. That perpetual grin of his, though, I do wonder if he wasn't a bit off if you get my meaning."

"Yes, I do think I know him," Paul said aloud to himself. "He was at Eton the same time I was there. Though he was an upper-classman, he was one of the few who didn't bully us lower slobs. He wasn't crippled then.

Wonder what the poor beggar is doing out here? Looked to be down and out, dressed as he was, like a farmer—and that pig.

"His hand was not damaged when he was in school, of that I am sure. If he is the fellow I am thinking of, he always had a winning way with him. Can't think why you should call him odious. And he most certainly wasn't in any way *off*, as you say. On the contrary, he seemed very sensible, very polite to me. He was all things civil and friendly. He helped us, didn't he? Could have taken his pig and disappeared, leaving us to fend for ourselves. You were a bit high-handed, I thought. Giving him your sass. The man couldn't help it if his animal had decided to wallow in the middle of the road. I'm certain he was there to retrieve the pig when we came barreling down the road straight for the poor silly thing."

****

In a huff, incensed, Pamela said, "Men, you are all hateful. If I was high-handed it was because you were being deliberately provoking. I was the only person present with any modicum of sense. My *high-handedness,* as you put it, was plain and simple level-headedness. You were going on and on about your horses, your carriage, and he was concerned for his pig and neither of you gave a thought to me.

"I was shaken, Paul. I was terrified. Did you console me? Did you give a thought to my shattered nerves? You did not. And, the farmer, it was clear to me, thought the entire episode highly entertaining. He was laughing at me, at both of us." Upon reflection, inwardly, Pamela could see the man had done nothing to warrant her displeasure save for his insipid grin, and yet she'd found him irritating. Now, he had become maddeningly unforgettable.

"Well, yes, I must say I would've found it devilish amusing too if it were not for my horses," Paul said, his head to one side, a smirk on his lips. "The pig really liked you. That was funny."

"These horses are not worth your concern, and if they were mine," Pamela said, "I would be rid of them as soon as possible. Foist them on to the first unsuspecting soul you find."

"They're a bit high-strung," Paul said. "I'll admit. But, after some schooling, they will do fine, better than fine, they will be wonderful. You'll see. I'll work with them every day. I took them out on the road too soon. They aren't used to this carriage, and to be honest, neither am I."

"Oh, there you go again. It's all about your horses and this silly carriage. What about me? Maybe I've caught a chill. Maybe I've sprained my wrist trying to get your addlepated equines back in line. Maybe I've hurt my neck, saving you and your precious team from disaster. Enough about your horses. Not one more word."

He shook his head and pulled his lips to the side in a dismissive gesture. "Well, I dare say you would have indicated by now if you had taken any kind of hurt."

There was no use talking to him. Pamela pressed her lips together. This morning had gifted her the much-needed diversion she'd craved. Not really the kind of adventure she'd set out to get, but an adventure all the same.

And the encounter with the farmer added a bit of a mystery. A mystery she intended to solve. She'd achieved her goal to drive Paul's team of whites. And she'd proven to herself she was very good at it, never mind her brother wasn't exactly profuse in his praise. Indignation aside, she considered the morning could indicate a possible turning point in her here-to-for dull existence during this holiday. She now had a project.

Pamela, not wanting her brother to know she'd paid much attention to the odious farmer, attempted to profess a minimum interest in his ramblings. She did wish he could recall a little more information. The good Samaritan was an enigma. Perhaps the next few months would not be so dull after all. She would now concentrate her time and energy on finding out all she could about the pig farmer. If he had indeed met with misfortune, then she wanted to know all about it.

Chapter Five

Once home at Pomeroy Chase, Paul handed the reins over to the groom and assisted Pamela from the carriage. Ignoring her, he immediately began a discussion with the groom on how they should go on with training his precious team.

Pamela was met by Chance, a giant, salt and pepper, rough-coated wolfhound who was supposed to be Paul's dog but had given his loyalty and preference to Pamela instead. Blood red tongue lolling and whip tail wagging, he came up on his hind legs to give her a slobbery greeting. "Oh, for heaven's sake," she said, although giggling, she wiped his greeting off her cheek and pushed his tongue away. "I've been gone less than a couple of hours. Do control yourself," she said and dislodged the hound's paws from her shoulders. The dog obediently went down on all fours but started a very thorough investigation of her skirts, sniffling, and snuffling. He even pawed at her boots.

Chance proudly trotting at her side, Pamela entered the house and made her way to the rose parlor toward the back of the hall where she was sure to find her mother and sister. She intended to make herself useful for the rest of the day. There were mirrors in the front hall. Pamela didn't bother to glance at them, completely dismissing the possibility it might be a good idea to change out of her muddy clothes and tidy her hair a bit before presenting herself to her parent.

"Ah, you're home," her mother said and bounced up out of her chair and set her sewing basket on the floor at her feet. One glance in her daughter's direction, she put her hand to her cheek. "Whatever have you been doing? Your cape…and…and your hair…and is that mud on your gloves and your nose? What is that smell? And Chance…I do not want that dog in here. We have fabrics and lace in here, and that beast, and you, smell of the stable. I've spoken to you about this before, Pamela. The least you can do is get that dog to lie down somewhere. He's so big. He takes up all the room."

Lady Alice was a small little lady with reddish, ash-brown hair with here and there a thread of silver running through it. She usually wore a mob cap or a lace mantilla, but today, she had nothing but combs drawing back her thick, heavy tresses away from her fair face and off her neck. Her figure was round but still very alluring, although her increasing girth was a constant worry to her. She was forever on a new diet, causing her to be slightly moody and ill more often than she should have been.

Pamela caught the wide-eyed question in her sister's eye and had the grace to look down at her skirts and her boots and put a hand to her hair to tuck a curl behind her ear. "Well, we had a brief encounter with a rather large pig," she said. "I simply thought I'd let you know we've arrived home. I'll go upstairs and change and get tidied up."

"A pig? Oh, my good heavens, Pamela," her mother said. Pamela turned to leave the room and waved Chance to follow her.

Lady Alice opened her mouth to ask more questions.

"Please excuse me, Mother," Penny said. "My eyes

could use a rest, and I need to stretch my legs a bit. I'll go along with Pam. Would you like some tea, Mother? I'll let Mrs. Springer know."

"Yes, yes," the lady said as she carefully sat back down in her chair. "I'll sit here and gather my nerves. I don't think I'm going to like hearing about this encounter with this pig. No, I don't think I will. With you, there's always something," she said to Pamela. "In town, it's balloon ascensions, archery contests, and galloping through the park, and here it's that dog and now a pig. Tea will help. Chamomile, please."

Pamela opened the parlor door as the chime of the mantel clock proclaimed the hour of half-past twelve. "Where is Paul?" her mother asked.

"He's gone to the stable. Where else," Pamela said.

Penny set her sewing aside, head down to hide her smile. She draped the sky-blue voile gown she'd been working on over the back of her chair. "The pearls are exactly what the bodice needed. You were right, Mother. And I think the gold satin will suit Pam very nicely, don't you think so, Pam? Mother thought the color might be too bold. But I think you can carry it off."

"I love the gold, and the satin is beautiful," Pamela said and came back to her mother's chair to give her a bus on her cheek. "You have wonderful taste, Mother."

Lady Alice waved Pamela away. "Go away, Pamela, you stink. No use trying to bring me up sweet. You children will be the death of me," the lady said. "Let Mrs. Springer know where Paul can be found. I'm sure Cook has our luncheon laid out. I'll see if your father will abandon his books. I expect you girls at the table in half an hour, presentable, hair combed, and then I want to hear about this pig and how it is you, Pamela, are covered in mud, or whatever that muck is." She waved her hand to shoo Pamela from the room. "And no dogs in the dining room," she said.

Chance on her heels, Pamela nodded and went out into the great hall. Penny caught up with her at the stairwell. The housekeeper stopped them, coming from the dining room. "Luncheon will be on the sideboard in the family dining room shortly. You look a mite disheveled," she said to Pamela. "Better not let your mother catch sight of you."

"Too late," Pamela said under her breath. "Mother says to let you know Paul is down at the stable. I'm going to change and get cleaned up. Mother has gone to the library to see if Father's going to join us for luncheon. Oh, and Mrs. Springer, some chamomile tea for Mother would be nice. Thank you."

Mrs. Clara Springer clicked her tongue against her cheek and walked away, muttering to herself.

Chance bounded up the stairs ahead of them. Pamela hugged the wall to let him pass and said over her shoulder to Penny, who had stayed well out of the dog's way, "The blue voile has silver threads, very nice. You'll look a treat. You're good at detail work, the fine stitches. I'm better at hemming, linings, that sort of thing. I don't have the patience."

"Never mind the gowns," Penny said. "I want to hear details. You look as if you've been dragged down the lane behind the curricle. Whatever happened to you? When you came into the parlor, your cheeks looked flushed, and your eyes were bright, bright like they get when you're angry about something. Did you get to take the reins? And where in the world does this pig come into the story?"

"I'll give you details once we are in my room and alone."

Inside her chamber, Pamela ordered Chance down off her bed and sent him to the rug near the fireplace. She draped her mud-encrusted cape on a hook on her wardrobe door and sat down to remove her boots.

Penny poured some water into the basin on the stand next to Pamela's vanity. "Thank you," Pamela said and used a towel to scrub her face, hands, and throat before drying off and dabbing a drop of Spanish lily toilet water behind her ears and between her bosoms. Penny selected clean underclothes, stockings, and a soft wool gown of deep sapphire from the wardrobe and laid everything out on the bed. She settled herself in the window seat and waited with her arms folded across her bosom.

Bent over, Pamela removed her soiled stockings. "Yes, Paul finally let me take the reins. Then, his team of fancy equines took exception to a farmer and his cart and bolted. His carriage and blasted horses are safe and sound, thanks to me. There was a giant hog in the middle of the road having a leisurely mud bath. I had to maneuver the carriage and the runaway team around the pig without going into the ditch. Which I managed to do quite handily, if I do say so myself. There was a farmer there. He'd come looking for his pig. He had this bucket of mash to entice the silly creature. I held the bucket and horse bridles as we maneuvered the carriage and team around to turn us back homeward. The pig, the muddy pig, a sow, soon-to-be mother of obviously a large brood, and I, bonded, you might say. You know how I am with animals. I can't stop myself from petting them."

Penny sat, eyes lit up with amusement, lips pursed for a moment or two before she burst out laughing. "You do have adventures. I don't understand how it is that you don't ever faint. I certainly would. But this one tops them all. I'll wager Paul was beside himself. I'm surprised he hasn't been sleeping down at the stable with his team of whites."

Pamela snorted dismissively. "I doubt you would faint," she said as Penny helped her change her gown. "You appear deceptively fragile, but I'm not fooled. You are tough, sensible, and you would never swoon no matter what. You are more apt to giggle than faint. I admire your ability to keep your tongue in your mouth under stress. I wish I could do that. As for Paul and his concerns for his precious team, he was despicable, contemptible, and thoroughly reprehensible. I will never forget how he behaved toward me in front of a complete stranger. He did apologize. But not until we were well on our way home.

"I dread explaining this to Mother," Pamela said, and heaved a weighty sigh. She held up her muddy cape and inspected it, then tossed it into a basket at the bottom of her wardrobe to be washed. "I'm certain she would prefer I faint. She's not going to be happy that I succeeded in persuading Paul to let me take the reins."

"Where did all this take place? You said you were on the road. Where did the farmer come from? Was he the farmer in the cart?"

Pamela sat down next to her on the window seat. "No. We didn't really see where he came from. We were near Copeland Manor, you know, the tree-lined lane with the lovely rock wall. He might have come from there. I'm ashamed to say we didn't even get his name. He was all things kind and helpful. We were lucky he was there. I don't know what we would have done with the pig if he hadn't been there, come to think about it."

Penny nodded and blinked, and Pamela experienced another helping of guilt. "I have been very selfish, haven't I? I haven't been very useful. From here on in, I will try to be of more help. We have your season to prepare for, and I know how exacting Mother can be. Funny, but you know Mother and Paul are a lot alike when they get fixated on a project. I've been her project for the last two years; now it's your turn. One thing is for certain: You will be the most beautiful debutante of the season. Mother will see to it. I think I'm a bit of a disappointment to her. After all her effort and hard work, I haven't really cooperated with her plans for my future. I haven't found a match, or rather, I haven't encouraged anyone to make the offer."

"I find the idea of dressing me up and putting me on display like a fancy bonnet in a store window rather insulting, if you must know," Penny said, picking at the folds of the soft, peach-colored, jersey wool skirt.

"Well, yes," Pamela said and laid her hand over her sister's moving fingers. "I felt the same way at first. But I know you, you enjoy the music, and the parks and the shops. Let Mother worry about how you look, which invitation to accept, which fete and ball to attend and who you must be introduced to, and all the falderal. You soak up the gaiety, the flavor of it all. Enjoy yourself, be yourself."

"I'm glad you'll be there beside me," Penny said and gave Pamela a hug. "Let me brush your hair. I'll braid it, and then I think we better scoot."

"Oh, good heavens, my hair. Yes, yes," Pamela said and popped up to get her hairbrush.

Chapter Six

"Oh, yes, the pig," Pamela said in response to her mother's question. Seeing the pig in her mind's eye, she sighed and nonchalantly helped herself to scrambled eggs and a scone, ignoring the ham on the sideboard. "It was in the middle of the road. We managed to get around it and come to a stop. The farmer was there. He had a bucket of mash to entice the animal back to its pen, I suppose." She shrugged her shoulders. "Anyway, I was handed the bucket when the farmer helped Paul turn the carriage around. The pig got a little too close, I guess and that's how I got mud on my cape. It was a very large pig. Enceinte female pig, if you will imagine."

Penny, seated across the table from her, stifled her urge to giggle and quickly averted her gaze as Pamela, head down, returned to the table. Pamela didn't dare meet her mother's dubious expression. Yes, it was what happened, minus the exciting details. Paul and their father had taken their lunch while Pamela was changing, so it was just the three of them at the dining table. Paul and Lord Pomeroy had excused themselves, saying they were off to visit one of the tenants. Pamela quickly turned the topic to gowns, fittings, and sundries.

"Miss Gillespie will be here shortly. We must get these gowns fitted today, so set your minds to it, girls," Lady Alice said.

****

"So, you finally wore your brother down and took the reins," Lord Pomeroy said to Pamela as they all came to the table for their supper. Pamela groaned and gave Paul a scorching glance. The afternoon had passed without one more word about pigs, mud, or complaints about dogs being in the same room with fripperies. Pamela had hoped to skate by with no more notice.

Chance, who had snuck in and stealthily belly-crawled under the big dining room table, lay at her feet. He shifted his weight, and Pamela stroked his ribs with her satin-slippered foot. "Yes," she said, and that was all she wanted to say.

"Paul said his flash team of prime goers took exception to a farmer's cart, and they bolted," her father said as he tucked into his roast beef to hide the smirk on his lips.

Lord John Pomeroy always wore a bland expression on his handsome face, but his merry brown eyes gave him away. Inside, he had a healthy sense of humor and was not above using it or expressing it. He was a well-built man, broad of shoulder and narrow of hip, a bruising rider, but an academic at heart. He was a family man who loved his children. To Pamela's dismay, now they were grown, he took great pleasure in all aspects of their lives. Hence, evidently, Paul had unloaded his budget and spilled all the details of the morning's events into their father's ear.

Pamela stayed quiet. Her mother set her fork and knife down on her plate. The clatter echoed in the silence that hung heavy in the room. "You said nothing of this," she said to Pamela's bowed head. "You did not tell me you had the reins," the lady said to Pamela.

Her accusing gaze traveled to her son. "How could

you, Paul?"

"There wasn't any traffic. It was quiet, and I didn't see the harm. And besides, you know how Pam is once she takes a notion into her head. I thought it best to let her have the reins and get it over with. The farmer's cart came out of nowhere, pulled by a great, hulking team of oxen, driven by a very loud and abusive farmer. Osborne, I think you know him, don't you, Father? My team didn't care for the cart, the oxen, or the man shouting curses at us, and they spooked. Then we saw there was a huge pig in the middle of the road," Paul said as he, too, forked in a mouthful of roast beef.

All was quiet. All of them waited to hear the rest of the story as he chewed and swallowed. "With Pam holding the reins, my horses going pell-mell down the road, she managed to get the carriage and horses around the silly thing and avoid the ditch. She put one wheel in, but all in all we came about, no damage done to my horses or the curricle.

"The owner of the sow showed up out of nowhere. He looked familiar to me, of my age or thereabouts. I think I know him from Eton. Be hanged if I can remember his name. He was very helpful. Got the curricle out of the ditch, the team turned about. Pam made friends with the sow. You see, the farmer had given her the bucket to hold while he helped me get the carriage out of the ditch, you know, the bucket full of the old girl's favorite snack."

Penny, napkin to her lips, brown eyes crinkled up at the corners, could not suppress her giggles.

Pamela put her palms on the tabletop. "Correction: I…I…turned the team around while you and the farmer guided the carriage out of the ditch. I led the horses around by their halters, with that pig following me around. We were near Copeland Manor. I could see the tiled roof. We did wonder if our helpful citizen had come from there," Pamela said in an attempt to divert her mother's attention.

"I believe Sir Simon-Loyd did have grandchildren, not that he recognized them," Lady Alice said, blinking.

Pamela hoped her mother's focus was properly piqued and diverted by the introduction of the manor.

"I remember his daughter. She was very pretty—dark hair, dainty. Mary, I think her name was. She came out about the same time as I," Lady Alice said. "A lively little thing. Her father disowned her. If I recall, she ran off to Gretna Green, married a broker for a tobacco merchant, I think. Big scandal at the time, as I recall. Forget his last name. Being in trade, Sir Simon-Loyd didn't think him good enough for his one and only child."

"I seem to recall someone mentioned Copeland Manor was undergoing renovations and improvements," Lord Pomeroy said.

"This is the first I've heard of this, John. Why have I not heard of it? I'm sure we would have noticed anyone new at church."

"Well, the renovations haven't been ongoing for very long, not even a year. Sir Simon-Loyd passed, I believe, just short of two years ago. The manor has been kept up with only the retainers and tenants doing the work, taking care of the stock and buildings while the old man's estate was being sorted. We were in London from the end of March until the end of June. Then we were off to Scotland for the summer until the fall season—same as the previous year. We could pay a call. Probably should pay our respects. After all, whoever the fellow was who helped you out this morning, we should give him thanks—introduce ourselves as neighbors."

"Did you say Simon-Loyd?" Paul asked. He swallowed hard his mouthful of potatoes and shook his head. "Oh, of course Smiling Simon. His last name wasn't Copeland, I'm sure, but I remember him now. Yes, the fellow was famous for always finding humor in things. Never a mean bone in his body, except on the field, of course. Bruising ball player, if I recall. On the rowing team, too. An all-round good fellow. He didn't finish Eton, though. He and his family left the country for the colonies. Definitely have to pay a call now. Poor devil was crippled, Father. His hand was horribly mutilated, and he had a slight limp. Nothing wrong with him when he was at Eton. Must have happened while in the colonies. He kept his deformity in his pocket most of the time. Sorry to say Pam and I were remiss in not getting his name. We both had other things on our minds."

"Like your costly cattle and your unwieldy curricle," Pamela said to the dinner roll upon which she was spreading butter.

"You rounded on the fellow, practically, accused him of placing his pig in the middle of the road just to put us in the ditch. Never mind you were racing down the road out of control," Paul said, shaking his fork at her from across the table."

Pamela moved up to the edge of her chair about to give a rebuttal, but Lady Alice put a stop to whatever she was about to say. "Children, please, no more of this talk of pigs and horses. Not at the table.

"Paul, you will apologize to Pamela. I suspect you

were less than gentlemanly, being concerned for your cattle and not your sister. The thought of Pamela, reins in hand, managing a runaway team of horses, going down the Great North Road, risking her neck, and your neck, is a vision I wish to discard from my mind's eye as soon as possible."

Pamela nodded in total agreement, then her mother added. "Pamela, you will apologize to your brother for pestering him into doing something so foolish as to let you have the reins in the first place. And for being churlish, less than ladylike in the presence of a complete stranger."

Pamela sat back, dabbed her mouth with her napkin and put it in her lap. "Paul, I am sorry I pestered you," she said, but inside, the apology cost her dearly. She had a tendency to keep all of her little defeats and surrenders fresh in her mind, which allowed them to haunt her, replay in her mind's eye in the wee hours of the night, and this was one of those times. She was sure she would replay this in her mind over and over, a different script with each rehash.

Paul apologized. Pamela barely paid any attention to what he said. She was thinking about the farmer and how and when she might apologize and lost her appetite.

Her mother had the floor now and by the gleam in her eye, Pamela would say her mother was plotting something. Something that would require all of their attention and participation with enthusiasm.

"I wish to give a party, a soiree with games, music and of course food. I know. I know society is thin right now. But we have the possibility of these new neighbors, and although we are a bit tardy in giving our welcome, we should do all we can to incorporate them into the local society. Perhaps the new resident of Copeland Manor is married. If he has a wife, I'm sure she would appreciate our including her in a bit of socializing. If not, then maybe he's a bachelor. We need bachelors right now. We lost too many when they went off to fight that annoying war."

Lady Alice shook her head as if to remove the sight of all the dead soldiers from her mind's eye before saying, "I believe the Smith-Mortons and the Davies family are home. I do believe I heard someone say the Abernathys would also be returning from Scotland soon. Duncan and James Davies are good friends with you, Paul, are they not? And the Smith-Mortons are launching their two daughters again this year. I saw them in church last Sunday. Then, I believe I heard the young Marquis of Fairfield and his bride are in residence. We met them last year at the Seaton's ball. All in all, I think we can entertain at least a half-dozen, maybe more, young people and their parents. We'll plan on holding our little soiree for, say, two weeks from today."

She looked around the table. Lord John hesitated, then tipped his head to the side. "I suppose we could. We won't be leaving for a month or two."

"Penelope needs practice," Lady Alice said.

"Practice? Practice doing what?" Penny asked indignation in her tone. "Every year, from the age of twelve, I've had dancing and deportment lessons, lessons on which fork to use, when and how to use the finger bowl, which glass to use for water, wine and how to extract the meat from a snail, and debone a squab."

"Well, giggling, if you must know," Lady Alice said, "you have a tendency to giggle. Your napkin stays in your lap, young lady. It's not for you to use as a mask to cover up your snickers and smirks. I also think you could use some practice standing in a receiving line. You, I've noticed, slouch and switch from one foot to the other. Your impatience shows. A lady must remain composed at all times. You have very nice table manners, I am proud to say," Lady Alice said, a gentle smile on her lips. "I'm very proud of you. You will do us proud. All of you, you all do us proud. Don't they, John?"

Lord John nodded and turned to his son. "Do you think you know this farmer, Paul? If so, I wonder if we shouldn't invite him to this soiree your mother is planning. And Copeland's heir, of course."

"It's strange we haven't seen them in church," Lady Alice said, then took a sip from her wine glass. "I think that's very strange. Tomorrow, when you pay your call, John, you must decide what is best. We don't know these people. We might not care for them at all. Yes, we'll be neighborly, pay a call, thank this farmer person for his aid, and suss him out if he is the long-lost grandson of Sir Simon-Loyd. Yes, find out what sort of neighbors they are."

"Don't think there's a family at the manor," said Lord John. "Surely, we would've heard if there were. Copeland's grandson couldn't be old enough to have much of a family if he's around the same age as Paul. If he had a wife, a woman would want to meet people, attend church."

Paul put in his two cents and said, "A man alone wouldn't care whether he met another soul or not, especially if he had wounds—been in battle. If he wanted to find a bit of fun, he'd head for London." Paul clamped his mouth shut. His father shook his head at him.

“Sorry,” he said. “But you know what I mean. There isn’t much around here that would provide the kind of diversion a man, a single fellow out for a bit of excitement and stimulation, with no family, kith, or kin might find save for the pub in Stilton. They serve a fine ale and rack of lamb there, but that’s about the extent of it.”

Chapter Seven

To serve herself a glass of milk from the pantry table, Audry sidled her way around the table to get past the stout housekeeper, and surrogate mother, Mrs. Dorsey.

"You'll sit yourself down young lady," Mrs. Dorsey said. Blocking her, hand on her shoulder, Mrs. Dorsey turned her about. "I can't stop you and Master Simon from taking your meals in my kitchen, but I can stop you from liftin' a finger and serving yourselves. Now, sit ye down, and I'll get you a glass of my special nog. Sit down in your chair and rest yourself."

Audry did love Mrs. Dorsey's special nog. It was eggy, sweet, and spiced with nutmeg.

"I'll have a glass of your nog too, thank you, Ellen. Add a splash of rum if you have it," Simon said and pulled out a chair at the work-worn, rough-hewn kitchen table.

"I really could get my own," Audry said under her breath. She passed around the plates and utensils and retrieved the butter dish and the salt cellar from the sideboard.

Mrs. Dorsey returned from the pantry with two glasses of her nog and set them down, one for Audry and one for Simon. "You can serve yourselves when I'm not about," she said and gave Audry's cheek a gentle tap. "Now, no skimpin' on your vittles, neither of yah. It pleases me you enjoy my nog, it's good for what ails you.

"You, young lady, are far too skinny in my estimation. I swear you are worn down to nothin' but skin and bones. I intend to fatten you up. We have the house in manageable order now. You needn't work so hard. It would be a fine thing to see you with some pretty gowns on your back. It's past time you start dressin' like the quality you are when we go to church.

"And that reminds me," she said and stopped behind Simon's chair. "You'd better start comin' to church, or you'll grow as heathenish as that place you lived in for far too many years. I wouldn't be a'tall surprised to see you chargin' about with a spear in one hand and nothin' but a loin cloth to keep you decent," she said quite seriously, but her words brought forth an uncontrolled round of laughter from her husband, Simon, and Audry.

"Oh, yes, well, laugh if you will," she said as she ladled out their supper of chicken and dumplings, starting with Simon's plate, then Audry's, before she set the kettle down on the table in front of her spouse and handed him the ladle. "You know tis true about Miss Audry here," she said and wiped her hands on her apron before taking her seat at the table. "You should be ashamed to keep her here dressed like a poor relation and not seein' any other young folks as she should."

Her husband Milo shook his head at her. She clamped her lips shut and helped herself to the dumplings in her kettle.

****

Simon sobered instantly and took a long, hard look at his sister. She'd even gotten taller, he thought. And yes, she was too thin, cheeks a bit sunken, wrist bones obvious, dark half-circles beneath her eyes. The gown she wore today was more of a sack, shapeless, gray, and drab, doing little to enhance the beauty of his sister's porcelain-like complexion, her wonderful, blue cat's eyes, and perfect, full lips and straight white teeth. Her luxurious, thick, naturally curly, black hair was drawn back into a tight coil on top of her head, a style for a woman of mature years, and yet Audry was but a girl of eighteen as of her last birthday in September.

He was three months short of being ten years older than Audry. She'd been five, he barely fifteen years old, when they'd sailed to Virginia with their mother and father. The only society she'd ever experienced were church socials and harvest celebrations. At fifteen, she'd been witness to the gruesome death of her parents and the destruction of their way of life. Mrs. Dorsey was right, it was past time Audry experienced some personal attention, a bit of pampering, a better way.

Audry had always been shy, and because of her trauma, Simon had perhaps been overprotective. She wasn't shy around the Dorseys, but he knew that when confronted with strangers in large gatherings, his sister could be withdrawn, unable to speak, overwhelmed even to the point of becoming nauseous. Since they'd arrived at the manor, she'd been kept busy. He'd been kept busy, and he had been remiss. He'd pushed aside his responsibility to bring his sister out of her shell. She needed some joy, some beauty.

The young woman he'd encountered this morning, and the young man, were the first people closer to Audry's and his age he'd met, although not formally, of course. Perhaps he should go to church as Ellen suggested and get acquainted with his neighbors.

As Simon thought these things, a sharp, searing pain

shot up his arm to remind him of why he did not go out into public. The fingers that were still on the end of his left hand twitched with the pain. He moved his hand between his legs to control the spasm but kept his face calm and unreadable to hide his discomfort from his sister and the Dorseys.

Partly to hide the pain and spasm, he leaned forward over the table. "Ellen is right. It is high time and a fine idea," he said to Audry. "Tomorrow morning, bright and early, you and Ellen will go shopping for new gowns and see a modiste to have some made up. You too, Ellen. I daresay it's been a while since you've had a new dress.

"I met two very nice young folks on the road this morning when I went chasing after Peg. The young man, I believe, is an old schoolmate from Eton. Don't think he recognized me. But I do remember him. I liked him. He was game but fair. I believe his name was Pat or Peter, no, maybe Paul Pomeroy," he said, a little too cheerfully, doing his best to ignore the pain in his arm.

Audry dabbed at the corner of her mouth with her napkin. "I don't need dresses. Goodness, I have several very good dresses, it's just that I don't wear them to beat the dust out of the carpets. And…brother mine, your lips have turned white, and I see your jaw has clenched up tight. It's your arm, isn't it? You pitched hay today. Too much hay. And you hammered and moved rails to suit that silly pig. You did too much."

He shook his head. "A little twinge, nothing to worry about. Ellen will dose me after we eat."

"I will," said Mrs. Dorsey with a nod to Simon.

"Good dresses?" Mrs. Dosey said, tsk-tsked, and shook her head. "I don't think so, miss. You've shot up and out some since your dresses were new. Styles have changed. This is 1816, not 1796. This is a civilized country, not a wilderness in some godforsaken land. Powdered wigs and whalebone are goin' out of style.

"And as far as you, sir, Master Simon, coming a little too brown with your, 'just a twinge. *Blarney*. Both of you work too hard. You will take a double dose of my tonic tonight and get a good night's sleep," Mrs. Dorsey said to Simon.

"I'll unearth the coach," Milo said to his wife. "I'll check the harness, and you ladies will go to town in style come mornin'."

Mrs. Dorsey gave her husband a quick kiss on the cheek.

"Now," Simon said and held up a hand to stop whatever protest Audry was about to give, "you have need of some fun, and buying new clothes is just the beginning. Come the sabbath, I will accompany you to church. Indeed, we will endeavor to seek out some of our neighbors, and we will introduce ourselves, emerge from our seclusion."

Audry studied him for a few pregnant moments, then shrugged her shoulders. "Very well. I want to hear about what happened this morning. I haven't seen you since breakfast. You said you met some people on the road this morning. Peg surely wasn't in the middle of the road?"

"That's just where he found her, miss," Milo said and snickered.

"I thought she might have gone to that grove of oaks across the road. But no, she was in the middle of the road wallowing in a mud puddle," Simon said. "I didn't have time to get her out of the way of the curricle. It was coming down the road at a far-from-safe pace, the team of white horses completely out of control. A young woman had the reins, doing all she could to slow the creatures down, bring them out of their panic. With skill and a good deal of luck, she managed to miss Peg by mere inches and only put one wheel of the curricle in the ditch. The young man, who was a passenger in the curricle, was greatly concerned for his team of prime cattle. They were winded and lathered, but that's all. We had little time to exchange names. Peg abandoned her mud bath for the bucket of mash and molasses I'd brought along to entice her home. As I needed both hands to help get the carriage wheel out of the ditch, I handed the bucket of feed off to the young lady. Peg instantly transferred her adoration to the young lady, of course. And the young lady started to stroke her behind her ears. And you know how Peg does love a good ear rub."

"If the young gentleman was tall with chestnut hair and a chiseled jaw, then that would be master Paul Pomeroy, from Pomeroy Chase, all right," said Ellen Dorsey. "The young lady, by your description of her havin' the reins and doin' a fine job of it, I'd say that would be his sister, Miss Pamela. Same chestnut hair, lots of it. Lovely girl, but she's a bit of a hoyden, or she was before her come-out a couple years ago. She cuts up a lark every now and then, but a good lass for all of that. She just jumps the traces from time to time. Nothing too outrageous. And there's another girl, younger, pretty behaved lass, Penelope, she's more of an age with our Audry.

"Yes, t'would be a good thing to become acquainted, be friends with the Pomeroy children. Fine people, the Pomeroy's. Treat their tenants right. They attend church. Lord Pomeroy was one of the few people who visited Sir Simon-Loyd from time to time. I remember he used to come over and play a board or two of checkers with the crotchety old gent. They'd share a bottle of brandy. My mother, God rest her soul, and I would keep them supplied with scones and honey."

Now the subject of the old traveling coach had been brought up it reminded Simon of some other chores, and soon he and Milo were deep in a discussion of the work that needed to be done. They'd taken care of Peg's accommodations, made her a larger crib, reinforced and revamped. But there was some planning that needed to be done before they could turn her out into a yard, especially if she had her little ones with her.

Audry helped Mrs. Dorsey clear the table and serve the men a slice of spiced apple cake. "I think we should make a list of the garments you'll be needing," Mrs. Dorsey said as she handed Audry some cake with a large dollop of clotted cream on the top.

She pointed the girl toward the table, her scowl indicating Audry should take a seat or have her ears burned with another scold. "It's more than dresses you'll be needin' I'm thinkin'. There's shoes, stockings, camisoles, under-dresses, bonnets, gloves. I've not touched a needle and thread to do more than patch and mend in a good long while. I wouldn't dare let myself hack up a good length of cloth. I used to be able to sew a pretty stitch, but these fingers no longer work like they used to. Now, Miss Gillespie, she's a proper modiste. Has a shop in Stilton. She's probably expensive, but she'd be the one to put together a presentable wardrobe suitable for a young lady of quality like yourself.

"The Pomeroy girls always look a treat, very stylish.

You're just as pretty, if not prettier, even in your old stuff gown. If your brother will get off his stumps and get you out and about, you'll soon outshine them all."

****

Audry smiled back at the woman, but her heart was not in this plan. Being in England was much easier than living in the colonies. The surrounding countryside, the farm, the warmhearted Dorseys had made her forget, or at least accept, her parents' death, but meeting people and mixing with other people her own age would be difficult. She couldn't make Simon understand, and she certainly couldn't make Mrs. Dorsey understand when she didn't understand herself.

New clothes would bring attention to herself. She liked going to church and sitting among the Dorsey family, fading into the woodwork. Hard work and lots of it had been her way to escape.

After the evening meal at the manor, Simon had acquired the habit of going to the front parlor to sit in the inglenook before the fire in the great stone hearth and enjoy his churchwarden pipe. Mrs. Dorsey literally pushed Audry out of the kitchen, so she followed Simon to the parlor and took a seat on the settee nearest the flames to warm herself while Simon filled the bowl of the long-stemmed pipe with tobacco.

Tobacco, when lit, smelled of Virginia and brought forth memories of home and her father and her mother, who also smoked a churchwarden pipe. Audry loved the smell but didn't indulge. She'd tried, but the smoke burned her throat and eyes and sent her into a coughing spasm. Simon had taken the habit of using the very pipe her father had used. Her mother's pipe sat in the pipe holder of the humidor on the occasional table before her.

She touched it and adjusted the angle.

Simon stood with his left hand thrust deep in the pocket of his wool trousers and one foot resting on the andiron. “Mrs. Dorsey is right, you know. It’s time you met some society. It’s no good you’re hiding away, head down, always doing some chore. The longer you avoid going out and about, the more acute your shyness will become. I don’t want that for you. Mother and Father would not want that for you. They would want you to have a home of your own, with children, love, fulfillment. It’s what I want for you too. If we were still in the colonies, you might have been married by now to some hard-working frontier man. You did attend socials when we lived there. You sang in the choir. You have a beautiful voice. We don’t live in the colonies now; we live here. We have neighbors, neighbors who are closer. They won’t eat you, Audry. They will be curious, probably a bit vacuous, perhaps, because of the lives they’ve been privileged to live, but they will admire you when they get to know you, I’m sure of it.”

Head bowed, hands in her lap, Audry said, “I don’t want to go into Stilton tomorrow. Maybe in a few days, I’ll go, but not tomorrow.”

“I know you don’t want to go.” He sat down beside her and laid the pipe in the brass tray on the table. “And I understand it is hard for you. It takes practice to be around strangers, people, and the only way to practice is to go among them. We’ll keep it slow at first and make a few good acquaintances. I think after you’ve gotten over the first few encounters, you will feel more relaxed. You’ll find, I think, there are many who feel exactly as you do, but they’ve had more opportunities to be thrust into the mainstream and have learned how to cope. You will, too. I don't want you to change. I love who you are. Stay strong, be confident in who you are, Audry. You have so much that other young women don't have. You've traveled, seen a part of the world others will never know or can imagine. Take heart, as Father would say, take heart and be resolute in your way and go forward, not backward." He took one of her hands in his, turned it over, and traced the callous on her palm with his finger.

She pulled her hand away, sat up a little straighter, and looked her brother straight in the eye. "We cannot afford gowns and the nonsense or for me to be a lady of leisure."

"Ah, so we get down to the practicalities and the reason I do love you so much. I would love to tell you to let me worry about what we can afford, but I know that would be wishful thinking on my part. So, I'll be truthful. Yes, we've spent a great deal of money on refurbishing this farm, the dairy, to make it work but…but it is going to start to pay almost immediately. It has started. And Peg is going to help us there. We have the dairy clean and producing to sell to the cheesemakers in Stilton. And the tenants are on their feet, working, and soon they will be showing a profit, which is more than they've been able to say for a very long time. Lambing season has already started, and soon we will go into shearing. We'll have wool for market as well as a litter of fine little piglets. I was going to tell you that you still have the trust Father set up. I thought we might use it as your dowry.

"Mr. Ledbetter has been busy. He sent me a letter listing his progress. He hopes to have it all settled and sorted before spring. I have some capital I've been holding on to. I originally thought to use it to get us into a place of our own. But now we have the Manor. We can use it for this very sort of necessity. And it is a necessity. You must resign yourself to being a young lady. You're an heir to Copeland Manor and you must present yourself accordingly, as must I. Sir Simon-Loyd disowned our mother, but as his grandchildren, I think Mother would want us to make him proud. I know Father would want us to succeed here. He always said it was a travesty what Sir Simon did to our mother, turning his back on her…on us."

Audry sat for a few moments and studied her brother's face. His lips were smiling, but his eyes begged her to bend to his will. She nodded. "And what of you, brother?"

"Me? What?"

"Do not gentlemen of quality also avoid hard labor? Are their hands not devoid of calluses and blisters? Do they not seek masculine entertainments and diversions? I, as a lady of quality, can hardly introduce my brother, manure on his boots, wearing a smelly pair of breeches and a slouch jacket as a proper gentleman. You will have to take yourself in hand, brother, for I will not allow you to bring disgrace to the family."

Simon, of course, laughed at her, but Audry remained pinched-lipped and very serious.

"What, may I ask, do you know of a gentleman's entertainments and diversions, little sister?"

Audry opened her mouth to tell him she knew quite a lot, certainly more than he thought she knew. She'd heard the sailors talking aboard the ship. While in London, she'd seen the dockside bordellos and heard the ladies hawking their talents. And she was also aware Simon did not partake of any of the offers he'd received from the ladies who worked those establishments, but she knew what went on inside those doors. She had a very good imagination. She'd been warned by Mrs. Murphy to stay clear of doorways and alleyways and be wary of men who approached her. Always be ready to run, Mrs. Murphy had told her. Drop everything, throw it at their heads, and run, was the woman's advice.

"Oh, very well," he said. "You've made your point, imp. But I do not plan to enter into society. You will, eventually, I hope when you marry a young man that I deem to be good enough for you," Simon said.

"So, you're going to be one of those," she said, her nose bunching up as if she detected a sour odor.

"One of those…?"

"Yes, an autocratic hypocrite, consigning me to society's whims and vagaries while you stay as far away from aristocratic machinations as possible. Come, come, you will surely be called upon to accompany me to any number of functions," she said and grinned right back at him. "Surely you would not cast me upon the vast social waters alone. I have no desire to be married. I've never thought of it. However, if I should, it will be my decision, and you will have very little to say in the matter. I will heed your advice, but I won't be dictated to."

She watched him closely. He tipped his head to the right and rubbed his left shoulder. "See," he said, "I told you, you are stronger than you think. I'm glad to hear you talk like this. It proves me right. You are ready, past ready, to get out of this house and mingle with people of your own age.

"But, as for me…I think I would make most people…society, uncomfortable," he said and came to his feet to gaze into the dying flames."

"At least your injuries are apparent. Mine are internal," Audry said. "I think both of us need to go forward, as you have said, as Father said. We've earned our scars, our wounds. We've become so consumed with our own survival that if we don't get out of our safe sanctuary soon, we'll become unrescuable recluses, and dementia will set in permanently. You have at least convinced me I should go into Stilton and buy those gowns, but I am also going to see if there is a good tailor in town, and you will go see him as soon as possible. If I have to mingle with the locals, so do you."

He didn't disagree. Audry sniffed back a stray tear. "Good, now that's settled, I will retire," she said and gave him an affectionate peck on the cheek.

"Goodnight, you sly puss," he said. She rose quickly and left the room.

Chapter Eight

Simon chuckled and shook his head. His little sister was maturing in more than one way. She'd just informed him she was her own person, and she could make her own decisions. He was proud of her. And yet, in a way, it made him very sad. He wished his mother were here to see and hear Audry stand up for herself. He poured himself a short glass of brandy and started to leave the room to go to his library. Before he reached the door, Mrs. Dorsey appeared on the threshold. "Ah, good, I'd hoped to catch you before you took to your library," she said and entered the room, head down.

"Ellen, I'm glad you chose to visit. I was going to speak to you in the morning, but I'll ask you now," Simon said and set his glass down on a side table. "Would you care to have a seat? May I pour you a brandy?"

"No, no. Good heavens no, thank you. I'll have me nog afore bed here in a tic or two," she said. "I won't take up much of your time."

"I always have time for you," Simon said. "Audry and I were discussing the changes we need to make. And one of the changes we should make is to get you and Milo more help. You were talking about sewing and the housework here, and I think it's time we find someone to help you. I'm hoping you might know of someone, a girl, I suppose, who might fit the bill. If she can sew and do household chores, that would be wonderful. And Milo, if we could get him some help, too, someone to look after the fires and help you with the heavy lifting. And someone to help in the garden and the upkeep of this old pile. Maybe someone who is good with a hammer and saw." He stopped talking. Mrs. Dorsey had started to fidget with her apron, gripping and folding it in her hands.

"I'm sorry," he said. "You wanted to speak to me, and I'm going on and on. Is there a problem? I haven't noticed there being anything amiss. I thought we were getting along."

Ellen shook her head. "We've no problems, Master Simon. Yes, yes, I think I know just the girl. She be my sister's oldest, Suzie Tidmore, be her name. She's a fine touch with needle and thread, and she's a good help in the kitchen. I know her mother would like to see her in a better situation. She be old enough now, six and twenty, married to a strong lad, Michael. He might like to come along. Milo, I know, thinks a lot of him."

"That sounds perfect," Simon said. "Do they live close by? Could we let them have the gatehouse? I looked in there a while back. Seemed a bit musty. Needs a good airing and a clean. The old furniture could be refurbished, I suppose. I think there's plenty of room for three or four families here. I walked through the east wing when we first moved in. I remember cobwebs and dust, but I didn't see any water damage or mildew.

"Do they have children? We'd have to think about that. I'm not saying I wouldn't want them if there were children, but we would want to make accommodations for children. Give them proper care. The gatehouse is close to the road but not visible. Might require a fenced-in space. We could manage that. I believe children climb rock walls. I know I did."

"They do have children. As it happens, they have two boys. They be three and five now, right little devils," Mrs. Dorsey said. "My sister sees to 'em most days. As it stands, Suzie walks to Stilton to work in one of the pubs every day. She walks home in the dark most of the time. We worry for her. And Michael is working long hours at the Bell Inn in the stable. If they could live here, it would be a dream come true for her mum, I can tell you. Right now, they share the cottage with my sister and her husband. My sister, Edna Ward, lives but a short distance from here on the other side of the fens on the Fairfield estate. Her husband, Wilber, was pensioned off when the Fairfield boys he tutored left for University. He was given a small cottage there. I'll see Suzie on the morrow and let her know you've made an offer. She'll talk to Michael. We should have their answer by the end of the day tomorrow."

He bowed in her direction. "I bow to your good judgment. You have complete authority to hire who you will." He stopped talking. The woman had shifted on her feet again. There was something bothering the good lady.

"But that's not what I wish to talk to you about, Master Simon," she said in a rush. "I come to give you an apology."

Simon pulled in his chin. "Apology? What on Earth for? You were quite right to steer me in the right direction where my sister is concerned. She needs young people, gaiety. She's been hiding here. I can see that now. I…we…I'm sure I want more for her. She deserves so much more. She's had enough ugliness, tragedy…sadness in her young life. Time she put all that behind her."

"Well, t'was not that, exactly, that I wished to apologize for. I'm not the least bit sorry for leading you, finally, to take a firm stand with your sister. I should have done that anyway. Never will I be sorry for gettin' your poor, lovely sister off her knees and on her way to being a proper young lady of quality as she should be. What I come here to crave is your pardon, Master Simon. Milo says it were wrong of me to question your religious persuasions, and the manner in which you choose to make your devotions. I had no right, and I'm embarrassed I pushed judgments too far."

Her admission was indeed shocking. Simon had all but forgotten Mrs. Dorsey's naked disapproval of his Sunday worship habits, or lack thereof, and pressed his lips together to stifle his propensity to laugh. He quickly turned his back to the good woman so she wouldn't see his amusement, for it would hurt her feelings greatly if she thought he was laughing at her, which he was, but with a warmth of feeling that held no ridicule.

"I see," he said after a pause to compose himself. "I do intend to take in Sunday services from now on, though, I must confess, only for the social benefit to our lives here. I accept your apology, but there was no need. I was not offended, and I could not be with any good advice you have to offer. Your opinion, Mrs. Dorsey...*Ellen*...is always gratefully expected and accepted. So let us forget this conversation. You continue to say what you will, when you will, and I will either take your advice or chuck it, but let us not change. I have known from the outset that you are in charge here. You oversee us all, and you are irreplaceable."

The woman blushed and smiled out of the side of

her mouth. "Perhaps, sir, some of the Lord's words will rub off on ye as soon as we get you into His house." Her words spilled out unchecked. She put her apron to her mouth, brown eyes crinkled up with amusement and embarrassment.

He knew she regretted her loose tongue, but he had to laugh at both of them now. "There is no stopping you," he said. "I have no wish to. I doubt any of us could. I'll go armed," he said with a grin. "I'll wear an armor plate over my heart, a helmet over my head, and cotton in my ears then," he said, shoulders shaking with barely suppressed mirth.

The lady started for the door, stopped on the threshold, turned on him, and said one word, her nose in the air, "Heathen."

Still chuckling to himself, he retrieved his glass of brandy and left the parlor. He crossed the halls and entered the library where he found waiting for him Mrs. Dorsey's bottle of tonic and a spoon beside a huge leather-bound ledger and a lamp lit with flame. In the yawning, massive hearth lay a few live embers. He poked at them, urging them to take heart, and laid some dry kindling over the top of the few remaining red coals.

Chapter Nine

Coal was dear in Huntingdonshire, and wood was even meaner to come by, but Milo had managed to keep the few rooms they used warm and well-supplied with both. The two wings of the house had been closed off for years. Sir Simon-Loyd had no need of the rooms, and now Simon and Audry had no use for them either. Simon thought it would be good to have at least the gatehouse occupied.

He and Audry had decided to take their meals in the kitchen with the Dorseys, not so much to economize but because the dining room was massive and drafty with high ceilings and wide windows that faced east, letting in the cold, damp wind that blew in off the fens that stretched out beyond the house as far as the eye could see.

The library was dark save for the lamp on his desk. The desk, the room, somber and isolated from the rest of the house, only one long, mullioned window, reflected the character of its former owner. Simon shivered thinking about his grandfather. He stood for a moment and stared at the gilded, ornately framed portrait of his ancestor, the father of his grandfather, the first Sir Simon-Loyd Copeland.

The man in the portrait had black, curly hair past his shoulders, piercing blue eyes, and a black mustache that did nothing to disguise his devilish, knowing smile. He was a well-set-up man, muscular. He was dressed in leather breeches, knee-high boots, a quilted woolen doublet that padded his arms and hugged his broad torso, and a black cape over one shoulder. He appeared a rogue, a risk taker. In his hand, he held a sheathed sword with a golden hilt. At his feet lay a large hound of some breed unfamiliar to Simon. Someday, Simon vowed, he would look up the history of this ancestor. He'd bet his pig he'd led a dashing life.

From time to time Simon did regret he'd never met his grandfather. He wondered if there was any resemblance between the man in the portrait and his grandfather. Had his grandfather smiled in that devilish way? Had he ever aspired to be a rogue, a scallywag?

And then, at other times, like right now, Simon felt relief he'd never met the man. Looking around him, he couldn't imagine the man who had wandered these dark, oppressive, cold halls ever smiling, ever laughing, ever loving.

Dark, open beams stretched across the ceiling and down the walls, forming bookshelves for volume upon volume of ledgers, books on tactical strategy, seamanship, and English history. The fire's light cast shadows on the ceiling and across the worn carpet on the floor.

Simon sat down in the throne-like, straight-back, hard oak chair at the desk. It made a soft, plaintive, creaking sound as if complaining about its age. He downed a swig of tonic, turned a page of the ledger and put his forehead in the palm of his left hand as he studied the figures in the volume before him. It wasn't long before his head grew heavy. He decided to rest his eyes. Folding his arms across the ledger, he laid his head there.

Just for a moment or two, he allowed, just a moment or two, he told himself.

****

A candle burning on her nightstand, Audry, sitting up in her big bed, laid her book of poems aside and went to her door. She opened it and listened for a moment or two, then went across the hall to Simon's room and knocked. She heard no sounds of movement and looked in. He wasn't there. She knew where to find him. She retrieved her dressing gown from her room and started down the stairs. The sconces were still alight at the foot of the stairwell. She heard the creak and squeak of the old floor. Leaning over the newel post on the stairwell landing, she saw Milo, candle alight, coming along the hall that led to the back of the house.

Milo stepped up the three steps from the back part of the house and onto the small landing before stepping down again to enter the grand entry hall.

"He's not in his room," Audry said.

No hint of surprise to hear or see her, Milo tilted his head, nodded, and set his candle down on a hall table.

"I left him in the sitting room," Audry whispered.

"Well, we'll have a look," he said. "Be my guess, he's gone to the library. Ellen spoke to him 'bout an hour or so ago. Let me check the door first. Batten it down for the night."

Audry looked into the front parlor, and it was dark, devoid of light save for a few embers in the inglenook hearth. She crossed the hall to the library. She could make out the slumped form of her brother seated behind the desk even though the lamp light was faint. She tiptoed across the room and nudged his shoulder, his good shoulder. He didn't even protest. His breathing was steady and regular. She hated to wake him. She tapped him on the head. He shifted his position.

Milo came to the desk. "I'll get the lad to his bed, miss." He came around and gave Simon a good shake. "Come on, lad. You've gone to sleep at your desk. We need to get you up to your bed."

"Simon, Simon," Audry said and touched his cheek. "Come along now. Milo and I will get you to bed."

Simon brought up his head and blinked in an attempt to focus. "Asleep? So I did. Blasted ledger worked better than a bedtime story," he said and chuckled. "That, and Ellen's tonic and a glass of brandy," he said and struggled to his feet.

Milo caught him and put Simon's right arm around his shoulder. Audry took up Simon's other side, careful of his wounded arm and shoulder. Between the two of them, they got him up the stairs and to his room.

"Here now, miss. I'll take it from here."

To Simon, Milo said, "I'll be your gentleman's gentlemen tonight, shall I, sir?"

Audry stood on the threshold as Milo deposited her brother on the bed and bent down to remove his shoes. She closed the door on them and retreated to her own room. She sat on the edge of the bed until she heard Milo go back down the stairs before getting under her covers.

****

Lying in the great bed, the one where his grandfather had spent his lonely nights, a candle casting eerie shadows on the wall and ceiling, Simon rubbed his left shoulder. His fingers roamed once again over the scars and dents in the muscle tissue that made craters in his shoulder and upper arm. He had nearly died of his wounds, and then, it had seemed that in order to save his life, he would have to lose the arm. But due to improper medical attention and the fact that Simon fought tooth and nail against the plan, the arm had been spared, but it was mutilated. Not only the digits on his hand but the muscle and tendons were damaged to a severe degree. It had been pure stubborn will. He'd slowly regained control and made his appendage strong and useful again, though it would never be the same as it once had been.

Unconsciously, he thought over the day's events, and a sly smile crossed his face. The vision of a pretty young woman, her glorious reddish-brown hair flying, brown eyes dancing with sparks of gold, cheeks flushed, swam before his mind's eye. He let forth a chuckle, recalling how Peg had advanced on the young lady. He had no business thinking about pretty young women with reddish-brown hair or women of any age, with any color hair. He wasn't whole. He wasn't anything any woman would want or need.

Chapter Ten

In anticipation of the visit to Copeland Manor, Pamela rose early and dressed in her cherry-red riding coat over her black wool skirt and warm jersey blouse and proceeded down to the breakfast room. She was the second to arrive. Paul, at the sideboard, filled his plate. Next to arrive, their father greeted them with a cheery good morning. Lady Alice followed him still in her night rail, robe, and slippers. Penny arrived late, looking half asleep, dressed for a cold winter's day in a moss-green gown of soft wool and a cream-colored sweater vest.

Her children knew better than to start a conversation before their mother had a chance to fill her plate and take at least four sips of her tea. "Well, you must postpone your visit," she said at last and added more treacle to her cup. "It's snowing."

Pamela's heart rate picked up. She looked down at her hands and held her breath.

"A few flakes," Paul said. "Not even sticking. Too warm—soon, turn to rain."

Pamela closed her eyes and allowed herself to take a breath.

"Well, if you must, then take the carriage," Lady Alice said and held her cup up for the maid, who stood hovering near the sideboard, to come fill it.

Lord John cleared his throat, declined to have his teacup refilled, and said, "I think we should ride, don't you, Paul? Less than a couple miles to Copeland Manor."

It was all Pamela could do to stay in her chair. She pressed her lips tightly together, for it would not do to appear over-eager at this point in the conversation.

"I think that's an excellent suggestion," her brother said.

"If it's a ride, then I'm definitely going along. I was going for a ride this morning anyway," Pamela said, as offhand as possible. "I should go. Apologize for my less than grateful acceptance of that fellow's assistance."

It was early afternoon before they were able to leave. Right after breakfast, Paul escaped to the stables to work for a while with his flighty, high-strung team. And Lord John went along. It seemed he'd taken an interest in the pair. Pamela spent the morning with her sister sewing sequins on a headdress that matched a gold ball gown. She was beginning to hate the color. And she really, really, really thought sequins ridiculous, unnecessary, and she was certain her stitches would come loose anyway.

Despite Lady Alice's protestations and predictions that they would regret their decision, they were able to start out right after their late luncheon.

The snowflakes were the size of goose feathers, wet and sloppy. Dark clouds were gathering to the north, and the birds were swooping and diving. Soon, her lovely shako hat with the ostrich plume in the black velvet band would be ruined. As it was, the blasted feather was drooping horribly with wet snow. She had to swipe it out of her eyes more than once. A puddle of melting snow was forming in the skirt between the top pommel and the leaping horn of her ladies' saddle. The snow was making her shoulders and sleeves soggy, creating a contrast from cherry-red to plum. The wet spot on her skirt wouldn't be too terribly noticeable, as her skirt was black, but just the same this weather was out to mar the sophisticated effect of her ensemble, and she did want to look her best. Pamela had no doubt she'd looked a fright yesterday: hair a mess, windblown, skirts muddy from that silly pig. She had hoped to make a better impression today. She refused to answer why. Why should she want to impress a grinning farmer? No, she didn't want to examine that question.

****

At mid-morning, Simon saw Audry and Mrs. Dorsey off with Milo driving the old coach pulled by the team of aging draft horses. He explained to Audry and Mrs. Dorsey that with the bank draft, they could spend up to two hundred and fifty pounds. If expenses were more than that, they were to instruct the tradespeople to send the bill to him, and he would see it paid directly. Not having made a lot of clothing purchases in the last couple of years, neither Audry nor Simon knew how much cash would be needed to replenish their wardrobes.

But two hundred and fifty pounds would strain the budget. Worried about cost and wondering if he'd given Audry enough money to purchase more than one or two dresses, he spent a few hours seeing to the regular chores: feeding, cleaning, talking to all the animals. It wasn't noon, but he was hungry and headed for the back of the house and the kitchen.

Mrs. Dorsey had left him a note explaining in great detail the food he could take for his lunch and instructions as to how it should be prepared. He took some of her advice and warmed the potato soup, locating it in the red kettle in the pantry right where Mrs. Dorsey had said it would be, and added more butter. But he didn't bother with the biscuits, even though all he had to do was put them on a baking sheet and brown them. Instead, he opted for a plain piece of cottage bread. On his way back outside, he nibbled on a cube of Milo's special recipe, his version of Stilton cheese.

He went back to work enlarging and reinforcing the pig cribs. Peg was due to deliver in less than a month. The plan was to give the family both an indoor crib and an outdoor, enclosed yard to provide room for them to roam a bit to forage. Boris, the father of the expectant brood, grunting and lunging, kept shoving Simon into the corners and, in general, making himself a big pest.

He finished patching the roof of the indoor pen and started to gather up his tools and take them to the barn when he heard the sound of horses. He thought it could be Audry and the Dorseys returning, but he didn't hear the sounds of a lumbering coach and old, jangling harness.

He stepped over the rails of the pen and went out into the barnyard to listen, and yes, he could hear horses coming up the lane. He looked down to the pig manure on his boots and trousers and the sleeves of his coat and quick-walked to the back of the house. He managed to shuck his boots, his coat, and his old sweater when the first summons rang at the front of the house. Stripped down to his collarless work shirt of homespun and wool trousers, he washed his hands and face in the cold water from the pitcher on the worktable at the back stoop.

The second sound of the bell echoed throughout the house. There was a pair of his old leather moccasins under the worktable. He slipped those on over his stocking-encased feet. He snatched a well-worn leather jerkin off the peg to the side of the pantry door and rushed through the kitchen. Up two steps, he entered a dark hall and passed the dining room. Wincing, hip screaming in pain, he leaped down three steps to enter the wide, paneled hall that opened to the main entrance of the manor.

The bell sounded again with an impatient, jangling ring. He could hear voices, none of them recognizable, and couldn't imagine who in the world could be paying a call.

****

The snow had stopped, none of it sticking, but making the ground slushy and sloppy wet. Paul held the reins of her mount, and Pamela slid to the ground from her saddle. Their father took the reins and tied them off at the hitching rail at the head of the stone walkway. Pamela had never seen Copeland Manor up close. It appeared a bit sad, white plaster here and there stained with black mold, the windows showing grime, dark, and neglected, deserted. Walking along a white stone path overgrown with dead flowers and herbs, the three of them approached the house. After ringing the bell to the side of the massive, brass-studded, and old timber door three times, it would seem no one was home.

Pamela, standing a little to the side of her father, stared in fascination at the stunningly handsome, unkempt, extremely virile man who, at last, opened the door. It was her farmer. He'd answered the Manor door. She hadn't expected that.

"Hello," her father said and tipped the brim of his hat with the touch of his gloved hand.

The farmer stood, mouth open for a brief second, then shook his head and smiled. Oh, the smile, his smile, a blend of humility and sarcasm lit up his blue eyes. That mocking smile and those blue eyes had haunted Pamela's dreams.

Leather jerkin, half on and half off, one arm, the one with the mutilated fingers, struggled to find the opening to the arm hole of the leather vest. Pamela had to resist the urge to help him and tightened her hand around her wrist.

"Hello, come in, come in, the weather is foul," he said and tugged the old, scabbed leather vest up to his shoulder with his right hand. He looked beyond them to their horses and said, "You're out for a ride? You must be cold to the quick. At least the snow has stopped."

Chapter Eleven

The farmer—her farmer, he'd answered the door in his shirt sleeves and trousers wearing strange slippers; they were beaded. She could see his stockings. His glossy, black hair curling over his high forehead and around his ears appeared damp, as if he'd just washed his face and neck. His homespun shirt was open at the throat, revealing a thin crop of black, curly hair and, beneath the hair, a scar. Not a line of old, white scar but the map of an angry red and purple scar. His blue, blue eyes danced with warmth and welcome. But it was the scar, the red, raised scar, that caught Pamela's eye. She couldn't see all of what was hidden beneath his shirt at the shoulder, but she could see enough to know that it must still cause discomfort.

Right then, a coach rolled into the yard and stopped right in front of the walk near their horses. The driver of the old, ornately decorated coach, his leather hat hiding his face, scrambled down and started to open the carriage door so the passengers could exit. First, he helped a dainty young lady dressed in an elegant traveling costume of deep slate blue. The lovely shako hat that matched the fabric of her traveling costume shaded her elfin face. She kept her head down but gave a furtive glance in Pamela's direction. Standing very still, arms folded at her waist, she waited for the woman who had alighted from the coach behind her. That lady, her arm around the girl's waist, propelled the girl, walking beside her as if shielding her, up the short walk to the entrance.

"Mrs. Dorsey," Lord John said and came forward. "Good to see you looking well," he said.

Pamela knew Mrs. Dorsey, of course, and she and her family were longtime residents of the parish. True, Mrs. Dorsey was looking very smart in a tartan wool cape of deep green and purple with a red stripe and a green bonnet to match.

"Lord Pomeroy, you've come to call and me not here to open the door to ye and welcome you in," said Mrs. Dorsey. "We've been gone to Stilton this day shoppin'. You must come inside. Can't have you standin' about out here. I'll get up some tea and my scones."

"Milo," Lord John called out over Mrs. Dorsey's head. "I see you got the old landau out and rolling. Haven't seen that grand old equipage out and about in a long while."

"Aye, she still rolls a treat," Milo said with a grin. "She's old and faded but well-sprung and built to last. The team of drays was eager to get back in harness, too."

Lord Pomeroy shook the man's hand. "Sir Simon-Loyd was very proud of it. Took great pleasure rolling into the churchyard in the grand style of a Sunday in that coach."

****

Embarrassed that he'd come to the door with his shirt open, scars exposed, Simon cursed the timing of this visit and fumbled with the toggles on his jerkin. The young lady, his intrepid carriage driver, Peg's friend—she'd stared at his scars and his feet. The moccasins, she'd noticed his footwear or lack of it. Simon couldn't remember ever blushing. Oh, maybe he had, as a boy, but he knew he was blushing now. He was sweating, too. Stange, he didn't even feel the urge to laugh at himself.

He didn't know what to do first: he should rescue Audry, but he had to see to the horses, no, he had guests, he should get them inside, no the horses, he had to take them to the stable, introductions, he should make introductions…he didn't know what to do. Mrs. Dorsey, bless her, saved him and said to her husband, "Milo, you might take Lord Pomroy's cattle with you to the stable, give them a rub, dry the saddles."

Milo set to unhitch the horses and tied them off to the back of the coach. Mrs. Dorsey nodded and turned her back on her spouse. She put her hand on Audry's waist to steer her forward into the house, "Now," she said, stepping around all gathered upon the entrance, "come in, come in and warm yourselves."

To Simon, she said, "Off you go. Encourage the fire in the front parlor to warm your guests."

To their guests, she said, "Let me take your wraps and hats, and we'll see if we can get them dry. I'll bring shawls, shall I, to warm the ladies." To Lord John, she said, "So good of you to call. It's been too long." She gave an encouraging nod to Simon, who stood stunned, in awe of Mrs. Dorsey's skill as a general.

"Yes, yes, please, come," Simon said. He took his paralyzed-into-silence sister by the elbow and waved his company forward. Audry's body was shaking. She gripped his hand like a drowning woman and walked with him to the front parlor. He was a bit shaky himself.

"I'm sorry I was tardy in answering the door and left you outside in this weather," he said as they crossed the grand entryway, their footsteps echoing in the great hall.

"I was in the barns. I'd just come in. I beg your pardon to be receiving you in a state of deshabille. I hope you will excuse me," he said and slid the heavy, paneled drawing room door aside.

"Milo and I have been working hard to bring the dairy barn and the cribs up to snuff." Flustered, he knew he was over-explaining but couldn't stop himself. "We hope to replace some of our milch cows. They'll expect a clean, orderly barn. As I understood it, milk production had fallen off considerably. I think we're making headway now. The dairymen and milkmaids, I've been told, are pleased with the changes we've made so far." He clamped his mouth shut, embarrassed for going on and on about his damn dairy. These people didn't care. They were being polite.

He took a deep breath and glanced down at Audry; she'd turned her head away. "Audry and Mrs. Dorsey have been working on the inside of the Manor house." He felt like a schoolboy, making excuses for his appearance, the condition of the rooms, everything. "We've not opened all the rooms yet, not with just the two of us here and the Dorseys to look after us."

Silent, nodding, eyes taking in their surroundings and smiling, his guests followed him into the formal parlor, the only parlor they had thus far refurbished. The room wasn't as cold as Simon feared it would be. The fire in the giant hearth was very much aglow. He motioned his guests toward the inglenook, and he guided a still-trembling Audry to a chair near the hearth while he added a few coals to the fire.

"Well, I feel we are the ones who should apologize," Lord Pomeroy said. He stepped forward and held out his hand. "We did arrive unannounced. I am your neighbor to your south, Lord John Pomeroy, from Pomeroy Chase. We've come, although belatedly, to welcome you," he said, his hand outstretched for Simon to shake.

"Welcome to Copeland Manor, Lord Pomeroy," Simon said with a slight bow. "Simon Lawrence at your service, and this is my sister Audry Lawrence."

Lord John stopped before Audry, took her hand in his, and gave her a bow and a smile before stepping back to say, "Pleased to meet you, Miss Lawrence."

To Simon, he said, "I believe you met two of my children yesterday. This is Paul," he said.

Paul stepped forward and shook Simon's hand, his good hand. Simon had his left hand, fingers clenched, stuffed down deep in his trouser pocket.

"We were very well met yesterday," Paul Pomeroy said with a winning smile on his handsome face. "We were lucky you were there. Thank you again for your assistance. I don't s'pose you remember me," Paul said, "but I think you were at Eton around the same time I was there."

"Yes, I believe so," Simon said. "I thought I recognized you yesterday. I wasn't sure. We were on the rowing team together, if I recall."

"That's right. I wasn't very good at it. You were outstanding."

"Well, we were children then. We've both changed some since then for the better. It was good fun. And I will always remember that."

Paul nodded in agreement.

"May I introduce you to my sister, Audry," Simon said to Paul.

Paul Pomeroy hesitated, then gave Audry a very careful bow. He stepped back, never taking his gaze from her bowed head. “It is an honor to meet you, Miss Lawrence,” he said, his voice low and intimate.

Audry straightened her shoulders, brought up her head, and then bravely offered the young man a shy, quivering little smile. Her voice barely above a whisper, she said, “A pleasure to meet our neighbors.”

Proud of her, Simon took a breath. There was a heavy silence for a moment or two, as if something important had just taken place.

“And this is Pamela, my daughter, my eldest daughter,” Lord Pomeroy said, cutting into the silence.

Pamela Pomeroy met Simon’s gaze directly. She didn’t flinch or portray hesitation in any way. “Father is right,” she said, “we should apologize for arriving on your doorstep unannounced. I’ve come along to make a special apology. I believe I was less than gracious yesterday. Rude, I think you would say. I came to apologize.”

He chuckled and shook his head. “Under the circumstances I thought you amazingly adroit both in word and deed. Very impressive. I accept your apology,” he said and offered her a slight bow, “even though I don’t think it necessary.” He took her hand, his gaze lost in her wonderfully gold-flecked, brown eyes. “Very pleased to meet you, Miss Pomeroy,” he said before he turned to his sister. “Miss Pomeroy, my sister Audry.”

Miss Pomeroy offered him a slight curtsy, then took the chair next to Audry and put her hand out to the arm of her chair. “Audry, very happy to meet you. I and my sister Penny, we will all, I am sure, become fast friends.”

Turning her attention back to Simon, Pamela said, “We are pleased to meet you, Sir Simon, and you, Audry.”

Taken aback at the use of the title, Simon rushed to make the correction. "I should explain," Simon said, "I haven't inherited my grandfather's, Sir Simon-Loyd's title, at least not as far as I know. The lawyers are still sorting all that out. Our father, Wyatt Lawrence, was third or fourth in line for the Baron Lawrence title. He was from Northumberland. I have no idea where that stands today. Our father was very aware he had to make his own way. It is really by chance that we find ourselves here at all. I didn't know, when we arrived in England a year ago, that our grandfather had been searching for his daughter, our mother, or his grandchildren. We had been living in Virginia. It was by chance that, when we lost our mother and father under tragic circumstances, Audry and I decided to return to England. We could have just as easily stayed in Virginia."

"Well, we, as your neighbors, are very glad you made that decision," Lord Pomeroy said. "And I'm going to go out on a limb here and say that I think your grandfather would be very pleased, overjoyed you've come home. Copeland Manor needs you.

"I used to visit your grandfather from time to time. We'd play a board or two of checkers. I'd supply the brandy. Mrs. Ayers, Mrs. Dorsey's mother, would supply the tea and scones. He never said much, but I know your grandfather was very lonely here. He was here in this big house all alone save for Mrs. Ayers and her daughter Ellen. And when Mrs. Ayers passed, her daughter stayed on. Ellen married Milo Dorsey. He was one of the dairymen at the time. Your grandfather regretted turning his only child away. And he was very angry and sad when you left the country. Everyone knew he was losing some of his faculties, memory loss, dementia, that sort of thing. He didn't know where you'd gone or why."

Simon shook his head. "I believe Mother wrote to him a few times. But after we left England for Virginia, I don't know if she did or not. She rarely mentioned him."

"Well, I'm interested in this pig. I understand she is quite large," Lord Pomeroy said, a twinkle in his eye but a serious set to his lips.

Chapter Twelve

The conversation between the men turned to the pig and the dairy.

With nothing to contribute to that conversation, Pamela turned to the shy young woman next to her. Upon introduction, Pamela thought she recognized the girl. She'd seen her somewhere before. But she couldn't exactly say where or when. Due to her slight frame and stature, at first, Pamela thought the girl to be younger than Penny, maybe fourteen or so. She had a delicately featured face, flawless complexion, and eyes the color of a deep blue sea on a stormy day. But upon closer inspection, Pamela thought Audry Lawrence could be a bit older than Penny. There was an old soul behind those eyes and the furtive glances. She'd heard the term, old soul, used before but never understood it until now. It wasn't innocence Pamela sensed in the depths of those orbs, it was apprehension as if she knew too much, seen, experienced too much. Her thoughts brought Pamela back around to the scars she'd seen on Simon Lawrence's chest. Perhaps his sister had scars as well. He had said they'd lost their parents under tragic circumstances. What exactly did he mean by that?

At first glance, as they entered this sitting room, she'd sensed the woman's touch, and her heart sank a little to think there must be a wife. The wood paneling was polished, the furniture dated and worn, but clean tapestry seat covers on the chairs, footstools, and settee were mended and placed well for conversations and arranged to take advantage of the warmth of the fire in the impressive inglenook. Now, to find there was no Mrs. Lawrence, but there was a sister, Pamela was inexplicably relieved. She didn't want to delve into all of the reasons why she felt relief. At the moment, how to put Audry at ease, was the question she asked herself.

"Shopping in Stilton is limited at best," she said. For lack of imagination to think of any other topic, she chose every woman's pleasure and quest—shopping, hoping to discover a likewise interest. "We are fortunate to have Miss Gillispie. She is reasonably priced and manages to keep up with the latest styles. I have no aptitude for sewing."

Audry tipped her head to the side and managed a tight, guilty little smile. "She seemed very nice. I…I mean, she was most helpful and kind. I have not one jot of knowledge or experience of what is the current style. I must defer to the opinion of others. I certainly wouldn't attempt to sew a fashionable gown. I wouldn't know where to start."

Pleased to have gotten a good response, Pamela continued in this vein. "I can't imagine following a pattern. I detest fittings. But we must. Ready-made gowns are rare. Miss Gillispie has a wonderful selection of fabrics for such a small shop. And she is remarkably quick to deliver. She does employ several local ladies in her shop. I've spoken to a few of them, and they all appear well treated and glad for the employment, unlike some of the modistes in London and how they treat their employees."

A sparkle lit up her wonderful eyes. Audry raised

her head and turned to Pamela to say, "She had this," she said, stroking the fabric of her corded skirt. "It's a traveling costume. It was one of three garments Miss Gillispie had on mannequins in her back room where her seamstresses were working. She said they were made by mistake. I didn't believe that for a moment. I think she makes a few dresses, coats, capes, and traveling costumes in advance in hopes someone like me will walk into her shop and, with a few alterations, they will purchase them. She said that once she saw my eyes, she knew she'd made them for me. Fustian, I say. There were alterations, but nothing major. I never hoped to have anything so fine as this, this traveling costume. And the dresses fit me so well. All of the garments are surprisingly comfortable, and I love the colors and fabrics. This traveling costume is lovely and warm. I might never take it off." The girl actually let forth a soft trill of laughter. It wasn't a girlish giggle. It was a genuine spurt of joy and wonder.

"Once the woman has your measure, you can be sure every garment she fashions for you will fit you to a T. And thank goodness, because fittings are no fun. Which, come to think of it, might explain the dresses you saw on the mannequins. They were, no doubt, made from a pattern and put together, say with a basting stitch, which would lend the garments to easy alterations. Interesting—and interesting that you sussed her marketing strategy. I'd never thought of it," Pamela said and reached for Audry's hand, the hand she had resting on the arm of her chair. They exchanged a knowing, womanly smile, and Pamela knew then and there she was going to love this young woman. Love her like a sister. The house, Simon Lawrence, her gentleman farmer, and now Audry, it all had come together—even the silly pig had become very important, important to her way forward.

****

Simon heard Audry laugh. The sound, the purity of it, took him by surprise. A lump came to his throat. He thought he might begin to weep. Paul Pomeroy was speaking, recounting their initial meeting. He had to fight his runaway emotions and pay attention. Miss Pomeroy had accomplished in a few minutes of acquaintance what he had been working toward for months and months—she'd gotten his sister to laugh.

On a purposeful mission, Mrs. Dorsey, followed by another young woman, hustled into the room. Mrs. Dorsey offered Miss Pomeroy a tartan shawl of red, blue, and green, declaring the parlor drafty and assuring her the riding coat was drying nicely. She then laid a knitted blue shawl over Audry's lap and winked at her.

The young maid, who followed Mrs. Dorsey into the parlor, balanced a tray containing the tea and scones. Simon had no idea who the young woman was. She set the tea tray down on the table in front of Audry. He didn't know how this young woman had gotten there or where she'd come from. He noted Audry didn't appear surprised or even interested in the young maid. She simply gave the young woman a little smile and a nod of approval.

"You know it's the heavy cream," Lord Pomeroy said, "it's the secret ingredient in Mrs. Dorsey's scones. Everyone knows the cream from Copeland Manor makes the best butter, always has—sweet and creamy. It's the feed, I've been told. Mrs. Dorsey's mother shared that little tidbit with me a long time ago." He came forward and took a chair close to the table where the tea had been laid out by the mystery maid and smiled at Audry.

Hands shaking ever so slightly, Audry poured his lordship a cup, offered him a saucer, and indicated he could help himself to the pitcher of cream, the treacle, and the rum in the silver flask, which, Simon presumed, Mrs. Dorsey had added for the pure extravagance of it. Audry placed a scone on a napkin and set it down on the table in front of Lord John. He nodded and took a big bite of it and closed his eyes in rapture.

Simon caught Mrs. Dorsey at the parlor door. The mystery maid skittered out, head down, and escaped into the hall. "Who is that?" he asked in a whisper.

"That is Suzie," Mrs. Dorsey said, whispering behind her hand.

"Where did she come from?" Simon asked.

"She was in the coach when we arrived," Mrs. Dorsey said. "I asked her to hold back out of sight until we were all inside. Poor girl, she couldn't wait to get out of that pub. She quit on the spot. She came shopping with us. She and Audry hit it off right away and helped to get your sister to decide on some very fine things. She even talked me into a new cape, a hat, and a dress. You'll probably be getting a bill from the modiste," she said, begging his forgiveness with her eyes. "We spoke to Michael. He's giving notice today. I think they'll move into the gatehouse tomorrow."

"Mrs. Dorsey, you have a sneaky side to you that both frightens and delights me."

"You have guests," she said, reminding him he had to play host.

The lump in his throat ached. A tear escaped out of the corner of Simon's eye. As Paul took a chair next to his father, Simon wiped the tear off his cheek and came forward for tea. Tea with his neighbors. Tea with his sister pouring, acting hostess, smiling, laughing again when she dribbled a bit of treacle on her fingers as she poured some of the syrup into her own cup.

****

Audry Lawrence sucked the treacle from her fingertips. Paul forgot to breathe. Her laughter did funny things to his insides—the sound of it was like music. He swallowed and closed his mouth. She didn't bat her eyelashes, or simper, or even glance in his direction. She was totally without guile. Everything about Audry Lawrence was genuine. She was shy, yes, but not in an artificial way. When she did speak, it was with a great deal of thought and purpose, no pretense. She was very specific and direct.

He didn't think she was aware of how beautiful she was. Her hair was thick, black as a raven's wing. It curled and waved in a heavy coil over one shoulder. She was slight of build, but there was a strength about her in the way she set her lips, the lift of her chin, the way she sat so straight, shoulders back, and those eyes, those bluer than blue cat eyes.

His father had surprised him with his interest in the dairy and the pig. He'd taken an interest in his team of whites, but Paul thought it his father's way of being polite.

This was different. His father had made certain Paul knew someday he would be the one to step into his shoes in every way. As the Lord of Pomeroy Chase, it was up to Lord John and his heir to see the needs of the tenants were met. And met with care and thought. There were families that depended on him. He would take up the mantle. He would be required to see to it the tenant homes were sound, children healthy, and the elderly properly pensioned. Lord John oversaw their lands and the crops, but Paul had no idea his father knew so much about dairy farming or that he was at all interested in raising pigs.

Chapter Thirteen

"Would you mind very much showing me this animal?" asked Lord Pomeroy. Pamela heard her father's question. She and Audry abandoned their conversation, interested, they waited for the answer.

"Certainly," her farmer said. "I've bred her with the British Lop boar that was here when we arrived. As I said, Peg is half Red Wattle and Gloucestershire Old Spot. We brought Peg with us when we left Virginia. She was only a few days old at that time. Her family was gone, too. We would have had to give her away, and after losing our parents, neither Audry nor I could do that. She did well aboard the ship—the crew took her on as, more or less, their mascot. We had her with us at all times. She kept growing and growing. Once we landed in England, she was a good size and as friendly and tame as a pup. Here, at Copeland Manor, she fell in love with Boris, and we have the potential for a fine litter of piglets."

Paul put his hand over his mouth to cover his smirk. Pamela shook her head as she and her brother exchanged incredulous glances. And Audry folded her hands in her lap and smiled. To Pamela, at least, it was obvious this man, her farmer, was besotted with his pig breeding, his dairy, and everything farm related. He was openly, and without reserve, a farmer and apparently, proud of it.

She'd known men, her brother in particular, who were obsessed with all things equine and carriage, but they also enjoyed society.

Something warned her this was not the case with her gentleman farmer. He was not the least bit interested in anything society had to offer. From his admission, it was obvious he cared nothing for titles. He'd answered the door to guests in his shirt sleeves. All he cared about was Copeland Manor and his sister. He did care for her, he cared a great deal. Pamela knew that by the way his gaze followed her, watched her, even listened in on her conversations, and the way he deferred to her in his manner. No, the man loved his sister, guarded her, and lo to the man who would dare to pursue her and win her heart.

This brought her around to Paul. Paul also followed Audry's every word and gesture. He was smitten. Perhaps she and her brother were both in danger of entering uncharted waters. She found the prospect enticing, challenging, and life-altering, whether for good or ill, Pamela could not say.

"I should be glad of your opinion," her farmer said. "It has started to snow again," he said, his gaze traveling to the floor-to-ceiling, mullioned windows. "We'll go through the kitchen, that will bring us closer to the barn and pig cribs. We'll see if Mrs. Dorsey has your coat and hat dried," he suggested to her father.

He turned and addressed her brother, "Paul, would you care to join us?"

Paul appeared startled by the invitation. He smiled and said, "I will decline to renew my acquaintance with Peg at this time."

"Miss Pomeroy? What say you?" her farmer asked, "Do you wish to say hello to Peg? I'm sure she would be happy to see you."

Pamela did not appreciate her brother's smirk or her farmer's dare, but she managed to smile and laugh off the playful challenge. "I will see her on another day. I'm warm and comfortable right here by the fire, thank you. You may give her an extra rasher of her favorite mash from me if you choose."

He bowed to her and smiled that dare-devil smile of his, blue eyes full of sparks of mischief. "She will appreciate your thoughtfulness," he said. "I will give her your regards."

Pamela nodded in return.

****

Paul waited until his father and Simon left the room, and then he approached Miss Lawrence. "I see you have a fortepiano. Do you play?"

She shook her head. "No, but I sing. Or I used to, in the choir."

"Pamela plays. She's very good. What say we have a duet? Do you know the words to 'Lavender's Blue'?"

Audry laughed. "I do, as a matter of fact. Simon tries to whistle that tune. He always gets lost and has to start over. Sometimes, he ends up whistling another tune altogether and mixing the two."

"Music, excellent suggestion," said Pamela. She rose from her chair, set her teacup and saucer aside, and made herself comfortable on the bench before the piano. She experimented with the keys, playing a few experimental chords, nodded, and began.

Audry opened her lovely mouth, and the most beautiful soprano voice came through. Paul nearly forgot to do his part. Soon they were in perfect harmony.

****

The second Audry Lawrence opened her mouth, and

her beautiful voice filled the room, Pamela knew where she'd seen the girl before. She'd seen her in church seated with the Dorseys. Why she had been there and not seated in the Copeland pew, Pamela did not know. She'd been dressed in a dowdy gray cape and bonnet to match. The cape hid her figure, the hat hid her lovely face, and Pamela had thought her one of the Dorsey family children. Of Simon Lawrence, there had been no sign. She would have remembered him if he had been seated with the Dorseys. It would have been impossible to ignore his smile, his presence. He resembled the Dorsey clan in no way. They were all rather short, rotund, ruddy-faced, and of a sober, unsmiling nature.

Why had these two people hid themselves here? Were they hiding? Or were they just anti-social? She rather suspected the former of Audry, possibly, and the latter of her brother. Time would tell.

They finished a round of "Blow Ye Winds," and Mrs. Dorsey appeared with a fresh pot of tea. She gave them an approving nod. "Fresh scones. I reckon Mr. Simon and Lord Pomroy will be in shortly. I have your wraps dried," she said and backed out of the room.

"Do you ride, Miss Lawrence?" asked Paul.

Audry poured a fresh cup of tea, added a liberal amount of treacle and cream as he had taken it before, and handed him his cup and saucer. "I do ride. Or I should say, we did when we lived in Virginia. We had to, it was the only way to get around. I will confess I'm not comfortable with a lady's side saddle—I wore breeches and rode astride. I've not ridden enough lately to get used to riding side-saddle. And Mrs. Dorsey won't allow me to wear breeches under any circumstances. Besides, we don't have any suitable mounts here. Simon and Milo make use of the dray horses when they go out to see the tenants. We did talk about the possibility of eventually purchasing suitable mounts for us. We have a lot to do here. Getting a horse to ride for pleasure, I'm afraid, is rather far down on the list of priorities."

"Maybe we could go for a ride. We have the proper saddles and mounts, don't we, Pamela?"

"Yes, we do indeed. Paul collects horses like most people collect pretty pebbles, always has. He has a fascination for saddles, harnesses, carts, carriages, anything with wheels."

"Oh, I don't know," Audry said. Her complexion had gone very pale, and she started to tremble, hands shaking. Pamela took the cup and saucer from her and the pot of tea.

"It would only be Paul and me and our sister, Penny. And we wouldn't go far. There's a lovely little bridge and copse not far from the Chase. We wouldn't encounter anyone. Oh, maybe here and there a sheep. You could practice riding in a lady's saddle. And I want you to meet Penny, our sister Penelope. I think you two are going to be fast friends. She hates riding side-saddle, as do I. Like you, we prefer to ride astride, but our mother objects. Father understands, but he defers to Mother."

"I will ask Simon."

"Yes, of course," Paul said.

"Your brother should come with us," Pamela said. "He might be interested in the copse and the bridge. I believe you can see Copeland Manor from the bridge. The view is something, it really is."

"But the weather?" Audry said.

Chapter Fourteen

"I'll have to speak to my steward about the boar. Need to introduce some new blood into our stock. And I like the look of Boris. Your Peg is a real beauty. And the dairy barn is looking very good. You've modernized. I think I'll send my steward, Jamison, over. He and Milo have known each other for a very long time."

Lord Pomeroy said, as they entered the entrance hall, "I definitely would like to purchase a male and a couple female shoats once they are weaned."

"You'll have first pick, to be sure," Simon said. "I'd be interested in seeing your dairy set up."

"Come to supper Sunday after church. You are going to church?" Lord Pomeroy asked.

Simon stopped in front of the drawing-room door. "Yes, Audry and I will be attending."

"You haven't been, we would have seen you."

"No, neither Audry nor I have wanted to go out into the public. Audry has been attending church with the Dorseys. But Mrs. Dorsey has convinced me I need to show my face as well. So, we will attend as the new residents of Copeland Manor come Sunday. It won't be easy for either of us."

Lord Pomeroy tipped his head to the side and grew pensive. He studied Simon and then said, "I don't know how you've come to have your wounds, but I assure you they in no way should stop you from joining society here.

There are many among us who have worse, more apparent afflictions."

Simon stood quiet, considering what Lord Pomeroy had said. He had sounded very much like his own father. He squared his shoulders and came to a decision. "Will you join me in the library for a moment?"

****

Pamela had gone down the hall to the water closet. She was on her way back to the parlor when she heard her father's voice. She was about to approach when her father and Simon entered a room across the hall from the room where they had taken tea. They both appeared very serious. She couldn't imagine what could be the cause. She moved down to the doorway in which they had disappeared and stood very quiet, ears straining to hear their conversation.

****

"The raid came in the middle of the night. I will never be convinced they were all natives. Some were white men with painted faces, I'm sure of it. The natives, I was told, don't normally attack in the dark. They were more likely to raid in broad daylight. Whoever they were, they set fire to the drying sheds, the stable and the barns, then the house. I joined the field hands to set up a defense. Father sent Audry and Mother to hide in the root cellar. Mother disobeyed, and she ran back into the house. Father tried to stop her. The shot they were using was anything metal they could find: nails, wire, barbs, anything. Audry saw both Mother and Father in the flames—burned to death.

"I was found, after the raid was over, in a ditch, wounded but alive. Our home, our plantation, was burned to the ground. Most of our field hands had scattered, but they and their families survived. I was taken to a neighbor's house, where they treated my wounds. It was a full week before I learned Audry was safe, but in shock, staying with the pastor of our church. She had found Peg, the poor little baby pig, wandering, crying, and she wouldn't let her go. I thought it best to leave, leave it all behind, and start over here in England."

Now," Simon said, "I'm telling you all of this because you've gone out of your way to pay us a call, and you did ask. I hope we go forward as good neighbors to one another. I did think it would be good if someone besides the Dorseys knew a bit more about us. I hope, for now, all I've told you will stay just between us.

"Eventually, perhaps someday, we, Audry and I, can speak of the nightmare openly. It all happened such a short time ago, in April, just short of two years. What happened, all of it, the smell, the sounds: gunshots, the fire, smoke, the screams. It all remains very fresh in our memories. It has caused both my sister and I to hide or, rather, retreat, each of us in our own way. Myself, by immersing myself in this broken down farm, and Audry, well, she threw herself into making the Manor house a home for the both of us. Working has kept us both exhausted, too tired to think, or do much else but eat and sleep so soundly we don't dream.

"Today, with you and Paul and your daughter here, I've seen Audry open up. She laughed. She sat with you, and she talked. You don't know what you've done, but I will never forget your kindness and the kindness of your children." Simon had to stop talking. He was on the verge of bursting into tears. His throat had clutched up into a hard, cold knot.

****

Pamela scrubbed the tears from her cheeks, tiptoed across the hall, and entered the sitting room. She went to the piano and started to play a wordless ballad. Paul and Audry were seated near the fire, enjoying their tea, she smiling and Paul evidently, being his usual charming self.

Shortly, her father entered the room. He had his coat on and hat in hand. "We should be going. It's getting dark. Pamela, it's raining now. Simon has sent for Milo to bring the landau around."

Pamela rose from the piano bench as Simon returned and entered the room. "The coach? That's very kind of you, Mr. Lawrence, but hardly necessary. A little rain won't hurt me," she said.

"You must allow me to see to your comfort. It would reflect poorly on me if I did not. I suggested to your father he and Paul also make use of the coach. So, you see, it wouldn't do for you to ride, and they would be warm and dry."

She opened her mouth, tempted to tell him to go to blazes, then laughed at herself. "You and my father, you are two of a kind. I'll have to guard my instinct to jump to conclusions around you, won't I, Mr. Lawrence?"

"I don't know what you mean, Miss Pomeroy," Simon said. He had to work very hard not to smile.

Lord Pomeroy clamped his lips shut, but his eyes were dancing. "You are an easy target," he said under his breath.

Mrs. Dorsey appeared with Pamela's cherry-red traveling coat and helped her put it on. "I've put a warm brick in the coach and lap robes," Mrs. Dorsey said.

"Very kind of you, Mrs. Dorsey," Pamela said.

"I've invited Simon and, of course, you, Miss

Lawrence, for Sunday dinner," Lord Pomeroy said. "Oh, and Lady Alice, my dear wife, is planning a soiree in a couple weeks' time. You will be receiving an invitation."

"Sunday dinner? That is the capital, Father," Paul said. "We were talking about going for a ride someday soon. Sunday after church would be perfect. We assured Miss Lawrence we had a mount for her and a saddle. And Simon, we hope you will want to join us. We don't plan on riding far. Of course, it all depends on the weather."

Pamela watched Audry's face, the girl had gone very pale, her eyes big and round. Simon came to her side and steadied her, his hand, his injured hand, beneath his sister's elbow.

****

Simon, Audry at his side, watched the coach head down the lane. "They aren't going to let us stay hidden now, are they?" she said.

"No, no, we opened the door, and it won't close. We can decline invitations. I would make our excuses. But I don't think we should. I don't know about you, but I didn't feel threatened or judged by them. To have them as friends and allies, I think would be for the best. It wouldn't do to insult them by declining an invitation for a simple Sunday dinner."

He turned her by the shoulders to face him and said, "I felt I had to explain. I told Lord Pomeroy. He, in a roundabout, polite way, asked why I hadn't attended church," Simon said in his defense.

"Everything?"

"As much as I could in words without screaming," he said.

"I need to go to my room," she said.

"All right," he said, and they went back inside and

found Suzie standing in the entryway.

"There's a warm fire waiting for you in your room," she said to Audry. "I've placed a nice hot brick at the foot of the chaise beneath the coverlet. And I've taken the liberty of unpacking all the things you purchased today. I hope I've arranged them as you would do."

"Suzie, thank you," Audry said and started up the stairs.

"Would you like me to come along? I could help you—see to your lovely traveling costume?"

Audry stopped at the landing and gestured for the girl to follow her. "You're going to spoil me."

"I'm going to see it as my duty," Simon heard the maid say as the girls went up the stairs.

"She sang today," Mrs. Dorsey said.

She'd snuck up beside him. Simon hadn't heard her approach, and he put his hand to his heart to keep it from jumping out of his chest. "What, sing, who?"

"Your sister and young Mr. Pomeroy, while you was in the barns with his lordship. Miss Pomeroy sat down at that old, out-of-tune fortepiano, and she played dead keys and all, and your sister and Mr. Pomeroy sang a duet. More than one, and Miss Audry was as happy as a lark. It did my poor old soul a world of good, I can tell you. No matter, neither of you might think so, but this day was good for the both of you," she said and walked away, sniffling and wiping the tears from her cheeks.

Chapter Fifteen

"I've never ridden in anything of this vintage before," Paul said. "The colors and decor are faded, to be sure, but isn't it well-sprung, though."

Pamela noted her father merely nodded his head in agreement, his gaze directed out the porthole of the elegant equipage, chin resting in the palm of his hand, obviously lost in thought.

She, too, had much to think about. She questioned her sanity. Among the list of her many admirers, Pamala couldn't recall her attraction to any one of them as being a physical attraction. Not like, not even close to, the physical attraction she felt in the presence of Simon Lawrence. When he spoke to her, it was the look in his eyes and the tone of his voice, not his words, that sent ripples of need and desire through her veins.

She had nothing in common with Simon Lawrence. He avoided society. She rather liked it. She knew nothing of farming. She did have a love of animals, and they seemed to like her, but to live on a farm day in and day out—no, she couldn't imagine that.

Heretofore, she'd been attracted to men with a sense of wit and humor, perhaps their station, certainly their willingness to play the game. Oh, yes, she did enjoy that. But there'd been no electric, sexual vibration involved. She'd been kissed more than a few times, discreetly, of course, and with her permission. But it had been the titillating thought of getting caught that inspired the cuddle, not hunger for feel and touch, desire. Simon Lawrence didn't play games. And he was very physical, in every way, earthy.

Paul had stopped voicing his admiration of the old coach, took a big breath, and sighed. "Audry Lawrence is an interesting young woman, isn't she?" Paul said. "She seemed almost skittish, afraid of us at first."

"She is very lovely," Pamela said. "She has a beautiful voice. If she so desired, she could sing for the opera, but she's too shy for that." Tipping her head to the side, she said, "No, not exactly shy. Even though she is very fragile in appearance, she struck me as being exceptionally brave in a quiet, stoic sort of way. Maybe apprehensive or uncomfortable would better describe Miss Audry Lawrence. I can't quite put my finger on it, but I do know she doesn't like to be the center of attention and never will."

"You be careful, both of you," her father said.

His remark surprised and puzzled Pamela. But he was right. She needed to think. She'd set her sights on her farmer. Could she forget him? She didn't think so, not now, not ever.

"I'm simply saying shyness can be brought on by all sorts of reasons, reasons we might never discover or understand," her father said. "Audry Lawrence is charming, demure, but underneath, she is thinking and observing. She is by no means dull-witted. On the contrary, she is wise and astute.

"It is for certain her brother doesn't suffer from shyness. He, too, observes and thinks. And I believe he's learned and intelligent. I like and admire them both. They have taken on an enormous task to bring the Manor back to life. Neither of them will have a lot of time to socialize or indulge in frivolities."

Her father looked directly at her when he said this last sentence. She winced and looked away. She felt ashamed of herself for the time and money she'd wasted over the last two years. Paul, when she dared to glance in his direction, also looked chagrined. The three of them continued the journey home in silence. Pamela, in thoughtful reflection.

****

Audry had sent Suzie away. Simon was right. They'd opened the door and there was no closing it now. Even Suzie, as much as Audry appreciated the girl's help, was an intrusion, a shameful extravagance. She didn't need help or want help. She didn't deserve help. She turned on her side and looked to her bed, where Suzie had laid out one of her new gowns. It was the color of a rosy, foggy sunset on an English evening in January. It was fine and elegant, beautiful. She didn't want to be seen as elegant or beautiful.

When Mrs. Dorsey had entered the pub then returned with Suzie Tidmore, Audry had recognized the girl from church. Suzie, most Sundays, sat in the back next to a very imposing, good-looking man of color who controlled their children, one on each knee. She'd learned the man was Suzie's husband, Michael. Soon, they'd be occupying the gatehouse. Audry thought that a good thing. Michael Tidmore looked like a man who could handle almost any chore given. She'd encountered many such men on their plantation. She admired them, their stamina, their fortitude, and their ability to forgive.

Her mother had loaned them books, even though it was against the law. That law didn't apply here, in

England, but still, Michael Tidmore obviously knew his place was in the back of the church. There were a lot of books in the library. She vowed to let Suzie know she could have her pick any time she wanted.

Eyes closed, in her dressing gown, tucked up beneath a lap robe, hot brick at her feet, Audry lay upon the old chaise lounge, her arm over her eyes, and commanded her mind to turn off. But when she closed her eyes, she heard Paul Pomeroy's warm, deep baritone voice blending with her own and saw his warm, brown eyes smiling at her, encouraging her to sing and forget.

Somehow, it felt like a betrayal to forget, to feel happy, to sing without care. She'd been perfectly content serving her penance here in solitude. Penance for what she couldn't say, other than she was guilty of having survived without a scratch while her parents had perished, and Simon had nearly died of his wounds while she'd hid, did nothing to help defend.

She shouldn't be thinking about Paul Pomeroy or anyone. He'd been kind to a poor little girl with nothing to recommend her save a head full of hair and a pretty voice. His smiles meant nothing. He was a man of experience, a man confident in his appeal. He probably gave his smiles to all the ladies, all the time with those eyes and that fascinating dimple in his right cheek that disappeared and reappeared when he laughed.

Thoughts shifting, Audry replayed all the awkward missteps of the day: spilling treacle on her fingers, then licking her fingers in front of company, and what about her clumsy attempts to converse?

Her mind traveled back in time, to home, to Virginia, the plantation, and a wave of homesickness swept through her. She groaned and rolled her shoulders.

Feeling sorry for herself was unacceptable. She had to snap out of it. Hadn't she enjoyed shopping? Yes, shamefully, she had. She could admit it had been more fun than she'd imagined. It had been satisfying and rejuvenating to reconnect with her feminine desire to be pretty and to feel fine fabrics against her skin.

She hadn't meant to talk so much, but when Miss Pomeroy started the conversation, her thoughts simply slipped out. She had expected to come home and share her experience with Simon, but to share it with another woman had come as a special treat. But right now, she realized she missed her mother. If her mother had been here, she would have shared her pleasure with her, and they would have laughed and gushed over the fabrics, the seamstress shop, and the quaint little village of Stilton.

****

Simon would have liked to retire to the library with a good stiff drink in his hand. Instead, he found himself in a complicated argument with Mrs. Dorsey. "Well, ye can't be takin' yer meals in my kitchen now," she said and meant it as her final word.

He shifted in his chair at the table. "I don't see what has changed. The formal dining room is too big and too cold. I want my meals hot, and to be seated where it's warm, and to share the meal with good company."

"Good company is one thing, but to share your meals with your servants is quite another thing. If word got out, you and Miss Audry took your meals here with us—well, you can't, and there's an end to it. It's, I don't know how to explain, it's—not done—unnatural," she said with such a tortured look on her round, rosy face he had to laugh.

"Unnatural? Oh, come, come now, Ellen, surely

that's going a bit far. Not done, I can see that, for we Englanders do have definite invisible lines of status in this country that no one is allowed to cross, I'll grant you. And I understand some of the lines must be maintained. Maintained while in public, but not here under my roof, *our*, our home, *your* home, and mine."

"Oh, for pity's sake," Mrs. Dorsey said and sank down in a chair at the kitchen table. "Yer don't understand. Tis Suzie and Michael, and their boys. They'll be here in this kitchen, probably eatin' at this very table. Now you and Miss Audry can't be like'n that. No, it won't do. It won't. Those children are five and three years of age. It's like eatin' at the table with a couple of squirrels. And Michael, he's a big man."

Simon sat down and chewed on what she'd said. What he'd heard was her kitchen wouldn't hold all of them at once, and she would be put to twice as much trouble if all of them ate in the same space at the same time.

"Yes, I see," he said, and started to talk aloud to himself, "Audry and I prefer to take our mid-day meal at around an hour before noon. We usually don't have breakfast together. She prefers to have something in her room, and I come in here and steal whatever it is you're serving and take it out to the barns. As far as the evening meal goes, we usually dine around seven or half-past in the evening, after I've had a chance to clean up. I hadn't considered those times might not suit you and Milo—your schedule."

He shut his mouth. He'd just come to a conclusion, and it wasn't a very good one. "Is having the Tidmores here going to cause you more trouble rather than lighten your load?"

Mrs. Dorsey looked as if he'd just slapped her. She huffed and rose from her chair, then sat back down and folded her work-worn hands tightly together on top of the table. "Now, listen to me. You are my employer," she said, meeting his gaze. "I don't own this place, you do. We are not equals. We never will be. I know, I know, we've been goin' on as if that were the case, but it tisn't. Today's visitors should have shown you that.

"Having Suzie and Michael here will be a blessing. After your grandfather passed, Milo and I stayed on. And we worked our fannies off to hold this place together, waitin' to see who'd show up. For a time, we didn't think anyone ever would, and then you and Miss Audry come along. And you work and share, and you aren't mean or stingy, and Milo and me can't believe our good fortune."

She sat forward in her chair. "This is my thinkin'. You and Miss Audry, you let us serve you. Suzie will bring the Miss her breakfast to her room then I don't have to do them stairs. You come in here, as you like, and sneak out of here with my griddle cakes, biscuits, what-have-you, and sausage in the mornings as you do, and I don't have to wash your breakfast dishes. At midday, Suzie will serve a repast for you both in the parlor in the inglenook, same with dinner in the evenings. Your grandfather used to have his meals there. It's not like I haven't done it before. He didn't care for the dining room either. You'll be served in the inglenook starting tonight.

"And, here's a thought: if you should happen to have guests, we'll open the dining room. Yes, as a matter of fact, Suzie and I will start on that right away. Michael will help. It should be opened up anyway. It's past time. We can take some of the extensions out of the big table and store them so it doesn't seem so formal and cold. Maybe set the table closer to the fireplace. And we'll see both the fireplaces are cleaned and the chimneys swept. The walls might need a bit of whitewash. Some fresh draperies and fabrics on the chairs wouldn't hurt. You'll see, it's going to be better all the way 'round."

Shaking his head, feeling banished, what else could Simon do? He agreed and left the kitchen. It had only been twenty-four hours, but a lot had changed. He'd met his neighbors. He'd sold two of his unborn pigs and made a promise to loan out his boar for a sizable fee. His sister had laughed and sang, and she'd made conversation with strangers. They'd acquired a maid and a groomsman. He hoped Michael Tidmore would be more than a groomsman; he hoped he'd be an all-around handyman. And now, he'd been kicked out of the kitchen, consigned to eat his evening meals in the drawing room.

All of this, he blamed on Miss Pamela Pomeroy, the beautiful, capable, amazing, kind Miss Pomeroy. If she hadn't been holding those reins in that curricle, if Peg hadn't taken such a liking to her, if he'd let Milo go get the silly pig in the first place, none of this would be happening.

Well, he might have thought to get Mrs. Dorsey and Milo help, eventually. This was a big house. His cheeks grew hot thinking back to how he must have appeared to his neighbors, standing in the doorway in his shirt and work clothes. He didn't know how many servants his grandfather had employed, but it was certainly more than four, probably more like a dozen.

Chapter Sixteen

Audry sat in silence on the settee before the inglenook. Suzie served her a helping of the lamb stew from the kettle on the cooking crane that hung over the edge of the coals in the fireplace. There was a platter of thick bread on the table in front of her, along with a dish of butter, small bowls of salt and pepper, a bowl of honey, and a carafe of cider. "Thank you, Suzie," Simon said.

"There's apple dumplings and clotted cream. So, save some room," Suzie said before she left the room and slid the drawing-room door closed.

Worried she'd spill stew on her new gown, Audry laid her napkin out carefully over her lap. "So, we take our meals here now. No more cozy meals will we share with the Dorseys." She tipped her head to the side, sighed, and took a bite of her crusty bread. She chewed and swallowed. "I think I know why," she said and scooped up a forkful of the savory stew.

Simon, a smile on his lips, said, "We were too long in the colonies. It's time we accepted the fact we are now of the gentry class, I guess." He, too, prepared a slice of bread with butter, took a bite, and followed it with a forkful of stew. "At least that's how Mrs. Dorsey explained it to me." He loaded his fork with another helping of the stew. "I see you're wearing one of your new gowns. The color suits you. It brings out the pink in your cheeks and the depth of color in your eyes. Do you like it?"

"I do like it. It is surprisingly comfortable, and with the added crocheted waistcoat, I'm warm enough. But it seems silly to wear it. There's only the two of us. It's too pretty, too fine. I could wear one of my old dresses and who would know. But Suzie laid this out for me, and I felt it would be churlish of me not to wear it. Here I am, all dressed up in my new finery, and now I come down to find we are consigned to eat in seclusion.

"And speaking of seclusion," she rushed ahead to say before taking another bite of her bread, "did you know Michael Tidmore is a man of color?" She laid her fork down on the side of her plate and dabbed at the corners of her mouth with her napkin. "This morning, when Mrs. Dorsey came out of the pub with Suzie, I recognized her from church. I'd seen her husband, Michael, with their children. He's a very attentive father. They sit in the back of the church. I have a suspicion this is why we find ourselves removed from dining in the kitchen. Suzie and Michael and their children will eat their meals with the Dorseys now, away from us, or rather we are away from them. I don't know who is trying to protect whom, but it seems a bit fishy."

Without hesitation, Simon said, "Ah, yes, right, that is a bit of a coincidence, and it explains a lot." He motioned for her to refill his plate with the stew. She got up from her seat, filled his bowl, and warmed her own with a shallow scoop from the kettle.

"Thank you," he said. "I hope the Dorseys don't think we'll object to Michael or the children. If it is as you and I suspect, it makes it all the more important they have the gatehouse. We'll surrender our place at the table in the kitchen and meals with Milo and Ellen if it makes the Tidmore family feel more welcome. I say let them take care of us, and we'll take care of them. Milo and Ellen and the Tidmores can sit with us on Sundays in the Copeland Pew as part of our household, if they so choose, which I hope they will. After all, we are to the Manor born, or is that manner born? I'm never sure. No matter, it's time we acted the part. It won't come naturally, I know that. We'll do our best. More like earn the label those *crazy colonists*."

Audry nodded in agreement. She pursed her lips together and tipped her head to the side. Lips twitching, eyes focused on the contents of her plate, she said, "To play the part then, you will go tomorrow into Stilton to the tailor and get yourself the proper attire. You answered the door in your shirt sleeves today. And you are still wearing your old moccasins, I see. That jerkin smells and looks as if it belongs in a museum."

Simon put down his fork and sat back. "Mrs. Dorsey is right. Our visitors have set us on a new path. It's time we—*I*—accept it. I don't think either of us are ready for what's coming." He shook his head and took a deep breath, then exhaled. "Very well, to embrace the future, I will go to this tailor you found, and I will have a suit of clothes made, proper clothes, for church or good enough to wear to, say, a Sunday dinner. But I refuse to wear clocks and tails or satin embroidered waistcoats. Plain breeches, a couple of linen shirts, two dress coats, and that should do it." He wrinkled his nose. "And a pair of new shoes for more formal occasions," he said and waggled his toes in his comfortable, warm moccasins.

"It's a start," Audry said, "that's what Mrs. Dorsey said today of my purchases. She said it's a start. You'll need a cravat or two and new stockings and underwear." She raised her glass of cider.

"Never you mind my underwear," Simon said. He raised his glass, and they made a silent toast.

****

Penny followed Pamela down the stairs. They'd arrived home late from the manor. Pamela had barely enough time to change her clothes before the supper bell rang. And her little sister wanted details and wasn't about to let up.

"In his shirtsleeves? Your farmer? The good citizen, he answered the door himself, in his shirtsleeves. How did you know who he was—I mean—what did he say?" Penny asked and stopped on the landing.

"Shhhh, keep your voice down. Yes, he answered the door in a plain-spun shirt and trousers, a work shirt. And I don't know how Father knew who he was. He just knew, I guess. Oh, for heaven's sake, I knew. We just knew, that's all," Pamela said.

She proceeded down a few more steps, Penny on her heels. She wished she could get Penny to shut up.

"Moccasins? He was wearing moccasins," Penny said. "I've never seen moccasins except in pictures in books. Did they have beads? Was he barefoot? Do you think he's an Indian?"

"No, he is not an Indian. Will you shush? They had beads, and he wore them over his stockings. They lived in the colonies, for goodness' sake, they have Indians there. He might have gotten them through a trade or something. I don't know. Now, shush."

"I heard that," her mother said, coming down the stairs behind them. "He didn't introduce himself. Your father assumed he wasn't a servant because he knows the

Dorseys and almost everyone in the parish, and the man who answered the door was none of those people." In a huff, Lady Alice marched down the stairs and went around them. "This is ridiculous." She said over her shoulder. "The man also wore an old jerkin over his homespun shirt and wool, tweed trousers. And he is a farmer through and through, and your father can speak of little else but the size of a pig and his hopes for expanding his pig cribs."

Penny practically jumped down the last few steps to catch up with their mother. "Did Father tell you he's invited Mr. Lawrence and his sister to Sunday dinner?" Penny asked as they made their way to the dining room.

Lady Alice did not respond. Shoulders squared, stiff, she took her place at the table and with precision, she placed her napkin in her lap. Paul and Lord John entered the room, and they also took their seats. A tense silence hung heavy over the room as they were served their meal. But, as soon as the servants made their discreet exit, Lady Alice cleared her throat, folded her hands in her lap, and said, "I, too, have invited guests for Sunday dinner. The Abernathys are home from Scotland. They paid a call while you were seeing this farmer person.

"Paul, Miss Abernathy was particularly sorry to have missed you. She almost came to tears. And Lord Dwight asked to convey his regards to you, Pamela. He looks forward to Sunday."

Pamela winced, now dreading Sunday when she had been looking forward to it. Dwight Abernathy was a popinjay, a fawning prig of the first order who continued to wear powdered wigs and lead paint on his face. And Lucinda, well, she was simply a nightmare. All Pamela could think at the moment was how poor Audry would cope. And Mr. Lawrence, what would he do if Lord Abernathy spewed one of his barely veiled insults in his direction? Neither Lucinda nor Lord Dwight were known to be empathetic. On the contrary, acid-tongued Lucinda and her pompous uncle were snobs of the first order. And as for riding, surely that was out of the question now.

"We will welcome this Mr. Lawrence person, and his sister, as the invitation has already been extended," Lady Alice said. "We cannot rescind the offer. But I do think we should limit our acquaintance with them. I've not seen either of them in church. Now, why is that? We've done our duty, welcomed them, and thanked them for their assistance; no need to go further than that. They don't sound like our kind of people. I'm sure they are very fine, honest, and hard-working, and they've been through a great trial, but we don't have to put them in our pockets, so to speak."

Both Pamela and Paul opened their mouths to speak. Pamela closed her mouth very quickly. She was about to tell her mother that Audry Lawrence did attend church. She'd attended with the Dorseys. But on second thought, she realized that information would probably make matters worse.

Her father raised his hand and stopped whatever she and Paul were about to say. "I believe you are being a bit precipitous in your judgment, my dear. I beg you to meet Mr. Lawrence and his sister before you consign them to your delete list."

Lord John went on to say, "We arrived unannounced. Mr. Lawrence had been outside working. His sister had gone shopping. Mrs. Dorsey went along as her chaperone, which seemed very proper to me. And Milo Dorsey, of course, had to drive the coach. There were no other servants to answer the door.

"I might be wrong, but I believe, just today, Mr. Lawrence increased the household staff. I think I recognized the Tidmore girl when she served tea. Mr. Lawrence appeared taken aback by her presence. I think I heard him ask Mrs. Dorsey who she was. I tried not to listen in on their conversation, but I'm sure that's what I heard. I would suppose where young Mrs. Tidmore goes, her husband will follow. If that's the case, The Bell Inn will be sorry to lose Michael Tidmore. He's kept the Bell Inn stables in very good order for a very long time. He started there as a child. He couldn't have been more than eight or ten when he started mucking out stalls and acting as a tiger to the passing nabobs with their fancy carriages."

Pamela pressed her lips tightly together. Her father had recognized the Tidmore girl. From where she would very much like to know. Could it be Suzie Tidmore had served him a pint at the pub, or had he noticed her in church? She was a very comely-looking young woman, full-bosomed, rosy cheeks. Her mother had not asked, but she didn't appear best pleased. Her clenched jaw spoke volumes.

Lord John softened his tone. "We were at fault for not sending a messenger to announce our intent to pay a call. That was rude on our part. You must sympathize my dear. Most of the servants and the grooms left the Manor when Sir Simon-Loyd passed away. Only the Dorseys and a few dairy hands stayed on. Simon Lawrence and his sister have only been living at the Manor for less than a year. Surely, we can give them a bit more time to come about."

Lady Alice looked to her children, then back to her spouse. She squirmed in her chair and adjusted her napkin. "Oh, I don't know." She huffed and waggled her head. "John, he answered the door in a state of undress. What does that say about the man?"

"He wasn't undressed," Paul said. "He had a shirt on and shoes, well more like slippers. But he wasn't undressed. He just wasn't dressed for company."

Lady Alice poked at her chicken breast and said, "I know, but—but will he, and you, John, come Sunday, will you please talk of something other than pigs and cows?"

For a brief second, all that could be heard was the ticking of the dining room clock, then Lord John burst out laughing, his children joined him, and Lady Alice relented and chuckled and dabbed at the tears in her eyes.

Chapter Seventeen

Looking out the window of his bedroom, Simon could see that it wasn't raining, but it wasn't bright and sunny either. The new day had dawned cold and overcast. He put on his canvas coat, snugged his stocking cap down over his ears, and started down the stairs. As he crossed the entrance, he could hear voices coming from the kitchen—children's voices.

"Sit still now, or you'll spill your milk, Jeremy. Yes, you may have more jam on your biscuit. Give me a minute," he heard Mrs. Dorsey say as he came through the kitchen doorway.

Simon removed his stocking cap from his head and took two long strides in time to catch the cup of milk from slipping off the side of the table. And he stopped the smaller of the two boys from dipping his fingers in the jam jar by grasping the child's wrists. "Now, who have we here?" he said to the older of the two children and placed the cup of milk at a safe distance from the child's arms and fingers.

"Auck, Master Simon, you gave me a start," Mrs. Dorsey said, her hand to her bosom. "Suzie's gone to the gatehouse to help Milo and Michael unload their things into the cottage. She'll be back soon. Meanwhile, I've got these two hooligans to care for, and I think I could use an extra pair of eyes in the back of me head, and at least two more hands."

“Then consider me as your extra eyes and hands. I’ll sit with the children, and you mind the stove,” he said and spooned more jam on the little one’s biscuit.”

“Ah, no, I couldn’t ask you to do that,” she said.

“You didn’t ask, I volunteered.”

“Well, let me introduce you, that young man there, with the jam all over his face, is Dennis, and the one there who’s wearin’ the milk as a mustache is Jeremy. I’ve got them here with me this mornin’ for a little while as my sister is at the cottage helping. It won’t be like this every morning. At least I hope it won’t,” Mrs. Dorsey said as she turned and set to flipping the sausages in her skillet.

“I was on my way to the gatehouse. It’s a big day for these two and for all of us,” Simon said and handed the glass of milk to Jeremy. “I hope the gatehouse is habitable. I should have looked at it closer.” He relieved the boy of the glass and set it back, away from the edge of the table.

Busy at the hob, her back to Simon, Mrs. Dosey said, “Milo thought it was in fair order. The roof needed some repair a while back, and there was a broken window off the back stoop, but he took care of that months ago before you and Miss Audry found us. Never you worry. If there’s things that need fixin’, Michael will see to it. He’s a good man. He’s quiet, he don’t say much, but he gets things done.”

“I look forward to meeting him,” Simon said. Mrs. Dorsey laid a couple of sausages on a plate, and a biscuit covered with her gravy and set it before him.

“You will,” she said, head down, and turned to serve the children a sausage each.

“Audry and I were talking last night, and we think we should all sit in the Copeland pew together. Suzie,

Michael, the boys, you and Milo, we should all sit together on Sundays."

Mrs. Dorsey shook her head. "No, we couldn't."

"Yes, yes we can, Ellen. And I think we need to show solidarity. Go forward as we mean to go into the future."

"You know, then?"

"Of course, we know. Audry recognized Suzie yesterday. She'd seen this little family in church. This is going to be home to all of us. I want it to be home, a place we can all feel wanted and cared for."

"Well, it hasn't been easy for Suzie. Mixed marriages are frowned upon on both sides of the fence, you know. And these boys face an uphill battle, I fear."

Suzie entered the kitchen from the back porch, breathless, cheeks pink with cold, eyes shining, a smile on her face which faded the moment her gaze landed on Simon. "Master Lawrence, good morning to you," she said and dipped a shallow curtsey in his direction.

"Good morning, yourself," he said. "Your children have been keeping me company. They are fine-looking boys. How's the move coming?"

"I think we're in. Michael's got the boys' room set up with their beds. And Ma's taking care of the kitchen. Milo was replacing a loose board on the back step. I rushed back here to serve Miss Audry's breakfast and see to my boys. I hope they weren't too much of a bother for you, Aunt Ellen. I didn't mean to be gone so long."

"Miss Audry would rather share her breakfast with these two handsome gentlemen than alone in her room," Audry said from the doorway of the kitchen. "I'll see to your children this morning, Suzie. You go, get settled in. I'll stay here and help Mrs. Dorsey if she needs it."

"Well, sounds like things have been sorted out here," Simon said and set to finishing off his sausage and biscuits. "I'll go see if I can make myself useful at the gatehouse. Do we need to take Milo and Michael some of your sausages and cakes?" he asked Mrs. Dorsey.

Suzie helped the woman fill a basket with some food. Simon held the basket and said, "I'll walk back with you, Suzie. No use arguing with either of these ladies."

"Keep in mind you are to see the tailor this morning," Audry said to him as he and Suzie left the kitchen by way of the back door.

****

Michael Tidmore was a good-looking young man. And he was everything the Dorseys had said. He was quiet, yes, but he was strong and eager to be of use, just what the manor needed. Simon found himself in the way and decided he would go into Stilton to the tailor, as his sister wanted him to do.

He rode one of the dray horses into town. Feedbag in place over the horse's nose, he tied the nag off on a hitching ring before a line of small shops along the main street. It took him a moment or two before he was able to move without pain or losing his balance. Riding in a saddle wasn't uncomfortable. He could stand the ache in his hip and back but finding his balance again once on the ground was the challenge.

The Braithwaite Tailor and Haberdashery shop and the Gillespie Modiste shop were side by side. They shared an awning. He chose the door with the top hat on the open sign. The tailor was in the back of the shop, but he appeared when Simon entered, and the bell over the doorway rang.

Simon wasn't sure what to expect, and he certainly wasn't prepared for what happened next. The tailor, a bald-headed, tall man with bony fingers and sharp facial features, greeted him with an overabundance of enthusiasm, almost as if he'd been expecting him. "It's a rare pleasure to serve a man with such a fine pair of shoulders. No extra padding will be needed for you, sir, no sir. It's going to be a joy to clothe you. I think I have just the coat. It's a good sturdy weight fabric of dark blue worsted, with a peppering of a gray tweed. We'll do a wide lapel of charcoal suede and the same suede for the flaps on the pockets, maybe the buttonholes too. I don't know, maybe that's too much. We'll see. But silver buttons, definitely. And I think the gray and wine-colored silk cravat. And I think we have a blue paisley somewhere and waistcoats. We need waistcoats. There's another coat here somewhere, I spotted it yesterday. It's black, cut out of a blended wool. Very fine, it was. A little adjustment here and there, and yes, I think it would do nicely for an evening coat. You'll want collars and a cravat. Not too high, no, not for you. New undergarments as well, I should think. And shoes, good heavens, I hope we have your size."

Simon stopped trying to get in a word one way or the other and surrendered himself to the fitting, the discussion of the length of the coat sleeves, the shirts and the shoes. He managed to put up with the poking and prodding for a full hour and a half, then he begged to be allowed to escape while the tailor's assistant made the alterations, which he understood would take at least another hour and a half to perform.

He stood outside the shop trying to decide where he could spend a quiet hour in comfortable seclusion when someone tapped him on the shoulder. "I thought that was you. I didn't recognize you in a proper hat and dressed in your cord coat. I've seen you as a beggar man, and then again in your shirt sleeves, but not this country squire look you have on today. Is Miss Lawrence with you?"

Paul Pomeroy stood there grinning at him, and Simon began to blush. He didn't blush, or at least he never used to. "I have several disguises," he said in answer to the man's challenging smirk. "Audry is at home. When I left her, she was taking charge of the Tidmore children. That family is moving into the gatehouse today. And it's because I answered the door in my shirtsleeves that, as my punishment, I'm here being mauled by Mr. Braithwaite. Audry insisted I do something about myself. We didn't really have very many tailors in the colonies or occasions to need one."

"Follow me," Paul said.

"Where?"

"Come along, I recognize the glazed look in your eyes. I've been there," Paul said and nodded his head toward the tailor's shop. "You need a cup of strong tea. There's a shop across the road. The girls are there. I've come from the farriers. Left my horses there to be shod. The girls were shopping for God only knows what. I told them I'd meet them at the tea shop."

"I…I don't want to intrude."

"Intrude, nonsense. We have a logistics problem, and we need to talk. I know what I want to do, but it will be up to the girls."

****

"Don't look," Pamela said.

Penny, of course, looked all around her but not out

the window of the little tea shop.

"It's Simon Lawrence, he's here, in town, he's crossing the street with Paul. They're coming this way."

Penny spun around in her chair and came to her feet to look out the shop window.

"Sit down. I said don't look."

"That—that man is your pig farmer?"

Pamela nodded her head. Simon Lawrence, his smile in place, walked beside her brother, arms swinging, shoulders back. Even though Paul was a handsome young man and a couple of inches taller than Simon, Simon stole the eye—powerfully built, his complexion weathered and a halting, easy swagger to his stride.

His black hair curled around the brim of his corded hat in a careless, fascinating way. His buff-colored corded coat complimented his broad shoulders, muscular arms, and narrow hips. Today, he wore tan breeches that stretched over his muscular thighs. His black hessian boots, up to his knees, fit snugly against his calves. He was a purely physical man, and he affected Pamela in a very physical way. But that was wrong, wasn't it? There should be more between a man and a woman than base animal attraction.

And there lay the rub. There was more, so much more. She admired his passion for nurturing, care, and sharing, his intelligence, his lack of artifice, false personification. He didn't try to be anything or anyone other than who and what he was. She'd played games too long. Could she be herself? Did she even know who she was or what she wanted? Was Simon Lawrence the answer?

Penny gasped and sat down. "Oh, my goodness,

Pam, I'm so sorry. What are you going to do?"

"What? Do?"

"Yes, what are you going to do? He's—he's so much more than anyone I've ever seen. He's not like your London beaus. He's nothing like them. He's better, a lot better, and you cannot play your games or fool around with a man like that. There's something in the way he carries himself, he reminds me of our father. You said they got along very well, didn't you? I think I see why. No, this is serious, isn't it?"

Pamela, licked her lips and nodded.

Chapter Eighteen

Fate was not going to allow him to ignore, or bypass, Miss Pamela Pomeroy. She'd raced into his life and there she was going to stay. He had to find a way to shield his heart against falling in love with her. She was of another class, that alone should be enough to discourage—*nay*—frighten him enough to keep him from thinking about her day and night.

He couldn't look away, she smiled up at him, her gaze full of uncertainty, the same uncertainty he was feeling. His resolve melted before the warmth he saw in her warm brown eyes. This made it worse, they both knew it wouldn't work, it couldn't.

"Mr. Lawrence, well met, join us," she said, her words saying the opposite of what her eyes told him. "Come, meet our sister Penelope."

Simon bowed before the young lady. "Pleased to meet you, Miss Penelope."

"Penny, please, I won't answer if you call me Penelope."

He chuckled. "I foretell that you and my sister are going to become fast friends. God have mercy on us all," he said.

"Amen," Paul said, and pulled up a chair for Simon to sit next to Pamela.

His knee brushed hers beneath the table, and a current of heat shot through him. She blushed and gathered the fabric of her cape and moved to the side to give him more leg room. He started to beg pardon, and she shook her head, silently, beseeching him not to bring it to anyone's attention.

"Indeed, we are well met," Paul said. He settled himself and reached for the little silver pitcher of treacle that sat on the serving tray. "As I was rounding the corner from the stables, I spotted Simon coming out of Braithwaite's. He appeared a bit dazed, as one is wont to be, having escaped the tailor. A strong cup of tea will set him straight again, I'll wager."

"I nearly stepped into the modiste shop when I first arrived," Simon said as Pamela poured him a cup of tea. She offered him a scone from the serving basket. He nodded, said thank you, and set it down on his plate. "The entrance to the tailor shop wasn't clear."

Pamela poured her brother a cup of tea. He applied a liberal amount of treacle to his cup, took a long sip, passed the pitcher down to Simon and sat back in his chair.

"They are man and wife," Penny said.

"No, they are not," Paul said, and finished off his cup of syrup-ladened tea.

"But they are," Pamela said, and refilled her brother's cup, then poured herself a cup of tea.

"Who are man and wife?" asked Simon, as he helped himself to the cream.

"Miss Gillispie, the modiste, and Mr. Braithwaite, the tailor, they are man and wife," Penny said.

The playful, twitchy smile on her pretty little mouth and the twinkle in her golden-flecked, brown eyes told Simon she was quite pleased with herself.

"This is the first I've heard of this," Paul said. "Why

ever? Why don't they combine their shops and use one name, for pity's sake? Why the separation and subterfuge?"

"The way Mother explained it," Pamela said, as she poured a bit more cream into her cup, "The shops were left to them by a distant uncle on Mrs. Braithwaite's side of the family. The Gillispie side, you understand. The uncle was a tailor, and his wife a seamstress, and he wanted the shop to remain in the family and offer those services. Mrs. Braithwaite, the current Mrs. Braithwaite, or Miss Gillispie as we know her, wanted to keep the Gillispie name over the door of the shop. Mr. Braithwaite, her husband, insisted the banner read Braithwaite's Haberdashery and Gentleman's Tailor. To save the marriage and their livelihood, they agreed they would each have a shop of their own, with their own banner. They put up a wall, created two entrances, and, as the story goes, they are now living happily ever after. They have two children, both employed. The daughter works for her mother, and the son works for the father."

"I can't believe I never heard that story before," Paul muttered to himself as he slathered butter and strawberry preserves on his scone. "Well, between the two of them, they do a raking good business here in Stilton, I can tell you."

"Is Audry seeing the modiste this morning?" Pamela asked.

"No, she's at the manor. The Tidmore family is moving into the gatehouse this morning. When I left the Manor, she'd come down for breakfast and immediately took charge of the Tidmore children. Seeing to it, their breakfasts didn't end up on Mrs. Dorsey's floor, being the main challenge, I should imagine. I dropped by the gatehouse to lend a hand but found I was simply in the way. Audry had insisted I see a tailor after yesterday. And here I am."

"After yesterday?" Pamela asked.

He smiled at her and chuckled. "Yes, I was told I couldn't attend church in my shirt sleeves and wool work trousers. It was explained to me that I had to do better."

"Ah," she said and laughed with him.

"Which brings us nicely around to those logistics I mentioned," Paul said.

Simon simply arched his brows and waited. The ladies dipped their chins, each suddenly becoming engrossed in picking up the crumbs on the table from their scones.

"I don't think we're going to be able to have that ride after church come Sunday," Paul said.

Slightly taken aback, as it had been Paul's plan to begin with, Simon wasn't certain what he should say. He started to say it was all right. They would go another time when Pamela interrupted. "We thought, instead of Sunday, we could plan our outing for either tomorrow or the next day. Jamison, our steward, promises sunshine for the rest of the week, with the possibility of snow moving in Sunday evening or Monday."

The sheepish look on Paul's face disappeared. He brightened, nodded, and, with enthusiasm, took up the thread. "Yes, the *weather*. The weather should be good, better than if we waited until Sunday. We'll send over a carriage, say around ten o'clock or at half-past ten of the morning. We'll get you fitted out and be on our way to the bridge in plenty of time to have a small repast for our luncheon."

Simon had a sneaking feeling he was being

manipulated. For what purpose, he couldn't say. It was January, and the weather was a concern, especially when it involved precious livestock.

The Pomeroy children were plotting; he hoped it was for a pleasant day's outing, but something told him there was more to it. The only way to find out the real reason behind the change of plan was to agree to *this* plan. After all, a nice horseback ride cross country would be a relaxing change from mucking out stalls and patching fences, and he knew his sister would love it. "If it's convenient, I would rather we make this ride for Friday. I feel guilty as if I'm wasting my time in town this morning.

"Tomorrow, I really do have to make sure the Tidmore family is comfortably ensconced. I've left it to Milo today. But I should spend the day tomorrow making sure everyone is—*well*—clear on how we'll go on. I don't want anyone to feel I've given up doing my part. I want to stay involved. Peg is about to deliver. Mrs. Dorsey is plotting a complete overhaul of our dining room. I would prefer to supervise. I fear if I'm absent for many more days, abandon the field, I'll lose ground, so to speak."

With a smile on her lips and a knowing twinkle in her eye, Pamela said, "Of course, Friday it is then. No need to explain. Like a runaway team, the Dorseys are in harness with the Tidmores. Have to hold on to the reins while giving them their heads."

"Exactly," he said. "Well put. Can't allow them to think I'm not paying attention, don't have a destination in mind."

She put her hand on his arm, his left arm, and leaned toward him. "You have much to do. We understand that.

The ride to the bridge isn't far. We won't be gone for more than a couple of hours. And, as I said to your sister, the view is especially fine. You can see the Manor from the bridge. You might find the perspective interesting. There's an old, abandoned gamekeeper's cottage near the bridge, so if the weather does turn, we won't be left out in the cold, so to speak. It's one of our favorite rides."

Simon had to swallow hard. He'd been following her lips as she spoke. He ached to kiss those lips, stop those words with his tongue. "The perspective, yes. I haven't gone much farther than the dairy barns thus far. I'm sure the weather will cooperate, if it is how you have ordered."

"Oh, it shall be as I order," she said with a superior nod of her head. "I have a way with the elements and runaway horses—and pigs." There was that electric current again. It ran through his body the likes of which he had never experienced before. His own laughter erupted more as a primitive growl.

For a few pregnant moments, there was complete silence at the table.

Paul cleared his throat. "Friday morning, let us hope, will be bright with sunshine. Very good thing we met up with you this morning. We had thought to send 'round a messenger, but this is better."

Paul and Penny began to argue between them as to which horse Audry might prefer. Penny declared they had two lovely ponies, both geldings, one a paint and the other a dapple gray.

The gray was more suited for a lady's mount, used to a lady's side saddle, and older, more sedate, Paul insisted.

Penny pooh-poohed that idea, saying the dapple was

old and tired, not sedate. And the paint was in need of some exercise and equally accustomed to a lady's saddle.

Paul waved aside her comments, saying he thought Simon might like to ride one of his favorite horses, his Arabian mare. She, according to Paul, was prime and up to the weight.

Simon didn't bother to explain to either of them that Audry had spent the better part of her youth on the back of a horse. She was a neck-or-nothing horsewoman.

Pamela, seated beside him, had grown strangely quiet. He was surprised she didn't have an opinion to add to this discussion. They shared a glance and without words, Simon knew, and he imagined that she knew, too. They were both set upon the same path. Where it would lead and how it would end, neither of them could know. But the course was set, and it didn't matter what horse they rode.

Chapter Nineteen

Simon found himself seated in the dining room, at the dining table, before a cheery fire in the huge, yawning grate. The heavy, black walnut table had been reduced from a twelve-foot rectangle to a six-foot square, the chairs arranged to seat two, possibly three, on a side. The arrangement was comfortable now, with three ornate wood-paneled screens surrounding it to contain the warmth of the fire. Being closer to the kitchen, the pork pie was good and hot, as was the tea. A sideboard was within reach of condiments and desserts. All in all, it was perfect.

"It was Michael's idea. He said he'd seen it done at the Bell Inn to accommodate a private party. There is still work to do. The fireplace at the other end of the room needs a sweep. Once that's done, the plan is to make it into a sitting room, where guests can gather before the meal and after the meal. I've never seen it done, but it sounds lovely and very practical. The drapes need replacing. At first, Mrs. Dorsey thought a good wash would do, but the fabric is moth-eaten and beyond repair."

"When I left, you were in the kitchen with the children. How did you get on?" he asked as he dived into Mrs. Dorsey's savory pork pie.

Audry laughed and shook her head. "They are adorable, irresistible, and in no time, they had me wrapped around their sticky little fingers. We visited Peg, we gathered eggs, and Jeremy showed me how to milk the goat. Edna, Mrs. Dorsey's sister, arrived in a pony cart to fetch them before lunch to take them home with her.

"I insisted on having my lunch with the Dorseys in the kitchen. Suzie had gone to the gatehouse with a meal for Michael. He was applying some whitewash to the walls. They started work on the fireplace right after lunch. It hadn't been used, so there wasn't a lot to do. I did try to help, but Mrs. Dorsey shooed me from the room. And once Suzie returned, I was resigned to reading my book before the fire in the drawing room with a tall glass of nog. I believe Mrs. Dorsey found some old drapes in a cupboard in the east wing. She's washing them and has hopes of getting them hung in here. I haven't seen them, but I'm sure they'll be fine."

"I stopped in at the gatehouse on my way home," Simon said. "The transformation is truly astounding. There are curtains on the windows, the walls are clean, as well as the floors. The faded, holey, overstuffed chairs and sofa were hidden beneath colorful quilts and throws. Even the windowpanes are clean. Michael assured me they were going to be very happy there. I told him he could have a milch cow and some chickens. There is a shed behind the gatehouse. I think it will hold a cow and some chickens. I'll take a closer look tomorrow. We both thought a fenced yard for the boys would be good. But he said he wasn't sure there was a fence high enough to contain his boys. I laughed at the time, but he may be right."

After a long silence, Audry said, "I'm relieved we won't be going riding after our luncheon on Sunday. E we get—uncomfortable—may we leave early?"

"I was thinking along the same lines. Regardless, yes, Friday, it's probably a better plan for our excursion into the countryside."

"Miss Pomeroy, she can be very persuasive," Audry said without giving him a glance.

"She certainly can."

"You—you—admire her?" she said, giving him one of her penetrating, mind-reading stares.

Simon sat back in his chair and dabbed the corners of his mouth with his napkin. "I—I'd have to be blind not to admire her. She's a beautiful young woman."

"It's more than that," she said and tipped her head to the side.

"It can't be more."

"Why not?"

"I'm in no position to consider I have a right to—to formally court anyone, least of all Miss Pomeroy."

"She admires you."

"Audry, how can you say that?"

"Oh, I know. She hangs on your every word. She stammers just a little when she speaks to you."

"Miss Pomeroy does not stammer."

"Oh, maybe not a stammer, but she has to lick her lips a lot, and she blinks, and her cheeks grow a little pink. Her eyes flash and sparkle. It's like she finds it a challenge to impress you. And when you speak to her, it's like there is no one else in the room. It's just the two of you, dueling, firing arrows with your gazes and words."

"If you noticed, then I must be more careful," he said down to his plate.

"I think you are wrong to say you are not in a

position. The position has nothing to do with love. Look at Mother and Father. He wasn't in position, and it didn't stop them. The love they had was deep and all-consuming. You could have that. You deserve that; don't let position get in the way."

"Audry, Audry, my dear girl, you are too much of a romantic for this world in which we find ourselves. All I know is this is not the time. I have a long way to go before I can ask any woman to be my wife. Pamela Pomeroy is not, and will never be, a farmer's wife. A farmer is all I shall ever be. And I will be proud of it. I find satisfaction here, doing what I do."

"And you, dear brother, are far too practical, too grounded. Give yourself the right to dream a little."

He had nothing to say to that. He did dream. His dreams were full of warm caresses, soft kisses, and sweet murmurs of ecstasy. A brief flirtation was all he could hope for. It would have to be enough.

****

A brief flirtation, that's all it could ever be, Pamela decided bright and early Friday morning. She would never be enough woman for the likes of Simon Lawrence. She was too vain, too accustomed to her comforts and privileges. He had things to do. She didn't have to do anything except think about what to wear to the next party, concert, ball, or ride into the country with a country squire so handsome he took her breath away.

Her riding skirt of hunter green fit snugly to her hips, flared, and split at the knee to reveal her black hessian riding boots. The black jacket and waistcoat followed the curve of her bosom. Her black, high-crowned leather hat, with a green plumb that matched the color of the skirt, enhanced her chestnut curls. Heretofore, she'd thought the costume very smart. Now, she thought it laughably ridiculous, impractical, and uncomfortable. Immediately, she shed the jacket and waistcoat. In her jersey, long-sleeved chemise, she traded the jacket and waistcoat for one of the jumpers she'd purloined from Paul's wardrobe.

The last time Paul had worn this particular sweater, he'd been a boy of fifteen, but the rust-colored, wool knit jumper fit her nicely today and would keep her a darn sight warmer than her fashionable, satin waistcoat. Both she and Penny had a couple of their brother's old, cast-off jumpers and breeches, garments their mother knew nothing about.

She searched the top shelf of her wardrobe for the buff-colored, suede riding coat she had kept for no other reason than she couldn't bear to throw it away. The suede was soft as velvet and the rabbit fur collar served to keep her neck warm. She found her fur hat and a pair of fur-lined gloves in a basket on the top shelf. The sun was out, but the temperature was anything but warm.

Penny entered her room, also dressed in one of Paul's old sweaters, a soft, heather gray jumper with tweed dots of red scattered through the threads, and a black riding skirt. Her black wool jacket lying over her arm, she said, "Ah, so we think alike. Better to be warm than fashionable." Crossing the room and standing before Pamela's mirror, she adjusted her black, sealskin cossack hat on her head. "They'll be here soon. Paul ordered Jamison to bring our mounts up to the house."

"Yes, I'm ready. I think I hear the carriage now."

"Mother and Father have gone out to meet them," Penny said, a note of warning in her tone.

"She is determined to dislike them," Pamela said as

she left her room and started down the stairs. "I do hope Jamison has locked Chance up somewhere."

Chapter Twenty

Beside him, Audry, fingers locking and unlocking, heaved a weighty sigh, her gaze taking in the countryside.

Simon had the reins of the one-horse shay the Chase had sent over. The groom, who had delivered the carriage, rode alongside on a sturdy-looking cart pony. “A horseback ride is just what we need,” Simon said and looked out his side of the carriage. “Good day for it, plenty of sun and not at all windy,” he said, looking out to the greener-than-green meadows, and gazing up at the white clouds drifting in a clear blue sky. “We both need some fresh air—do something that doesn’t require us to do more than enjoy the scenery,” Simon said. With his free hand, he reached for her to hold her fingers still.

“I know you’re trying to distract me,” she said, “but I have an uncomfortable feeling we are headed for—I don’t know what, exactly. Nothing unpleasant, I don’t think, but unexpected, different—I don’t know, but it’s making me skittish. I’ve got butterflies flapping around in my stomach, and I don’t know why,” she said.

Simon thought possibly the anticipation of spending the day in the company of Paul Pomeroy might have something to do with the fluttering of those butterflies. He hated to admit it, but spending the day in the company of Pamela Pomeroy had produced a few butterflies in the pit of his stomach as well. He wasn’t sure how he felt about that.

He told himself to never mind how he felt, denial was his only choice. Head tipped to the side, he said, "Could it be we're simply excited? It's all right to be excited, to be happy, to enjoy a day's ride cross country on something other than an overweight, swayback, dray horse. Nothing unpleasant about it. We're going riding across a few fields to partake of an alfresco with some new friends."

"Oh, you know very well what I mean. These new friends live a very different life than we do. Look, look at that," she said and pointed to the grand Palladian home constructed of golden stone blocks situated on a slight rise to the left side of the road. Before the manse proper, the lawns that sloped down to the road were trimmed and manicured, the cedar hedges sculptured into urns, cones, and stacked balls. Rock walls contained three mounded flower beds, and one displayed a grand, three-tiered fountain. The grand, double-door entrance to the interior of the home was protected by four stone pillars that supported the balcony above.

Simon reined the carriage horse to turn off the main road. The groom went ahead. They proceeded through an ornately scrolled iron gate and up a granite paved lane to Pomeroy Chase mansion.

A dog, a very large dog, came charging down the drive. Barking, it circled the carriage. The groom's horse came up on his hind legs, then sidled. The groom kept his seat and cursed the dog. And the barking dog raced ahead of the carriage up the drive to the entrance.

"That dog, he's huge." Laughing, Audry and Simon said at once, "he looks just like the one in great, great grandfather's portrait."

They could see there were people standing before the entrance to the home. Simon recognized Lord Pomeroy and Paul. There was a lady standing between them, a woman, not Pamela, and not her younger sister. "Looks like we have a welcoming committee."

Audry saw them, too. "I hope they are welcoming. I hope the dog is welcoming," Audry said, doom in her tone. "I recall encountering a few lordly ladies in London, and again when I was with Mrs. Dorsey while visiting the modiste shop. They turned up their noses when they passed us as if we smelled of rotten fish."

"I doubt Lady Pomeroy will be of that ilk. From what I can discern, she and Lord John have raised three very accepting, intelligent, personable children to maturity. Lord Pomeroy was all things kind and gracious. I expect his spouse to be the same. By the way, you look charming in your riding costume, and that is a very fetching hat. Is it mink?"

She felt the soft fur of the collar of her red riding coat and then the crown of her hat and shook her head. "No, I don't think so, rabbit maybe, or fox."

"Well, it is very attractive and warm, I should expect."

Paul, to Simon's relief, made sure he was there when the carriage pulled up and came to a stop between the pillared entrance.

"Chance, sit," Paul ordered and waited for the dog to go down on his haunches before he offered his hand to help Audry to the ground.

"Sorry, never mind the dog," Paul said. The dog barked in protest. "Oh, well, might as well introduce you to him first. His name is Chance. This is Audry, Chance. Mind your manners. Don't worry, he won't bite. He's excited," Paul said and tried to shove the exuberant, barely contained dog out of the way with his knee.

Propelling Audry forward, Paul said, "Come, meet my mother. Mother, Miss Audry Lawrence. Audry, our mother, Lady Alice Pomeroy."

Simon couldn't help it, he had to scratch the dog's chest, reward him when he got out of the carriage. The animal was doing such a beautiful job of controlling himself when it was obvious he wanted to jump up and lick them, give them a proper welcome. Simon stepped around the dog, and the dog came to his feet and leaned against his leg.

To give Audry support, Simon placed his hand beneath her elbow as she made a curtsey. Flushed and flustered, she managed to say, "Honor to meet you, Lady Pomeroy."

Paul rushed ahead with his introductions. "Mother, this is Simon Lawrence. Simon, our mother, Lady Alice Pomeroy."

Lady Alice drew herself up, sent a critical gaze toward Simon, offered him a weak smile and said, her hand held out for him to take, "Welcome to Pomeroy Chase, Mr. Lawrence."

"Lady Pomeroy, pleasure to meet you," Simon said. Holding her hand gently with his good hand, he managed a courtly bow. He turned and bowed to Lord Pomeroy who stood next to his good wife.

As soon as he stepped back, Lady Pomeroy cocked her head to the side and zeroed in on Aurdry's delicate visage. "You have your mother's eyes," she said, taking everyone present by surprise.

"You look just like your mother," she said. Arms outstretched, she drew Audry into an embrace. Holding

Audry at arm's length, Lady Alice studied Audry's features up close. "It really is uncanny how much you resemble her. At least in my memory of your mother, you look like her. She might have been a few years younger than you are now. You both have that age-defying, elfin quality about you. We were presented at court together, you see, along with three other young ladies. We weren't close, but I shall never forget your mother. She was so full of life. Like a sprite, she lit up the rooms with her laughter and smile. She had beautiful eyes, so deep blue. Mary, her name was Mary. She loved to dance. Her mother, your grandmother, was ill, unable to accompany her to London. Your grandfather left Mary's debut in the hands of one of his distant cousins, I believe. They weren't very vigilant or caring. She created a few raised eyebrows, I tell you. So full of high spirits. Was she happy in her life? Did she dance?"

Audry nodded. "She was very happy," Audry said, her words choked with tears. "She and my father loved to dance, especially when they thought no one was around. I caught them dancing down the aisle of the drying shed more than once."

"Then I am happy for them. I am truly sorry for your loss. And that is how you must remember them, always dancing in each other's arms. When Mary fled to Gretna Green with her young man, I was very concerned. And then, when we didn't hear from her, we could only speculate. All of us who were presented at court that season, had promised to stay in touch. But we didn't know what had happened, you see. Now you are here, and we are neighbors. I hope she and you know how this pleases me. Sometimes, one does wonder if those who have gone on, somehow, do they guide us to connect down here?"

****

Nothing could have surprised Pamela more. Seeing her mother take Audry Lawrence in her arms left her feeling a bit lightheaded. She waved Chance to come sit by her side. Her hand going to his ears, she calmed him and composed her own jumbled reactions. Her father's sober expression did not reach his eyes. Those eyes fairly glittered with amusement. He quickly averted his gaze and put up his chin.

Audry, trembling, nodding, said, "Lady Pomeroy, you are too kind."

Simon bowed before Lady Pomeroy. "We are indeed fortunate to find ourselves with such welcoming neighbors," he said, his gaze traveling from the lady before him then to the expressionless man standing at her elbow.

To Audry, Lady Alice said, "Well, we'll talk more when you come back from your ride. You'll stay for tea to warm yourselves before you return home?"

Audry nodded, and Simon said, "Thank you, yes. I'm sure tea will be most appreciated. Audry and I have been looking forward to today's outing. We are grateful for the generous offer of the use of your stable." That grin of his in place, eyes dancing, he said, the subject coming out of nowhere, "Forgive me, Lady Pomeroy, but I'd appreciate some gardening advice."

Paul directed Audry to Penny and made the introductions. Confused by Simon Lawrence's interest in gardens, Pamela's attention was drawn to her mother and the ongoing conversation with Simon.

"Your garden beds are splendid," she heard him say. "Sadly, the country garden in front of the Manor has been allowed to go wild. I can't tell the difference between the weeds and the flowers. I did recognize your hydrangeas, and I think I see valerian. Our mother loved hydrangeas."

Once again, Pamela was taken aback and surprised. What in the world was going on? The man seduced everyone. How Simon Lawrence had sussed that gardening was her mother's passion and all-time favorite subject, she did not know—but he had. First, her father returns from the Manor and can talk of nothing else but pigs and dairy farming, and now her mother and her gardens. The man was uncanny.

Chance at her side to help hold her upright, Pamela thought she felt the earth shift beneath her feet.

Brown eyes sparkling with golden flecks, Lady Alice said, "I have a wonderful book on the subject of all things herbal, flowers, shrubs, and trees. I'll find it while you are on your ride, and you may take it home with you to study. Many of the cuttings we have here on the Chase were taken from plants from the Manor. Every spring and fall, we have a garden fair in Stilton. We all share cuttings, seeds, and produce. The tenants depend on it, you see."

"I have a lot to learn," Simon said, blue eyes flashing, a playful smile lighting up his face. Her mother was not immune to that smile or those eyes any more than Pamela. The lady giggled, or at least it sounded like a giggle.

****

"Have you ever?" Penny asked while Paul helped Audry adjust the stirrup to her ladies' saddle.

Pamela knew exactly what her sister referred to. "No, I have not. He is what I believe some would call a spellbinder. I never would have thought Mother susceptible to spells and hypnosis, but there you have it. None of us are immune to a master."

"Well, we certainly have underestimated Mr. Lawrence's ability to charm. And I think Paul is underestimating Audry's horsemanship. Did you see her talking to Lancelot after he did his little protest wave and dance when the groom brought him up the drive from the stables?"

Pamela nodded. "She slipped him a piece of apple from her jacket pocket, Lanny, that is, not Paul. Paul doesn't need to be bribed with treats to attend Miss Lawrence. Haven't you noticed he's besotted?"

Pamela laughed into the collar of her coat and straightened the hem of her riding skirt over her boots. "She slipped Lanny another nibble once she was in the saddle. She mounted all by herself and hardly needed the block at all. I say the girl is absolutely fearless. She didn't wait for Paul to give her a leg up. Lanny stayed perfectly still. He will give her a well-mannered ride. You were right to say the paint would suit her better."

Penny cleared her throat. "I noticed Chance has abandoned you. He's attached himself to Mr. Lawrence."

Penny's saucy smirk said she thought her remark pretty cute. Pamela shrugged her shoulders, refusing to take the bait. But Penny wasn't through with the pokes just yet. "I know you don't really need to use the block either, and yet you allowed Mr. Lawrence to give you a lift."

Pamela huffed dismissively. "He gave you a leg up, too."

"Yes, he did. He's terribly strong, maimed hand notwithstanding. And doesn't he look at home in the saddle—very rugged."

Pamela had noticed the slight wince on Simon's face as he had mounted the mare. She thought it as well this morning's ride would not be a long one. "Enough. Let us ride."

Chapter Twenty-One

Simon tried to shake the feeling it was wrong that things were going along so well. Feeling pretty good, he really wanted to enjoy this outing, the ride along the farm tracks across downs dotted with grazing sheep. He'd felt a slight twinge when he'd mounted, probably because he'd over-extended his leg, forgetting for a second he had injuries. But now he was in the saddle, there was very little discomfort. Enjoyment, pleasant day, good company, it couldn't be this simple, this easy, this right, could it?

Lady Pomeroy's reaction to Audry had given him goosebumps. Audry had taken it well, but surely it had come as a shock. He'd thought to give his sister a chance to recoup by diverting the subject to the safe topic of gardens, little knowing he would hit on the very subject that would ingratiate them even farther into the fold.

The only dark cloud might be in the form of Paul Pomeroy. He needed reining in. He was being way too familiar with his sister. He'd touched Audry's ankle. Actually, his wandering hand had gone a little higher to her calf as he carefully and thoroughly adjusted her stirrup. Perhaps a little man-to-man warning would be in order.

The real thorn needling him was this, why hadn't anyone told them Lady Pomeroy had known their mother, that they'd had their come out together? They could have prepared themselves a little better for this meeting. And about this meeting, this welcome, Paul had said a ride; he hadn't said anything about a formal receiving line.

Simon suspected Pamela Pomeroy of manipulating, orchestrating? But then, Lord Pomeroy wore a very satisfied expression on his face. Was this part of the plot—why the need to change the day of their ride? Why didn't they want it to be Sunday? Simon had some questions for Miss Pomeroy. He had to get her alone. Today was as good a time as any.

He couldn't tell if Audry was having a good time or if she was just being polite and pretending to enjoy her ride. She appeared animated, smiling, and laughing, which was certainly a change for the better. Her painted pony was a bit fresh, in Simon's opinion, but he was the right size for her. Not that Audry couldn't handle almost any horse she might encounter, but she wasn't used to her saddle.

She was making him nervous. As soon as they went through the paddock gate, she set her mount into a fast trot, then an all-out gallop. Paul and Penny were keeping up with her, Paul on his dapple gray and Penny on her sleek, black Arabian, all appeared to be enjoying the race. Chance, barking, giving chase, encouraged the riders.

"You look worried," Pamela said as she came alongside. Her mount was a chestnut gelding with a star blaze and white socks. Clearly, his sorrel mare and the gelding were friends. They whickered and bobbed their heads and set their gaits to match.

Simon smiled automatically, but he wished he could stop doing that, stop giving away his secret attraction to the woman. “So, you read minds, too?”

She chuckled. “Hmm, no, I read expressions, brotherly, concerned expressions. I’m familiar with them. You see, I have an older brother.” She tipped her head to the side and offered him a cheeky little smile. “Let me guess, number one worry: you’re worried your sister will fall off her horse and break her neck because she is unused to a lady’s saddle. Number two worry: you’re concerned, no,” she said, her gaze narrowing in on his eyes, “no, not worried, you perceived you witnessed my brother taking liberties with your sister’s person. And you are considering having a little talk with him on the subject.”

He wanted to laugh. He really did. She was spot on. But he couldn’t give her the satisfaction of admitting she had read him correctly. Instead, he went directly to what was eating at him. “Did you know your mother knew our mother? If so, why didn’t you tell us? A little warning might have been nice. It came as a big shock. Your mother’s… revelation has brought up all kinds of…of…memories. Audry has been through enough. She really wasn’t prepared for your mother’s reaction to meeting her. And neither was I. Audry does resemble our mother in many ways. But she is not our mother in temperament or demeanor. Audry is very much her own person.” God, he thought he might choke on his unshed tears. He had to look away, and when he did, his hip gave him a sharp twinge.

Gritting his teeth against the spasm in his hip and shoulder, Simon wished he’d kept his thoughts to himself. He shifted his weight and corrected his seat in the saddle. The only sounds to be heard were the clip-clop and snuffling of their horses as they rode side by side along the farmer's track down over a pasture that would take them to the bridge and the gamekeeper's cottage.

Pamela cleared her throat and spoke very carefully. "The day we met you and Peg when we almost ran her down, Paul told Father, in detail, what had happened. I had given Mother an abbreviated, much-redacted version of the incident, sensing she would object to my part. Once the entire story was out, we all speculated as to who you were and where you'd come from, as residents of a small parish are wont to do. Strangers always evoke curiosity.

"Father has lived at Pomeroy Chase his entire life, he knows everyone, their families, their history. Mother is very active in the community with the tenants. We concluded you had come from the Manor because of where we found Peg. I think you will discover there are many people here that remember your mother. Her home was here. She attended church here. She was born here. The Dorseys knew your mother very well, I'm sure. They no doubt have seen the resemblance, too, but being the polite servants they are, I perceive they've said nothing.

"Mother recalled she had made her come out with Sir Simon-Loyd's daughter. She remembered her as being very beautiful and that she'd married a man to whom Sir Simon-Loyd disapproved. Much more than that, she didn't say at the time. Your mother's presentation at court, all of that was before our mother met my father. What she did today took all of us by surprise. I'm sorry if it has upset Audry…and you…I'm sorry. I have no control over what my mother will say and do. I'm sorry," she said and spurred her mount to move on without him.

****

Well, now Simon felt like a complete fool, a fool for overreacting. Of course his mother had lived here, so why shouldn't people recall her looks, her demeanor? He and Audry needed to be reminded of that. He wanted to urge his mount into a full gallop, catch up with Pamela, apologize, but he didn't dare, his shoulder and hip had gone into cramp. Sweat had formed on his upper lip and brow. He closed his eyes and prayed no one would be around to witness his pain-riddled, awkward dismount.

Ahead of him, the dog trotting alongside, he watched Pamela cross the arched stone bridge and turn up a narrow path into a copse. Smoke curled and clung to the trees from the chimney of the gamekeepers' cottage. Gracefully, Pamela positioned her horse next to the rail before the cottage and slid from her saddle to the ground. She straightened her skirt, waved Chance to heel, and they entered the cottage. She didn't give Simon the satisfaction of a glance.

In not so gracefully a fashion, Simon was able to dismount. He was grateful no one was there to watch. He bowed his head against the horse's neck to steady himself. Squaring his shoulders, taking a deep breath, he limped up the short path to the stone-arched entrance to the cottage.

The heavy wooden door stood open. To gather his composure, he stood in the doorway a moment or two and allowed his eyes to adjust to the dim interior. Chance came over and licked his hand.

Audry left the warmth of the fire to greet him, her beautiful face alight with excitement, joy, and a hint of tears forming in her blue eyes. "This is what these people call an alfresco," she said and stifled a snicker behind her gloved hand. "Penny said Rudy, that's the boy setting out the food for us, wants to go to Paris to learn to be a chef. For now, though, he has to work in the kitchen at the Chase. Lord Pomeroy is encouraging his ambitions."

Against the far wall, a teenage servant, a boy, stood placing silverware and napkins in a row on a table constructed of old doors covered with a linen tablecloth. Upon the table were five game hens roasted to a golden brown, each on its own platter, surrounded by an assortment of vegetables arranged in the shapes of woodland creatures. In the center of the table was a tower of tarts: apple, berry, and lemon decorated with sugar-coated berries. At the end of the table, there was a pot of tea kept warm by three votive candles in a holder beneath the pot, cups and saucers, a pitcher of cream, and one of treacle. It was a buffet feast. Five chairs and an occasional table had been placed before the rustic fireplace for the diners.

In many ways, this cottage reminded Simon of Virginia. The floor was of stone and clay. The walls were river rock, and the roof was thatched and sagging. There were bird droppings in the corner beside the fireplace. The beams that stretched across the one-room hovel were rough, honed black with age. The windows at the back of the room were missing their glass, but the fireplace was grand, with a warming oven above and one on the side, two swing arms for kettles. Their very first home in Virginia had been very much like this cottage. He and his father had built their cabin on the land the company had designated for the plantation. But they needed shelter that first year and the one-room cabin was all they had time to build.

"This place, does it remind you of Virginia?" he asked. Audry nodded, and her eyes grew misty. "Are you all right?" Simon asked her.

"Of course, yes," she said and shook her head. "I miss Virginia, but I don't want to go back there. This place reminds me of the happy times. The times we worked and played together. Are you all right? Your brows are furrowed. Is it your shoulder or your leg?"

He nodded and shrugged his shoulders. "I'm fine, a little twinge, nothing more. Don't worry about me. I have a good mount, and the day is fine."

She patted him on the chest. "Good. You were right about the horseback ride. Lanny was, is, precisely what I need. He's lovely. And I don't even mind the lady's saddle. It is surprisingly comfortable. I think Paul made it more so by adjusting the stirrups for me."

"You and Paul? You like him?"

"Yes—I like him, of course," she said, but her blush said so much more. Ducking her head, she went to the serving table to retrieve her luncheon.

Resigned, he nodded and turned to stand in the doorway of the cottage, his aching hand in his pocket knotted up in a fist. Chance laid down at his feet. From the doorway, Simon could make out the steeply tiled rooftops of the Manor. Feminine fingers wrapped around the wrist of his mutilated hand, and he sucked in his breath. "I told you one can see the Manor from here," Pamela said.

Without looking at her, he asked, "Who owns this cottage?"

Her head nearly resting on his shoulder, she said, "It is shared between the Chase, Fairview, and the Manor. No one really owns it. There has been some talk of converting this cottage into a school for the tenant children. For those tenants who choose to send their children to school, the children are taken all the way into Huntingdonshire three days a week. And it's very expensive. Because of the distance and the time away from home, many children don't go to school at all. We all maintain the cottage and use it from time to time, like today. There is a gamekeeper, but he doesn't live here. He lives in Stilton and checks on the wildlife during hunting seasons."

"Why did you change the day for this ride?" he asked her.

She hesitated before making her reply. "Ah, well, unbeknownst to us, Mother also invited some people for Sunday dinner. We didn't know—how could we—when we proposed our ride for Sunday. With more people present on Sunday, we didn't think we should plan a ride. The people she invited are not the horseback riding-the-back-lanes-of-the-countryside, alfresco luncheon type. Besides, we'd much rather have you and Audry all to ourselves."

Her hand on his wrist, her head less than an inch away from his shoulder, he knew this was the excuse he'd been hoping for, but he found it difficult to declare a resounding retreat and waffled. "Maybe we should forgo the Sunday dinner if your mother made other plans for the day."

He looked down at her, and their gazes met and locked. He put his hand over hers. "I must apologize. As I said before, I wasn't thinking. All of this," he said and waved his free hand to the scenery and the horses, "is unexpected. I'm having a difficult time believing in it, in any of it. We lived where no one knew us, or cared where we came from, our families, our ancestors. To be here where everyone knows our history, knows things about our family that we don't, is strange. It's new and will take some getting used to. Maybe an intimate Sunday dinner isn't the best idea. Perhaps after a bit more time, we could, but not now."

She shook her head and tucked in even closer, her hip touching his thigh. "Yes, I can understand. It must all be rather overwhelming and sudden, I suppose. If it's any solace, Father didn't warn us either, and I'm pretty sure he knew what Mother's reaction to Audry would be. After his meeting with your sister, he knew Audry was the spitting image of her mother. He didn't say a word. Now, I look back on the conversation at the table, all he said was that he hoped Mother would withhold her opinion until she met you and your sister.

"You see, Mother was concerned that you and Father, seated at the same table, would dominate every conversation with your interests in farming. Father is very wily. You could back out of Sunday dinner, but I hope you don't. Really Simon, Paul, Penny, and especially me, we hope you will come, sit at our table, be our special guests as our new neighbors, as our new friends. Besides, we need you to save us from ourselves and the pair Mother has invited. I warn you now, they are insufferable prigs."

He laughed aloud this time. "Miss Pomeroy, you are incorrigible."

"I know, I've been accused of that many, many, many times."

****

From the small, grimy window of the cottage, Pamela had watched him dismount. His jaw tight, eyes squeezed tightly shut, complexion gone bloodless. She sensed Simon Lawrence was in a lot of pain and wondered if anyone else had noticed. She thought Audry had. She'd gone up to her brother immediately when he entered the room.

Pamela had deliberately stayed close as they rode down the lane, ignoring Paul, Penny, and Audry as they urged their mounts into a race. She noticed when he'd mounted back at the Chase that it took a great deal of will and fortitude for him to get in the saddle. Oh, yes, Simon Lawrence was strong and very stubborn.

Chapter Twenty-Two

"I thought you'd gone with your brother and the girls on the hike up the hill to admire the view," Simon said.

Seated on a bench at the table, facing the fire, Pamela shook her head. "Chance and I decided to stay here. Didn't feel much like hiking after that big meal. Although, I think I have room for a tart. Is there a lemon left?"

Chance, sound asleep and snoring, had stretched out before the fire like a long, wooly rug. Simon didn't question why, but he spoke very softly so as not to wake him. "I helped Rudy pack up what remained of our lunch. He's gone back to Pomeroy Chase. But yes, I asked him to leave the tarts." From the basket on the table, he selected a couple of napkins.

"I was interested in his goat cart. I think we should have one at the Manor. There might even be one somewhere. I'll ask Milo. We have goats; we just need the cart. Might have to make one. I know we have wheels. I've moved them out of the way several times over," he said and brought her a lemon tart on a napkin and an apple tart for himself. "There is tea left, too. Probably cold by now."

She took the tart from him and shook her head. "No, just the tart is fine." She moved down the bench to make room for him. "Please sit down. I broke my arm once. I was seven. I'd attempted to fly off the roof of the potting shed. I had on a cape. I spread it out like a bat's wings. I was sure it would work. I landed sideways. My neck hurt more than my arm. I can't imagine how much pain you must be in."

He sat beside her on the bench, their hips touching. "I really don't want to talk about it," he said.

"Oh, I'm aware of that. No need, just know that I know."

"There you go, being incorrigible again."

"And you are stubborn, stoic to a ridiculous degree, and thoroughly the most intriguing man, *person*, I've ever encountered."

"Intriguing?"

"Yes. There is nothing artificial about you. How do you do that?"

"Why does that make me intriguing? Are you implying I'm naive or simple?"

She laughed at that. "Hardly, neither, far from it," she said and took a good-sized bite out of her tart. Covering her mouth while she chewed and swallowed, she said, "I believe you know exactly who and what you are. And you are very comfortable with who and what you are, and you do what you do expertly. Most of us have not an inkling who and what we are, or who and what we want to be, but you know. I envy you."

He finished off his tart, removed her tart from her fingers, and set it down on the table. He brought her up to stand before him and cupped her face with his hands. "I know this: I want you. I adore what I see. I love your incorrigible spirit," he said.

He kissed her as she had never been kissed before. It was deep, bone-melting, earth-shatteringly, passion-fueled.

She swayed, and Simon wrapped his arms around her waist. "I shouldn't have done that," he said, his breath warm against her ear.

"Oh, but I'm so glad that you did," she said, her hands braced against his chest.

"All the more reason why I should not have taken advantage," he said.

"You can't take it back," she said and giggled. "I won't let you."

He let her go to stand to the side of the hearth, careful not to disturb the dog. "If I were an honorable man, I would go immediately to your father and beg for your hand. I am a coward and a fool, and I don't care to humiliate myself by doing any such thing. I have nothing to offer you. Your father knows, and I'm sure he wants more for you than to be the wife of a poor, crippled farmer."

His reasoning was sound. Pamela knew he was correct, and yet, she didn't consider him crippled, and the prospect of never sharing another kiss or embrace with Simon Lawrence was unacceptable. She came abruptly to her feet. Chance rolled over and raised his head while she paced the room. She stepped over the dog and grabbed Simon by the lapels of his coat. "Very well, let's have an affair. We can meet here. This will be our love nest."

"Incorrigible," he said and set her at arm's length. "You can't be serious."

She gave him a gentle shake.

"No, you don't know what you're saying."

Shaking her head, she opened her mouth to protest.

His hands over hers, holding them to his breast, he

said, "No. Your brother would call me out and shoot me dead, and I wouldn't blame him. No. This has to be the end."

Pamela didn't say it out loud, but she answered in her head: *this is the beginning. It has to be.*

****

The day proved something of an eye-opening revelation for Paul. Audry Lawrence was what he wanted. She was courageous, beautiful, hardy, funny, and so very loveable, and she had a voice like an angel. How in the world he could have thought Lucinda Abernathy his ideal, he couldn't say. He knew, without a doubt, he would ask Simon for permission to court her. His mother's reaction to Audry had surprised him and delighted him. He would have her. He was certain Simon couldn't object. He'd wait, of course. After a brief courtship, he would ask permission to make his offer.

They'd kissed behind the tree. He shouldn't have surrendered to temptation, but he had to taste those lips. She'd tripped over a root and had nearly fallen. Both of them laughing, he'd caught her, but when she found her balance, she came up on her toes, begging for his kiss. Her lips were a bit stiff at first, but they'd limbered up with a bit of massage. She had participated as a willing innocent should—not with expertise, but enthusiasm.

****

"I think it only fair I warn you," Penny said. She and Audry were walking arm in arm down the track back to the cottage. Paul, ahead of them a few paces, was singing a marching song, arms swinging.

"Warn me?"

"Yes, he sings all the time. Come Sunday he'll enlist you into singing in the choir. I'm sure of it."

"I love to sing. We sang a duet at the Manor. He has a wonderful voice," Audry said.

"Ah, of course you would say so," Penny said and laughed. "You are a perfect match, I should say."

"Match?" Audry said.

"Yes, match. Mother's approval pretty much sealed the deal."

"I don't know what you are talking about."

"Audry, how would you like to be my sister?"

"Penny, you are being ridiculous," Audry said. "I'm not going to listen to you. You spout nonsense. I've never had a sister, but, as sisters go, I should think you and I would suit very well."

"So, you are going to pretend that you are not equally as smitten with my brother as he is with you?"

"Really, Penny, this conversation is embarrassing."

"While I was pointing out the church spire, you both disappeared behind that big oak tree, and he kissed you, didn't he?"

Audry felt the rush of heat all the way up to her ears and cursed herself for blushing—it was a certain giveaway. He had kissed her, and she had kissed him back. Oh, it had been a dream, a wonderful dream. The whole day was a dream. Audry expected to wake up any minute and discover she was alone in her big, cold bed. "Does your brother do that often—kiss girls behind trees?" she asked.

"He does not. At least, I've never known him to do such a thing," Penny said. "And I have known him for seventeen years. He's been soppy over a few girls, but as far as I know, he's never kissed any of them. None that I've heard of." Penny came to a sudden stop and shook her head before taking another step. "I suppose he has.

After all, he's almost ten years older than me—a man. Actually, I've never thought of it before. I wonder…."

Audry had told Simon she'd never thought of marriage. But today, today she could think of little else. The promise of a life with Paul, Penny, Pamela, and their beautiful mother and kind father, living at Pomeroy Chase—that was the stuff of fairytales. It would be perfect, and Simon would be close by. She could see him whenever she liked.

Paul's singing stopped as they approached the cottage. Audry and Penny entered the cottage, and instantly, Audry sensed something was amiss. Unsmiling, brows puckered in deep thought, Simon stood at the hearth, his back to the door.

Pamela, at the table, packed a basket with the tea kettle and a few tarts. "Ah, you're back. Good," she said. "Mother will have a fresh pot waiting for us at the Chase," she said. Chance following her, his head and tail down, Pamela went outside to her horse.

The oppressive air was palpable, and none of them spoke. Audry assumed Simon and Pamela had had an argument of some sort. Paul helped her mount her pinto. With a wink, he said, "My sister sometimes has that effect on men." He patted her hand and went to help Penny mount. Audry watched Simon bring his horse around to the front step and waited to be sure he could manage without assistance. She took note he very carefully swung his bad leg over. Shoulders hunched, he gripped the saddle horn for a bit longer than usual.

Paul took the lead, the basket in his lap, and they started out for Pomeroy Chase.

Chapter Twenty-Three

Reins in hand, seated in the one-horse shay, Simon set out for home after their tea with Lord and Lady Pomeroy. On her lap, Audry, seated next to him, had the Gardener's Guide to a Green Thumb.

He was exhausted. It had taken everything he had to keep up the appearance of someone whose heart was not bleeding. He wanted Pamela in the rawest way a man can want a woman, but he knew damn good and well it was not to be. She, however, he also knew, was not about to give up.

Ignoring her had proved impossible. She'd deliberately sat next to him on the settee in the drawing room as they enjoyed their tea, her knee brushing against his, her shoulder rubbing against his arm. Audry was of little help. She'd handed Pamela the gardening book, which gave Pamela the opportunity to turn the pages as her mother pointed out the plants and chapters that might interest him.

Anxious to be away, a hasty and easy escape was not to be. Delay arrived with Paul, who tagged him on the way out the door, taking him aside to let him know he wanted to speak with him tomorrow. He asked permission to pay a call. Simon couldn't say no. Audry stood very close by, and he was sure she was listening in on their conversation. Pamela also had been listening, and she too said she might tag along. She had something to discuss with Mrs. Dorsey. Simon couldn't imagine what that might be. He shuddered to think.

They'd no sooner set upon the main road when Audry said, right out of the blue, "I think I should tell you that Paul kissed me today. He's going to ask your permission to pay court, I'm pretty sure."

Simon cringed. Paul Pomeroy was doing the honorable thing, as opposed to himself, who, because he couldn't bear the humiliation, would not be doing the honorable thing. "Do you want him to court you? One kiss is not a contract for life," he said aloud and internally accused himself of being a bloody bounder and a hypocrite. "I can turn him off. If it's not what you want."

She laughed at him and tapped him lightly on the knee. "Not want a handsome, wealthy, kind, generous, caring man, who loves to sing, to court me with the intent of eventual marriage, what kind of idiot do you take me for? Of course, I want his suit. I enjoyed the kiss, by the way. It was my very first."

"Well, be careful. Don't give away too many kisses. I'm happy for you. I like Paul. I worry this has come on rather suddenly. There is no rush."

"What about you? You and Pamela? You argued, I take it?"

"No, we didn't argue. She's a lovely woman. I told you before, I admire her. Please let it drop, Audry. Please."

They rode in silence for a while. He didn't want her to think his heart was bruised, so he forced himself to make conversation. "Lady Pomeroy revealing she knew our mother as a girl came as a shock to me and to you, I believe. Pamela reminded me that our mother grew up here in this parish. Mrs. Dorsey and Milo knew her as a child, as a young woman. They didn't say anything, of course. Maybe they should have. Lord Pomeroy, when he met you, he didn't say anything either. We are going to attend church, and there are going to be people there who knew our mother, knew our grandfather and grandmother. We have a history here about which we know very little. It's an odd situation. It makes me want to go back into hiding."

"I don't. Not anymore," Audry said.

Simon had nothing to say to that statement. He was left to search his mind for a neutral topic, then remembered he had more to share. "Oh, and we are not the only guests for Sunday dinner. Lady Pomeroy has invited two other guests. It is why our ride was moved forward to today. From what Pamela said, the guests would not have enjoyed a horseback ride cross country, or a luncheon served in a rundown gamekeeper's cottage. I believe the term she used to describe them was 'insufferable prigs.' I did offer to opt out of the invitation, but she asked me not to. From what I could gather, we are to provide a buffer of some sort. I'm not sure how we are to do that, but we will go and do the best we can."

****

The day after their ride, they'd barely finished their lunch when Paul showed up on the Manor doorstep. Suzie escorted Paul into the library, where Simon had gone to do some calculations. The mantle clock struck one of the o'clock precisely, as Simon directed Paul to have a seat before the desk.

Wasting not a second, Paul said, arms straight and hands braced on his knees, "I've come to ask your permission to pay court to Miss Audry." Seated on the edge of his chair in the cavernous library of the manor, his voice, as well as the ticking of the mantle clock, echoed in the ensuing silence.

Simon folded his hand over his twisted fingers. "This day has come sooner than I had expected," he said. "When we came here, I thought Audry and I would remain, for the most part, reclusive. I had accepted that someday, far down the road, someone special would come along, give her all that she deserves, and I would lose her." He got up from behind the desk and went to the floor-to-ceiling windows. Hands in his pockets, he spoke to the English countryside. "I have reservations," he said. "You, I presume, will be leaving for London in a few months. What then?"

Paul hesitated, then joined him at the window and faced him. "Last night, when I spoke to Mother and Father, I told them, and my sisters, of my intentions. Father raised this very question. I have my own residence in London, in Grosvenor Square. I would make Audry my wife before the season begins, and we would have our honeymoon in London. I suggested to Mother she take Audry under her wing for the season. Penny is coming out. She and Audry get along. Pamela will be there for both of them. Mother agreed. They both, Mother and Father, appeared to be relieved at my choice. Pamela and Penny, of course, applauded my good sense."

Simon shook his head. "I want Audry to be happy. I know you would make her happy, but there is a problem. My sister is not going to do well in London. She knows nothing about what it entails to maintain a residence in London's environs or entertain an up-and-coming lord. She would be required to socialize. Until a few days ago, she was petrified of strangers. Thanks to you, and your family, she has found friends that make her feel less threatened. She would never, never be able to endure a season in London attending balls, routs, concerts, theaters. No, I shudder to think of the damage it would do to her nerves. You have known my sister for less than a week. You know nothing about her. Nothing."

Paul made a circuit around the room and came back to the window. "Then tell me about her. I want to know. I sensed she was afraid that first day we met her."

Simon heaved a weighty sigh and considered what he should and shouldn't say. "She's always been reticent, not shy exactly, she simply gets uneasy in a crowd, the noise, the closeness of all the people jostling. Think of her as one of your horses." He shook his head at himself for reducing his sister to this level, but he had to make the man see what he was asking his sister to do. "She's never going to be at home in a crowd. She will be loyal and sweet-natured but do not try to put her in tight spaces with a lot of movement, flashing colors, and vibrations. She will freeze, panic, she might get sick to her stomach or buckle. And then she retreats into herself, ashamed of her weakness. She shuts down and goes silent and unseeing. No, Paul, you can't do this to her. Don't try. Accept her for who and what she is, or walk away."

Simon faced him and extended his hand for Paul to shake, "For now, you have my permission because I know it is what my sister wants. She has a dowry, it's pitiful, but it is something. For now, let us take it slowly. You pay her court, see if this is something that will last, and we'll talk again in a month. Tell her about your home in London, what her role would be in your life, what her life could be if she becomes your wife."

"Thank you, Simon."

"I believe Audry is outside the door. Mrs. Dorsey said she would serve tea in the parlor. You have about fifteen minutes of alone time with my sister before I send Suzie to chaperone. Leave the door open."

"Yes, yes, thank you."

"Paul," Simon said to call him back, "your sister, Pamela, said she was going to come along."

"She went with Milo to say hello to Peg. She brought her some acorn squash from our root cellar that our cook was going to toss. Then she said she was going to see Mrs. Dorsey in the kitchen."

"Why?" Simon asked himself and made his way to the back of the house. He stopped short of the kitchen doorway. He heard Pamela's voice. He was ashamed of himself, but he decided to eavesdrop as his presence might inhibit the discussion, and he wanted to know what his incorrigible Miss Pomeroy was up to.

"If we had a school close by, do you think the tenants would allow their children to attend?" Pamela asked. "It was Audry who set me to thinking about it. She mentioned she'd had a lovely morning playing with the Tidmore boys. She'd played number games with the older boy. The child said his grandpa was teaching him. Audry showed the boy some old maps she'd unearthed from the library here. He was very interested."

Simon heard Mrs. Dorsey set what he presumed to be cups and saucers down on the table, and then he heard her pull a chair out from under the table. "I know my sister would be glad to have a school. Her husband, you know, he was a tutor to the Fairfield boys for a number of years. Edna was a parlor maid at the Hall at one time."

"What? This is the first I've heard. Well, now that is

very interesting."

"What is all this about?" asked Mrs. Dorsey.

"Maybe you know we had luncheon yesterday at the old gamekeeper's cottage. Mother had mentioned that, at one time, there was talk about converting it into a school for the tenant children. I think it could be done rather easily. Between the Manor, the Chase, and Fairfield, we have enough resources, books, chairs, and tables, but what we don't have is a schoolmaster.

"But, the more important question is, would the tenants allow their children to attend? I've heard the private school in Huntingdonshire is expensive. I know many of the children are needed to work their lands. I thought if we limited our hours at the school to, say, four hours, three days a week, and sent reading and study material home with the children, it might work well for everyone, parents and children alike. We'd have to discuss cost, upkeep, and a stipend for the schoolmaster."

Mrs. Dorsey appeared unable to speak and took a deep breath before saying, "Bless you, Miss Pamela. I think that sounds like a beautiful dream. Would you like me to take this idea of yours to my sister's husband?"

"Would you? His name is Wilber Ward, isn't it? Your sister is Edna? I know I've seen them in church with you."

"May I ask, does Master Simon or Lord and Lady Pomeroy know what you are about?" Mrs. Dorsey asked.

"No, not yet. I thought I should do a bit of investigating first. To see if the plan would be feasible."

Simon stood in stunned silence in the hall outside the kitchen, eyes closed, a tear rolling down his cheek. God, he loved this woman.

****

Paul, on the way home from the Manor, told Pamela that Simon had given his permission but with reservations. Repeating some of what Simon said, he told Pamela why Simon didn't think he should expect Audry to endure or enjoy a London Season. Paul hadn't told Audry what her brother had said. Pamela thought that was a mistake.

"I think you should know Audry and Simon have been through hell," Pamela said. "Father doesn't know, and neither does Simon, but on our first visit, I overheard Simon telling Father some of the terror they'd been through."

Paul groaned.

"Yes, I know, I was snooping. Anyway, their plantation was set upon by raiders in the middle of the night. Their home and their warehouses were set on fire. Simon was wounded by shrapnel. Their father rushed Audry and their mother to a root cellar. Their mother ran back to the house, now engulfed in flames. The father rushed in to stop her, and both of them were incinerated right before Audry's eyes. Audry was found and taken in by the local pastor. It was a week before either of them knew that each had survived. That experience alone would leave a person's nerves damaged. And if she was already someone who found it difficult to be surrounded by a lot of people, then it all might get more so after the trauma. All I'm saying is, and what I think Simon has told you, is if you truly love her, Paul, you must get to know her, and love all the parts of her, even the flaws you would wish you could erase, or heal, but cannot."

"She hasn't told me any of this," Paul said.

"You've only known Audry for a few days, Paul. I

realize you loved her at first sight. And I do believe that can happen, and that it is very real. But where and how will she fit in with the life you are destined to live? You both must find a way, a way together."

For all the good advice she had given Paul, Pamela had none for herself. She was still at a loss as to how she was going to get out of participating in another season in London. She had found her passion, and within that passion, there was a project that would keep her where she wanted to be. She wanted to be with Simon, living and working with the people who kept the Manor, the Chase, and Fairfield afloat. She wanted to make their lives better, and she wanted to make Simon's life sweeter and give her own life meaning.

****

"The gamekeeper's cottage, there was talk of converting it into a school. What happened with that?" Pamela asked her mother over their supper.

"The subject does arise now and then. But there is a problem. Many of the tenants' children are expected to work their lands, and the time allotted for classes is a contentious one, to say the least. And the expense of sending them away from home daily discourages most of the tenants. Then there is the problem of finding a schoolmaster or someone qualified to act as a schoolmaster."

Pamela, to control her enthusiasm, pressed her lips together and held her tongue while her mother spoke. She nodded, paused, and then said, "I was speaking to Mrs. Dorsey today; she said that her sister's husband, Mr. Ward, at one time, had been a tutor to the Fairfields. He was pensioned off and given a cottage. I didn't know that. Do you remember anything about Mr. Ward being a tutor?"

"I'd completely forgotten about that. Yes, I believe he was. That was a long while back, though, Pamela," her father said.

"Has the new Lord Fairfield been included in these discussions?" she asked.

"The subject has come up more than once. I'm sure the late Lord Fairfield had been apprised of the possibility. As for the young Lord of Fairfield, he would know Mr. Ward. He had him as his tutor before he left for university. He most probably would also know there was talk of a school for the tenants. Why do you ask, Pamela?"

"I recently recalled, while we were at the cottage, that not long ago it had been suggested to make better use of the gamekeeper's cottage, that it could be converted to a school. That's all. Simply thinking. If we here at Pomeroy Chase, Copeland Manor, and at Fairfield, all of us defrayed the cost, supplied the books, maps, and tables, and contributed to a wage for a schoolmaster, it might be possible to provide the tenant children with a free school. Not a full-time school. I thought possibly a school with limited hours and take-home lessons could work. I don't really know, but I'm looking for the possibilities. Would Lord Fairfield object to the plan?"

Her father cleared his throat. "Let's ask him when we see him tomorrow in church. Lady Fairfield has taken charge of the children's choir, I understand. She might have some suggestions."

Chapter Twenty-Four

Lord Pomeroy approached Simon after the service and invited him to follow him to an antechamber. “Lord Fairfield, meet Simon Lawrence of Copeland Manor. He’s Sir Simon-Loyd’s grandson, recently home from the colonies,” Lord Pomeroy said, leaving the door slightly ajar behind him. “Simon, this is another neighbor, Lord Robert Fairfield, of Fairfield Hall.”

Simon hadn’t expected the Lord of Fairfield Hall to be quite so young. He looked to be younger than Paul, maybe the same age as Pamela. “It is a pleasure to meet our neighbors, Lord Fairfield.”

He and Audry had been introduced to many of the parishioners before the service. Audry had stayed her usual quiet self at his side, nodding and smiling when addressed. There were a half-dozen squires who were interested in his pigs. A marquis, who had dominated the conversation about the dairy farming business, was confused as to who he was and where Copeland Manor was located until Lord Pomeroy explained Simon was Sir Simon-Loyd’s grandson.

Vicar Bodine’s wife purposefully welcomed Audry, declaring she had the look of her mother about her. Audry was looking splendid today in her new frock of winter-green brocade with white and pink rosettes and her bonnet of pink velvet. She had turned many heads the moment the old Copeland Manor coach pulled up into the yard before the church, and Milo came to help her alight.

During the service, the vicar announced their presence to one and all. Audry visibly shrank during this exposure, sliding behind his shoulder in her attempt to go unnoticed. Both he and Audry had enjoyed the hymns and appreciated the quality of the choir, but the vicar's sermon on the virtues of temperance had nearly put Simon to sleep.

He was able to convince Mrs. Dorsey, Milo, and the Tidmores to sit in the Copeland Manor pew with him and Audry. It was a long pew, and he'd been told by the vicar that it had sat vacant far too long and that he was pleased to see it occupied at long last. Three-year-old Dennis Tidmore grew restless during the long-winded sermon and insisted on crawling under the pew. His father caught him. And the boy, once held firmly in his father's arms, went to sleep. Jeremy, leaning against his mother, also closed his eyes and snoozed the sermon away in quiet repose.

Before the services had started, Paul had asked Audry to join him and sit with the church choir, but she declined, stating she needed a bit more practice before joining. Paul accepted her excuse with good grace and offered to come to Copeland a couple of times a week to practice the hymns. Simon suspected this ruse as a means to proceed with the courting of his sister—choir practice, indeed.

During the introduction to the young Lord Fairfield, Pamela quietly entered the antechamber, closed the door behind her, and came to stand beside her father. "Lord Robert, I've been speaking with Lady Kathrine," she said with a bright smile on her lips and a sparkle in her lovely brown eyes. “She’s doing a wonderful job with the children’s choir. She tells me, for the most part, they are tenant children.”

“True,” the young lord said. “She’s very fond of all of them. They’ve practically moved into the Hall. Now they come twice a week at mid-morning to practice in our music room. Nanny gives them biscuits and milk. I told Kathrine that’s what they really come for, not the music.”

Pamela laughed politely. Her father nodded and she put forth her proposition. Simon, who had supposedly no inkling as to what she was about to say, kept his mouth shut and stood back to watch her operate. Between Lord Pomeroy and his daughter, they had cornered poor Lord Fairfield right and proper. Simon admired their maneuvering tactics. They were experts. He must keep that in mind going forward.

Pamela fluttered those beautiful, big brown eyes of hers and said, “Speaking of the children, we were at the gamekeeper’s cottage the other day, and I recalled that at one point, it was suggested it be transformed into a schoolhouse for the tenant children. As I understand it, the sticking points have always come down to two things: would the children be allowed to attend, and could we find a schoolmaster? I was speaking to Mrs. Dorsey, and she reminded me that her brother-in-law, Wilber Ward, had, at one time, been a tutor for you and your brothers. She informs me Mr. Ward isn’t averse to the idea of a small school where he could take up his profession once more.

“He’s been instructing the Tidmore boy in mathematics. If we, at Pomeroy Chase, and at Copeland Manor, and you at Fairfield could supply the tables and chairs and books from our own libraries, and with Mr. Ward as a schoolmaster, who is willing to discuss the possibilities, we could open a proper school come fall, after harvest time, of course. A school for the children of our tenants for very little cost to us and of great benefit to all."

Simon had to suppress his urge to clap and cheer. She'd put forth her proposal succinctly and reasonably. Young Lord Fairfield stood blinking, obviously slightly dumbfounded by all the information she'd laid out. He sputtered a bit. "You know, this is exactly what Lady Kathrine has been going on about for months now. Not in this much detail, but she has lamented there is no proper school for the tenants. We are newly married, you know, and I'm unused to the ladies and their interest in all things local. I say it is a capital idea. Our library is overflowing with tomes, maps, books on shipbuilding and mining, codes for this and that, literature, old diaries, and even old sheet music. I'm sure our attics have enough furniture to supply a dozen schoolhouses. But…and here is the but, I don't know if the tenants will go along with it. They depend on their offspring to help with the livestock and the crops."

"Yes, I know. And I understand it is a hurdle we will have to address. I thought a school where students attend two or three days a week for a few hours and take-home assignments they could do at their own pace might be the answer. We would have to provide slates, chalk, and materials. I think it would benefit the parents, too. They might learn right along with their children.

"No one would be made to attend the school; it would simply be available with no charge. Or could we, perhaps, give the tenants an incentive to send their children to school by giving them a credit of some sort for shoes or fabric? Or, oh, I don't know, surely there is something they need that we could put out there to entice them to take advantage of receiving an education for their children."

"I better find my wife," Lord Robert said. "You've, no doubt, set her lively mind off onto another quest. I'll be glad to get her back to London and balls, shopping, and the theater, and me back to Parliament and leave the country behind. Consider Fairfield in favor of your proposal. I will leave the organizing to you. Keep me informed. Let me know what you need. Lady Kathrine and I have accepted your good wife's invitation to your soiree, Lord John. We'll talk more then, I have no doubt," he said and rushed off for the back of the church and the choir room.

"Lord Pomeroy," Simon said, "may I have a moment or two to speak with your daughter," he said, his hand going beneath Pamela's elbow.

Lord Pomeroy offered him a slight bow. "Certainly. I must find my lady. We have guests arriving at the Chase. Don't be long, Pamela."

****

Pamela went along without resistance to the yard beside the church where the old landau from the Manor awaited Simon and his sister. Simon glanced around. She presumed he wanted to be sure they were alone. "I, too, am in favor of a school, if you are worried I would try to dissuade you from pursuing your latest hobby."

She bristled and folded her hands at her waist, chin up. "This is not a hobby. I take this mission very seriously."

"Really? And what happens once you are back in

London? How do you plan on orchestrating this…*your mission*…from afar?"

Pamela hadn't planned on telling him, or anyone, because she hadn't told her mother or her father that she wasn't going to London for the season.

Simon was decked out in his new clothes today. There was nothing special about the cut of his dark blue suit coat, or his cloud gray breeches, or the carelessly knotted, blue satin, paisley cravat at his throat, but the blue of the coat set off the blue of his eyes, the cravat accentuated his weathered complexion, and the coat emphasized the breadth of his shoulders, and the breeches the narrowness of his hips. His total lack of artifice only made the understated costume more striking.

He mistook her silence as her answer. "Ha, so you hadn't thought of that, had you? You will rush in and get everyone all excited, set things in motion, then leave us all in the lurch."

She opened her mouth to scream at him, tell him how wrong he was, then she thought about what he'd really said. He'd said, "Leave us in the lurch." He was speaking of himself, she realized, and her heart cried for him. "I have no intention of leaving anyone in the lurch, not you, not our tenants. Nor will I be leaving anytime soon to go anywhere. I know where I am meant to be. I will stay right here, and you will see me as often as I can possibly manage. I will not leave the field. I want you, Simon Lawrence, and I will have you as my husband. We are meant to be. I don't care how long it takes. I know where I belong. I belong at your side. I will be a farmer's wife. I will," she said and moved toward him, came up on her toes, and kissed him lightly on the mouth.

Simon put his arms around her. Pamela was sure he was about to pull her into an embrace. Instead, he moved her away and stepped back, his hands quickly going deep into his pockets.

"Simon," Audry said as she and Paul came around the corner of the church, "Lord Pomeroy sent us to fetch you. He says there's room in the Pomeroy carriage for all of us. It will save Milo with a trip."

Chapter Twenty-Five

Watching Lord Abernathy eat and try to talk at the same time was nauseating. Pamela had never noticed before how repulsive the man was. He even smelled bad, like horse liniment, old horse liniment. His coiffed and curled wig beneath the light of the chandelier appeared more dirty yellow than white. He'd painted his lips a grotesque shade of orange, and his mouth was now smeared, lip rouge mixed with copious amounts of the butter and honey he'd slathered on his dinner roll.

Lady Pomeroy brought her kerchief up to her nose as he expounded on the horrible blizzard they had survived at Christmastide while visiting his friend, Laird Baltock, at his castle in Scotland. "I said to Lucinda, 'Darling, we have to get out of here, or we will simply freeze to death,' is what I said, didn't I, sweeting? The Laird begged us to stay, of course. But as soon as the roads cleared, we left post-haste. And when I say cleared, I really mean ice and packed snow so hard the wheels of the carriage barely made a dent. They were expecting another blizzard to arrive within the week.

"Still, although frozen nearly to death, we made it to Northumberland and a distant cousin's rather rundown manor, encountering only a few flurries. One of the coachmen lost some fingers. Horrible, we were nearly put in the ditch." He shuddered. "The fingers came off right in his glove. He was no longer of any use, of course.

We left him behind and hired a fellow, a dusky-colored fellow. They are tough, hide like leather, and are impossible to freeze. The inns along the way were abysmal, as usual. I shall never travel again in winter, never."

"I swear my Christmas punch turned to slush two seconds after it was poured into my glass," Lucinda said. "I rather liked it. Somehow, it strengthened the potency of the brew and gave one an instant rush. Perhaps that's how the Scots endure their climate. They are preserved in their meads and ales. I, for one, prefer the French. They have a lovely wine with bubbles. I adore bubbles."

"You are bubbles, my dear. You are effervescent," Lord Abernathy said. "Isn't she, Pauly?"

Seated between Lucinda and Lord Abernathy, Paul swallowed, rolled his eyes, and nodded.

Addressing Simon, who sat across from him at the table, Lord Abernathy said, "So, you lived in the colonies. You have the look of a colonial about you: shaggy, sunbaked, and brawny." He shuddered as if repulsed. A derisive snicker escaped his stained lips. His beady, brown, bloodshot eyes held unchecked disdain.

Pamela had to resist the urge to tip the man's chair over and kick his painted face out the dining room door.

Simon smiled at the man, actually smiled, with his eyes. "Yes, living in the colonies does tend to make a man of you."

Oh, that was a beautiful response. Pamela pressed her lips together to keep herself from cheering.

"Your father was in trade, if I recall," Lord Abernathy asked and sniffed. "Tobacco, is that correct?"

"Yes, our father was a broker for Wellburn/Holekum distributors," Simon said. He laid aside his knife and fork, folded his hands on the tabletop, and looked directly into Lord Abernathy's disgusting visage. "I recall seeing the name Chauncy D. Abernathy, of North Berwick, Scotland, attached to several shipments—any relation?"

Pamela gave another point to Simon.

"My father," Lord Abernathy said, more as a cough into the high points of his collar.

Simon continued. "I seem to remember there was a problem with their account. I'm sure it all got straightened out," he said. Head down, he picked up his knife and fork and proceeded to dice the cutlet on his plate.

Pamela gave him another point. But it set her mind to thinking. Lord Abernathy and Lucinda didn't have a residence of their own in London, they bounced around staying with relatives and other members of the haut-ton. Now they were here, staying at Fairfield. They hadn't attended church with Lord and Lady Fairfield.

A few tears, a few words of deep disappointment, and Lady Pomeroy had extended the pair an invitation to Sunday dinner. If Pamela were to parse what Lord Abernathy had just said about their Christmas, their exit from their friend's castle, and their journey, she would say they were nothing short of vagrants looking for a free roof to lounge under until the London season began. Did they hope to make Pomeroy Chase their next hostel? Or did they have a more permanent arrangement in mind?

Lucinda was seated on Paul's left, Lord Abernathy on his right. They had him surrounded. Pamela was seated directly across from Lord Abernathy, and Simon sat between her and Penny. Her mother and Audry were seated at one end of the long table, and her father at the other end. She wondered if her mother had designated the seating arrangement or had Lucinda and Lord Abernathy taken matters into their own hands.

The conversation drifted into the entertainments to be enjoyed in London during the spring season. There was little anyone at the table could do to stop their guests from expounding on their experiences.

The meal ended when Lord Pomeroy put his hand over his wine glass and signaled the wine steward to remove all libations.

As they started to exit the dining room, Pamela heard Lucinda ask Paul to show her their mother's orangery—she was interested in any orchids their mother might have. Paul hesitated, then made his excuse to his father, who had invited him, Simon, and Lord Abernathy to join him in his study for a smoke and a brandy.

Pamela, Audry, and Penny followed Lady Pomeroy into her parlor. Pamela went to the window. "Mother, I think we should go to the orangery. Lucinda was interested in your orchids. Perhaps she has questions."

"I doubt that," Lady Pomeroy said. "I'll wager the child doesn't know an orchid from a dandelion."

"All the more reason to go, introduce her to your lovely flowers. After all, she's taken an interest."

****

Paul guided Lucinda into the mullioned glass, hot house where his mother's collection of exotic and precious flowers and citrus trees flourished. Lucinda took a few steps into the room, fanned herself with her kerchief, eyes blinking, she absently surveyed the room.

"I believe my mother has some lovely orchids over here somewhere. As I understand it, the light from the morning sun is best over here," Paul said.

Lucinda had stopped to smell the blossoms on a lemon tree. She glanced up at him and offered him a weak, sad little smile.

Paul proceeded to the east corner of the room where his mother's prized orchids could enjoy the morning sun. Lucinda made several detours to admire blooms and fragrances. There was an exit close at hand. It led to the recesses of the house where the servants gathered. Paul had a strange feeling he was being led into a trap and was grateful for the possible exit. He didn't know what kind of trap or how the trap was going to work, but he knew enough to stay at least three paces away from luscious little Lucinda. If necessary, he would take this opportunity to let her know he was now courting Audry Lawrence. He felt he owed Lucinda that much. They had been close throughout the last two seasons.

"I need you, Pauly. I need you to marry me," Lucinda said. She didn't try to touch him. She simply looked pitiful, big, blue eyes wide, beseeching, flooded with tears, pouty, pink, full lips trembling. "I'm going to have a baby, Pauly," she said on a whimper.

Flesh exposed by the low decolletage of her gown, her hands clasped in prayer, Lucinda snatched one of his hands and pressed it between her warm, creamy, full bosoms. "You will be my baby's daddy. You will make a wonderful daddy. I know you will."

****

Pamela, Penny, Audry, and Lady Pomeroy arrived in time to hear Lucinda's announcement. Penny wanted to burst into the room and tackle lying Lucinda. Lady Pomeroy, to Pamela's astonishment, put out her arm to stop them from making their presence known. She put her finger to her lips, and they stayed well out of sight behind the big potted palm at the entrance to the glass-paned, enclosed orangery.

"Does Lieutenant Collin Prescot know you're seeking an alternate father for his child?" Paul asked.

They all heard Lucinda's pitiful wail. She sniffed back her tears and said, between gulping sobs, "He's gone and gotten himself married over the anvil. Seems he spread his seed over a very wide field."

"Ah, you know Lucinda, I don't believe I can, or should, oblige you in this request," Paul said. Jerking his hand away, he turned to exit via the servants' door. She grabbed him by the arm and spun him around.

"You don't have a choice," she said, her voice a nasty snarl, pouty lips curled into a sneer. "If you don't marry me immediately, I will spread the word you ruined me and took advantage of me repeatedly. I will drag your reputation down into the mud and your family's name along with it."

Lady Pomeroy waved them forward. "Miss Abernathy, I will send for your carriage to take you wherever you want. I would hazard a guess you and Lord Abernathy have worn out your welcome at Fairfield. If you are thinking of spreading this lie, I warn you it will be three against one."

"Five," a masculine voice said from the other side of the room. Lord Pomeroy and Simon stepped away from a wall. "I have taken the liberty of having a servant pour Lord Abernathy in your carriage with Simon's help," Lord Pomeroy said, a sly smile twitching on his lips. A footman entered the room, Lucinda's cape and hat draped over his arm. "This gentleman will escort you out," he said and waved Lucinda to leave the room.

"Oh, John, I'm so glad you were here," Lady

Pomeroy said as she threw her arms around her husband's neck.

Simon didn't speak until the young woman had been escorted from the room. When he did speak, he spoke to Pamela.

"Abernathy can't hold his liquor or his tongue. He started giggling and singing a dirty little ditty on the way to your father's study. He tripped when he entered the room. Then he thanked me for helping him get back up on his feet and passed out—sank down to the floor like a big sack of—of," he looked around him at the highly intelligent, interested ladies present, stopped himself from saying what he was thinking, and adjusted his statement, "something sloppy and stinky. Use your imaginations."

The ladies laughed at him, even Lady Pomeroy.

Lord Pomeroy draped his arm around his son's shoulders. "You, my boy, should take a lesson. Never allow a lady to lead you down a garden path."

Chapter Twenty-Six

"Are those the kind of people one can expect to encounter in London? I mean, will they be at the balls and routs?" Audry asked. Paul beside her, they followed Lord and Lady Pomeroy through the house back to Lady Pomeroy's parlor.

Paul placed his hand beneath her elbow as they crossed the entry hall. Their footsteps and voices echoed against the domed ceiling. "There are a few be-wigged and powdered ladies and gentlemen who receive invitations, but for the most part, the foppish prigs, like Lord Abernathy, prefer gambling dens and private clubs rather than crowded ballrooms filled with watchful, protective matrons and young people dancing. Their ladies sit on the sidelines, sip ratafia, and gossip. Lucinda managed to find her way into society through her hosts. Looking back on it, I can see that now."

"You…you liked her?"

"I did, yes. She had quite a following. Flattered, I was among the list of her admirers. Yes, idiot that I was."

"If someone like Lord Abernathy asked to dance with Penny, would you let him?"

"Protocol wouldn't allow me to interfere if he made such a request. Penny could refuse and make an excuse, but it wouldn't be allowed for her to refuse his request and then accept another's request. All ladies, and all the gentlemen, are expected to dance with all present, no matter who or what. And only two dances are allowed with the same partner, or there will be talk."

"What kind of talk?" Audry asked. "I mean, if the gossips were to speculate there might be a romance, isn't that what the London Season is for? As I understand it, isn't it where the gentry assemble to look for a spouse and make a match? Don't they call it the marriage market?"

He stopped their progress before entering his mother's drawing room. He laughed at himself. "It doesn't make a lot of sense, does it?"

Audry shook her head. "I don't think I want to go to London. It's so lovely here. And, I should think, in the spring and early summer, it is beautiful."

"There are other entertainments, other than balls and routs during the season that are very worthwhile. There are museums and art galleries, and the Cathedral choir alone is worth the stay. There are theaters, musicals, and lovely rambles through the parks. Don't let one foppish idiot color your opinion. And I would be at your side every minute."

"Every minute?"

"As your husband, yes, every minute," he said, coming down to press his lips to hers.

****

First thing the next morning, Simon employed Michael to help him locate a crate that could be fashioned into a cart with a bench that would accommodate two people if needed and an axle. But it took some digging to find two wheels the same size and with spokes that weren't cracked or completely broken.

The goat for the cart took a bit of doing, as the only goats they had were not inclined to be harnessed or used to pull anything. They tried three of them. Two simply sat down on their haunches and refused to move. The third one, a large ram, refused to take direction and had a tendency to go trotting off to eat whatever treat it perceived was in the nearest ditch or hay pile. Michael thought the two stubborn goats could be trained to pull the cart if he could find the right incentive.

Simon returned to the Manor late for lunch. Tired and smelling like a sweaty goat, he started for his room to get cleaned up when he heard the sounds of singing and a piano coming from the front drawing room.

"Mr. Pomeroy and his sister arrived a few moments ago," Suzie said, peering over the balustrade at the foot of the stairs. "As Miss Pomeroy was with them, I didn't think I'd be needed. You missed your noon meal. Where would you like it served? We kept it warm for you."

"Would you mind very much bringing it upstairs? I have to get cleaned up."

"Right away, sir. I'll be up directly."

Less than an hour later, scrubbed, clean clothes on, hunger abated, and thirst quenched, Simon headed back downstairs with no intention of encroaching on the choir practice or seeing Miss Pamela Pomeroy. On the contrary, he must avoid her. But the music coming from the front sitting room did not sound like hymns, none that he'd ever heard. There was a bounce to the tune echoing throughout the hall. The words being sung were not reverent. They were almost bawdy in their liveliness.

"*Some think the worrrld is made for fun and frooolic.*"

He recognized his sister's voice. The male voice could only be Paul's.

"*And sooo do I, and sooo dooo I.*"

Their voices blended in perfect harmony.

"Some think it welll to be all melllannnchooolllic, to pine and sighhh, to pine and sighhh. But I, I love to spend my time in singgging some joyous song, some joyous song. To set the air with music bravely ringgging is far from wrong.

Simon went to the sitting room door and stood in the doorway. Audry and Paul, with eyes only for each other, were dancing and singing as they skipped around the room in a lively jig. Pamela, smiling and laughing, obviously enjoying herself, sat at the piano as master of the keys.

"Some think it wrrrong to set the feet dannncing, but not I. But not so I. Some think that eyes should keep from coyyyly glannncing, upon the sly, upon the sly, but oooh to me the mazy dance is charrrming, divinely sweet. Divinely sweet, and surrrely there is naught that is alarrrming in nimble feet, In nimble feet.

"Ahhh me 'tis strange that some should take to sighhhing, and like it well. And like it wellll. For meee I have not thought it worth the trrrying. So cannot tell. So cannot tell. With laughter and dance and song the day soon passses, full soon is gone. Full soon is gone. For mirth was made for joyousss lads and lasses to call their own. To call their own."

Breathless and giddy, the couple stopped in the middle of the room, laughing, and they embraced.

"I've never heard that particular hymn sung in church before," Simon said and stepped into the room.

"And you won't," Pamela said.

"I told Pamela I didn't really know how to dance, not the formal kind I imagine practiced here in England," Audry said, still laughing. "We had reels in Virginia.

They were fun. Paul says many of the reels are simply versions of the cotillion. The reels they perform are set to a more sedate, less animated pace. So maybe I won't find them as intimidating as I thought. Pamela says that at the soiree her mother is planning, there will be dancing. If Paul will show me a few steps and some changes, I might not feel so out of step," she said and laughed at her own pun. "Paul says he had some dance instruction at Eton. You were at Eton, too, so you had instruction as well."

Paul says, Paul says, oh, Simon wanted to bellow like a jealous fool. He bowed his head and gathered his composure. "Ah, yes, I remember it well," he said. "At an all-boys school, we had to partner with each other. Most of the time, we ended up in a wrestling contest. And what about the hymn practice?" Simon asked.

"They can do both," Pamela said."

"Practice singing hymns or wrestling?" he asked.

She banged a sour chord on the piano, and said, "brothers," under her breath, and got up and headed for the door.

Suzie interrupted the conversation, entering the room with a serving tray containing tea and scones.

"Where are you going?" Simon asked Pamela.

"I asked Mrs. Dorsey to show me to the attic. I'm looking for items we might want to use in our school."

"Don't bother Mrs. Dorsey," he said and opened the door for her. "I'll come with you. About time I had a look around. Suzie, you will keep my sister company," he said without giving the maid a glance.

Chapter Twenty-Seven

Pamela followed Simon down a narrow hallway, up two flights of stairs, another hallway and they were in another wing of the Manor. "The nursery, I think, is up here," he said and opened a door to the left. "We might look in here first. I believe I saw a small desk, some books, of course, and a child-sized table and chairs. I came up here when we first arrived. I haven't been here since."

The room was lit up from the daylight streaming in from the long rectangular, mullioned window across the room. "It is a lovely room, but it's so far removed from the rest of the house," Pamela said without thinking.

"That was my first reaction," Simon said. He wandered over to a bookshelf against the wall at the front of the room. "There are some children's books here with pictures of farm animals, another with woodland animals, and another with sea dwellers. The illustrations are a little yellowed, but the pages appear in good condition. Also, some wooden puzzles with letters, numbers, and colors."

"Don't get angry, but I'm going to ask you a rather personal question," Pamela said and crossed the room to inspect a low child-sized table, one that could be used to lay out several projects and accommodate several children.

He laughed at her. "Consider me braced, fire at

will."

She smiled at him and shook her head. "Your mother, could she read and write? I ask because I was shocked at how many debutantes could do neither. I thought it ridiculous, but some families don't believe in educating females."

He crossed the room and picked up a small box constructed of twigs and covered with little pebbles and snail shells. The brown glue was messy, in clumps, the rocks dull, covered in dust, definitely the work of a child.

"Yes, she could read," he said. "She loved to read. She told me once that she could read by the time she was five or six. Mother wasn't a great writer. Oh, she could write and write and write, but she admitted she was terrible at spelling. A Miss Donnely, I think her name was, a nanny, who was very righteous, dour and strict, taught her. Miss Donnely, she supposed, was turned off. Mother remembered the nanny wasn't there for her twelfth birthday. Nanny always made sure she had cake. Her twelfth birthday was the last birthday she could recall.

"What about Audry?" Pamela asked.

"Our father taught her to read and write and do sums. She is a very fast learner, eager, he used to say. He continued with my education as well, giving me assignments that had to do with the brokerage accounts. I don't care for accounting. I've always preferred working with my hands. Audry loves poetry, but I prefer adventure stories. What about you?"

Pamela was drawn to the child's desk in the corner. It faced the wall. Any child sitting in it would see only a blank white space. She turned it around and opened the surface to the compartment beneath. Inside was a dried, wilted flower tied with a faded, dirty, blue hair ribbon. Pamela picked it up and wound the ribbon around her finger.

"We had tutors. Three of them. I love adventure stories and history." She handed him the flower and ribbon, opened the lid to the little box he had in his hand, and put the abandoned treasure inside.

"I don't need to see the attic. This room, if you don't mind, has several pieces we can use. But I won't take them if you'd rather I didn't. There is something very sad about this. There is light and all manner of things, books, tables, and chairs, but it feels very lonely. If ever I have children, I wouldn't put them so far away from me. I would want them close, perhaps even in the same room with me all the time. Your grandmother, she was ill, wasn't she?"

"Mother wasn't sure, but she thought her mother had miscarried several times. She wasn't allowed to see her more than once a day and never allowed to stay longer than half an hour. Grandfather said Mother's exuberant nature disturbed her mother's nerves."

Pamela couldn't stand it another minute. She put her arms around him and held him close for several seconds. He put his arms around her waist, and they clung to each other.

"Take whatever you think can be of use. Mother would want you to have it for your school. I know she would. If she were here, she would be in here right now loading up the books, dragging furniture down those stairs. Dismantle this pretty prison."

****

Simon needed fresh air. On the way out the door, he could hear Audry singing and Pamela playing the piano.

He was jealous. He had to admit it. He was jealous of Paul. Paul could make his sister laugh, sing, and dance. He should be happy for her, and he was. He was unhappy with himself. He loved Pamela Pomeroy, and he thought she wanted to love him. If they were living in Virginia, this would be a simple matter of time. There would be a courtship, some family gatherings, possibly a house raising and that would be that. Here, he couldn't even court her. He had nothing to offer.

He went directly to Peg's pen. She could barely waddle from one end of her crib to the other. Her appetite had gone off the last few days. He and Milo attributed the weather to her lack of enthusiasm. To entice her, Simon prepared her a small pan of her favorite feed with a dribble of molasses for garnish.

"You can't hide," Audry said from the doorway of the shed. "You can come back inside now. They've gone home. It's starting to snow. Mrs. Dorsey sent me out with these," she said, holding up what was left of a full head of cabbage and some turnip tops. "Pamela said you hadn't gone to the attic. You went to the nursery. I've been in there."

"When?"

"Oh, shortly after we arrived. I go there now and then to sit. I found a book of nursery rhymes. I have it in my room. Mother drew some pictures in the margins. There is a kitten she illustrated in several different poses. He lives in the dairy barn, and there are a lot of cows around. And flowers, of course, always flowers. When Lady Pomeroy described our mother as a laughing sprite, I couldn't quite imagine it. But I think I know now she'd been set free from this place. She'd found love with Father. Love should do that, don't you think? It should free one from their fears. Maybe not free, but at least diminish one's fears and doubts to a manageable size."

"Is that what Paul has done for you?"

"I'm going to allow him to try," she said, her gaze locked to his. "I can't stay with you forever, Simon. You'll always be my brother, and I love you, but we both have to find our own lives and make our own families. You love this place, the farm. Your Peg, she's gotten so big, she scares me, and the dairy barn smells. I'm afraid of the chickens. I do love being in the kitchen with Mrs. Dorsey, churning butter and baking bread. Those things remind me of Mother."

"You're only eighteen, Audry. Eighteen years isn't forever. I beg you to slow down. Paul will be a member of Parliament someday; he'll be a Lord, and if you wed, you will be a Lady. Society would expect you to be seen, possibly influential, definitely gregarious."

"I think I would rather enjoy that. My silence and reticent manner would be uniquely my own. I will don a mantle of mystery to disguise my failings. Many will crave to be included in my circle. I shall be discerning in the company I keep around me—no sycophants allowed."

He dropped Audry's offerings in the pen with Peg. The sow snuffled and ruffled the leaves of the cabbage and turnip tops but preferred the pan of feed with the rich molasses drizzled over the top.

Speaking to Peg, he said, "Ah, no need to worry about you then," sarcasm in his tone of voice and a snide set to his lips.

Audry put her hand out to his chest and gazed deeply into his eyes. "I am very mindful of my weaknesses, whether I marry Paul or if I don't marry at all," she said.

"I am not as naive as you would suppose. I know you worry about me. I was in a bad way not so long ago, and I can't promise I won't relapse. No matter what happens, and that includes Paul Pomeroy's tentative intention to take me to wife, I want to be better. I don't want to be your delicate little sister or anyone's delicate anything. In memory of my mother, I will strive to be stronger."

He put his hands over hers. "I will continue to worry."

"I know. I will endeavor not to give you anything to worry about."

"I would appreciate that," he said.

She patted his jaw. "Now I've assured you I am aware of my shortcomings. What are you going to do to keep me from worrying about you?"

"Well, to start with," he said as they left the shed, "I don't wish to attend the Pomeroy's soiree. I would be extremely uncomfortable, out of place, and ineffective as a scintillating guest. You have convinced me you are perfectly at home in the company of the Pomeroy family. You will go, sing, play games, dance—enjoy yourself. I will stay here, have a wonderfully quiet evening before the fire, savor a glass of Mrs. Dorsey's nog with a generous splash of rum added, and fall asleep without a care in the world."

Audry linked her arm with his. "That's not what you really want. How silly of you. I know you. You are overthinking this. You want to go to the Pomeroy's party. You can't stay away from Pamela. You want to see her. I know you do. Besides, you must escort me to these functions. It's your duty. Me thinks you protest too much."

"You found the works of Shakespeare in Grandfather's library, didn't you?"

Chapter Twenty-Eight

The snow lasted for two days. Paul still managed to visit the Manor to continue the hymn practice, but Pamela hadn't accompanied him. By the end of the week, Michael had two goats trained to harness. He said they were friends, and one wouldn't go without the other. Now the snow had melted, Simon wanted to give the little cart a run to be sure it would be safe for Audry to navigate, or the dairy maids, or whoever needed it. Milo gave him directions to the gamekeeper's cottage by way of the farm tracks that would keep him on Copeland Manor land.

The goats trotted along fine until they reached the fens at the bottom of the hill, it was soggy, unstable, and starting to overflow into the pasture with melting snow water. Simon urged the willing and game little team of goats to follow a narrow track beside a rock wall that bordered a side pasture. He was headed for the knoll where he thought the cottage lay on the other side of the rise. Ahead of him, he saw the bridge and urged his team forward.

Before he could prepare his inexperienced team for the attack, Chance came racing across the bridge, barking, circling. The goats took exception, reared, and tried to butt him. The cart tipped sideways, the bench came out of its mortise and tenon groove, and Simon slipped off the box with it to the ground. The goats, dragging the cart, challenged the dog.

Simon could hear her, but he couldn't lift his head to see Pamela. She was calling her damn dog to sit.

"Simon, oh, my God, are you all right?"

"They like carrots. In my coat pocket."

"What?

"Coat pocket, carrots for goats. Get them to stand."

It took Pamela a few moments to round up the goats, coax the team to stand and right the little cart. Simon was grateful to be left alone, ignored to get himself up in a sitting position on his own steam. Pamela, dressed in a dark cotton skirt, a gray wool jumper, and a heavy canvas apron, a blue scarf tied around her head to keep her hair out of her face, looked like a peasant woman. He had to blink several times to assure himself he wasn't seeing things.

Chance, standing over him, started to lick his face. Pamela called him to sit. The dog went down on his haunches, panting, looking pleased with himself. Pamela had the team by the harness and had turned the cart around, bringing it back over to him. While the goats enjoyed their carrots, Pamela asked, "Do you think you can walk, or do you need to ride? Oh dear, the seat, it's broken?"

Simon got to his knees, then to his feet, brushed the mud off his coat front and the sleeves of his coat, and straightened his knit cap. "It's not broken—just came out of its slot on the box." He took the board and pounded it with his fist back into place. After taking a deep breath, he said, "I'll walk, thank you. What are you doing here?

She handed him the tack to one of the team and took Chance by the collar. "The thatchers are here today. They've removed the old thatch and are in the process of laying down the new. I wanted to patch up the fireplace. I saw the bird droppings when we were here. Jamison showed me how to mix up the slurry with clay and grit. I'd just got started when I noticed Chance wasn't inside the cottage. I stepped outside and saw him charge across the bridge. I'm sorry, but he does love you. He was happy to see you. Better that he likes you rather than hates you," she said, turning her smiling brown eyes at him, knowing full well he couldn't resist. He laughed and nodded in agreement.

"But that doesn't answer my question: why are you here?"

"I told you; I'm patching up the fireplace."

"You surely have people who could do that."

She pursed her lips and huffed. "Yes, I have people who could do it, but I want to do it. So far, I haven't had to lay out any cash for anything. And I hope to continue trading as opposed to laying out cash as long as possible. I've traded six laying hens and a rooster to the Riley brothers for the thatch and the roofing. Their hens froze. And their rooster is old. I was able to acquire the hens from one of our tenants who needed a pair of boots for her little girl. I had saved mine. They were practically new. When I bought them, I was thirteen, and I grew out of them almost immediately. I also gave her a cape and some gloves I no longer wear."

One of the young men on the edge of the roof waved at him. Simon tipped his cap and entered the cottage. The broken windowpanes at the back of the cottage remained broken, but the windows at the front of the cottage were clean, and the droppings beside the fireplace were gone. It was clear to Simon someone had been cleaning, and he had a pretty clear idea who that was.

There was a bucket full of caulk in front of the hearth. A trowel lay on the mantle. "I'll take care of this," he said.

"Fine," Pamela said and left him to it.

When Simon turned around to see where she'd gone, she was behind him, slathering whitewash on the wall. "We need to find replacements for those windows," he said.

"I found some in a shed out back. But I don't know if they will fit, and I have no idea how to get the old ones out or the replacements in."

Simon smiled to himself; once again, this place reminded him of Virginia and how they had worked together. "Couple more cracks, and I'll have this taken care of. Then I'll go see if we can use the windows you found."

"I did ask Mr. Dorsey to help Jamison with the privy," Pamela said. "I'm sure it needs some serious care. We can't have the children falling in. But I think it can wait until the weather clears. I don't expect everything to come together all at once. But getting a new roof was a priority. I want to start bringing furniture in here. I've asked Mr. Ward to drop by next week. I need his opinion."

Simon had made use of the privy on the day of their ride, and yes, it needed some serious renovations. Funny how easy it was to talk to this woman. They were at home with each other. He smiled to himself and wondered what Lady Pomeroy would have to say about the subject of this conversation. Was she aware of her daughter's ambition to take on every part of this project?

"You are being very quiet over there," she said. "I think I can guess what you are thinking. You are wondering if my mother knows what I'm up to? Father suspects. He hasn't said anything. But Jamison probably reports to him. Anyway, so far, Father hasn't stopped me."

"I doubt the condition of privies comes up very often in conversations with your mother," Simon said. "But I do wonder what she would say if she knew that you feel free to discuss them with me."

"She would be shocked, absolutely shocked and dismayed, I should think. Where my behavior is concerned, she is often shocked. This project is one of my less dangerous undertakings, but considering my mother's delicate sensibilities, I would guess she would say this new obsession of mine is inadvisable, unseemly, and unnecessary, I'm sure. I suppose I am a trifle rebellious. I don't want to hand over this project to the tenants. I want to see this through. I want to do this for them. They shouldn't have to do all the work all the time. My mother would try to talk me out of it, stop me. So, we won't tell her, will we," she said and made one last, wide sweep of whitewash to her wall, and dabbed here and there where she'd missed.

He heard her toss her brush in the paint bucket. "I'm done here for today. I'm going around back to see how they're coming with the roof. How are you doing?"

He padded in and smoothed out a long gap at the top of the hearth with the trowel. "I think that's it. If you have a cloth, we can put it over this bucket of caulk to save it. There might be a use for it outside."

"Good idea. I hadn't thought of that. I suppose there is more to do outside."

****

The roof wasn't quite finished. The shed proved to

be a good source for window replacements and plenty of flat stones to replace the cracked stones around the well and pump outside. With very little effort, the window frames, riddled with rot and woodworm, practically fell apart and were easy to remove. They replaced them with the ones they'd found in the shed. They used the caulk to shore up the size gap. By the time they had finished, the roofers had gone home, and it was starting to get dark.

"How did you get here?" Simon asked her.

"I walked," she said. Chance, outside the door, had fallen asleep next to the goats who were grazing among the tall grass at the corner of the cottage.

"Get in the cart. I'll take you to the Manor. We'll send Michael to the Chase to let them know you're having supper with us, and we'll see you home."

"That's not necessary. I'm perfectly able to walk home. There's still plenty of daylight left."

"It would be nice if just once you didn't argue with me. I'm inviting you to dine with me at my home."

Brows raised, she pressed her lips together in consideration. "Oh? Sounded like an order to me," she said and tipped her head to the side.

He started to say something, but before he could correct his offer, she said, with a playful smile and a giggle, "But if it's an invitation, then I accept."

"Good, now get in the cart." He shut his eyes and took a breath. "Or, rather, your chariot awaits you, my lady," he said and bowed from the waist and swept off his cap to her.

She curtsied, closed the cottage door, and got in the cart. She moved her skirt aside to make room for him. Chance woke up. With a flick of the reins over their rumps, the goats set forth at a trot down the lane and crossed the bridge, turned to head north toward the Manor, Chance leading the way.

Chapter Twenty-Nine

Simon shouldn't have been surprised to find Paul at the Manor, in the music room, alone with Audry, but he was. They weren't singing. They were cuddling on the settee by the fire. When he and Pamela entered the sitting room, the couple sprang apart. Audry adjusted her skirts and Paul set his cravat straight, both of them blushing and breathing heavily.

"Who gave you leave to paw my sister? Where is Suzie? She has been told not to leave you alone together," Simon said.

Paul came to his feet and pointed at his sister. "Pamela? What are you doing here? Why in the world are you dressed like that? What have you been doing?"

Taking a few long strides across the room, Simon marched over to confront the man making love to his sister. "Never mind *your* sister, Mr. Pomeroy, I asked you a question."

"Brothers," Simon heard Pamela say over his shoulders.

"We were mutually pawing," Audry said and snickered.

"I will deal with you directly," Simon said to her. "But first, I want some straight answers from you," he said and poked Paul in the chest with his finger.

Audry stepped in front of Paul, arms out to the side to protect him. Blue eyes flashing with sparks of defiance, chin up and out a mile, she said, "I sent Suzie back to the kitchen to help Mrs. Dorsey as I had invited Paul to join us for supper. And while we were left alone, I took advantage and seduced him."

Simon had to suppress his urge to laugh. Oh, his sister had come a long way in less than a full month. He was proud of her. Her mother would be proud of her. But he couldn't allow Paul Pomeroy to think he could make love to his sister right under his nose without his objecting. Then again, the man had already offered to do the honorable thing, and by the look of it, the sooner, the better.

"I assume you have invited Pamela as well?" Audry asked a challenge in her tone. "And I could ask you, *brother mine*, what have you two been doing? I think I see mud there on your sleeves and grass stains on your trousers. You both look a trifle windblown and disheveled. What I don't understand is what is that white stuff on Pamela's fingers and nose, where did that come from?"

Paul took Audry's hand. "You're not helping," he said to her out of the side of his mouth.

Suzie popped in the door. "Supper is laid, Miss Audry. Oh," she said and bobbed a curtsey to Simon and a nod to Pamela. "Should I set another plate?"

"Yes, please, Suzie," Simon said without looking at her. "And I think we need to send word to Pomeroy Chase that we have purloined two of their residents. Oh, and I should tell you that you have a very large dog in residence at the gatehouse. Michael and your boys have taken quite a shine to him. His name is Chance. He belongs to Miss Pomeroy. She'll be taking him home with her. So, this is temporary. He's a big puppy, not a mean bone in his body. The boys are safe with him."

"That's all we need, is a dog," Suzie said under her breath. She nodded and said, "Yes, sir, right away. I'll send Michael."

"Master Simon," Milo Dorsey said, moving aside to allow Suzie to exit the room. "Tis Peg, I think it's her time."

"Oh, of course," Simon said and threw up his arms in surrender. "Wonderful. And I've just sent Suzie off to find Michael to send him to Pomeroy Chase. We might need him. See if you can stop her."

"I'll go," Paul said to Simon.

"I should go home," Paul said to Audry. "I'll return, bring back the carriage for Pamela and her dog."

"I'm not going anywhere," Pamela said. "Peg needs me. She needs a woman, not useless, hand-wringing men about her."

Simon started to argue with her, then stopped. "That's not a bad idea. She is fond of you, and she trusts you. I think we're going to need all hands for this one. And—luckily, you're dressed for it," he said and laughed.

"We need to move Peg to the birthing pen," he said to Milo.

****

Milo, walking alongside Simon, left the room and started out to the hall, leaving Pamela to tag along. They didn't see Paul and Audry's lingering, passionate parting, but Pamela did, and she shook her head.

Simon continued with his concern for his pig. "We can't have her giving birth where she's at. She and her brood need to be in the birthing pen; it's warmer and drier there. Also, quiet and out of the way where she won't be disturbed."

"I tried," Milo said. "She won't move. I tried everything, even biscuits with butter. She won't move, I tell you."

Simon turned back to see that Paul and Audry were locked in an embrace. Pamela held her breath, waiting for the explosion.

Eyes narrowed, jaw tight, fist bunched, Simon stopped and took a step toward the lovesick pair. "Will you two stop that," he said, his voice loud and echoing into the rafters. "Paul, go home. Let your parents know Pamela is here with us. Audry, let the man go now, please."

"Do you have an old blanket or coat that you no longer need or wear?" Pamela asked Milo, ignoring her brother and Simon's ineffectual objections to the overt displays of affection between his sister and her brother.

Simon turned to enter the hall that would lead to the back of the house with Milo alongside. Pamela had to skip to keep up. "A rug or carpet might do," she said. Both men stopped short and looked at her as if she'd lost her mind.

"For nesting," she said as if they should know what she was talking about. "She's going to want to nest. I read something somewhere that most animals like to nest before giving birth. Even humans. We prepare a bed for the baby, blankets, and layette. A blanket would be the best. Maybe we'll need more than one," she said after pausing to give it some thought. "Peg is rather large. She most likely will give birth to at least ten piglets, maybe as many as a dozen."

Mrs. Dorsey came rushing down the stairs with Suzie behind her, who had a couple of wool blankets in her arms.

"I haven't yet told Michael he's needed to go to the Chase," Suzie said. She sounded more than a little breathless. "I'll go straight away," she said and handed the blankets off to Milo, who looked startled and confused.

****

"No, wait, Suzie," Simon said, "no need for Michael to go now. Mr. Pomeroy is going to the Chase. He'll bring back a carriage for Miss Pomeroy. We're on our way out to the sty. Hold our supper for us. This might take some time."

"I thought to make rugs of those as they're full of holes," Mrs. Dorsey said, pointing to the blankets, "but I think Peg needs them more than we need the rugs. It's going to be a frosty night. Will you be joining me in the kitchen, Miss Pamela?"

"I'm going to see if I can be of any help," Pamela said.

Sputtering, "You'll be doing no such thing," Mrs. Dorsey said. "A pigsty is no place for a lady. Especially if the pig is about to give birth. We won't allow it, will we, Master Simon?"

"Master Simon has nothing to say to it," Pamela said. "I am going out to the sty. I will make myself useful if allowed. Peg, I'm sure, would thank you for the blankets."

Nose in the air, Pamela relieved Milo of the blankets and headed for the kitchen and the back stoop, which would lead to the farm buildings in the back of the manor. Milo and Simon were left with nothing to do but follow her.

Chapter Thirty

The moment Paul walked in the door at the Chase, his mother rushed him, wrapped her arms around him, and wept. "You're home, oh, Paul, thank God you're home. We can't find Pamela anywhere. Your father sent Jamison to the gamekeeper's cottage to find her. That's where she said she'd be. Why would she go there, Paul? Why? Jamison said he saw her and that monster dog heading down the track right after luncheon. He returned not long ago and said no one was at the cottage. No one. Oh, Paul, where can she be?

"Your father confessed he knew where she's been going for the last couple of days in this terrible weather we've been having. But she's not at the cottage. Chance is with her. We can't find him either. We have people out looking for her now. You've come from Copeland Manor, I presume. Did you see her along the road?

"Oh, Paul, where can she be?" Without giving him an opening to reply, his mother began to walk around in circles, twisting her kerchief, then dabbing at her nose and eyes, wailing over and over, asking the fates why she was being punished.

She came to a halt in front of him, eyes flooded with tears, she shook her finger in his face. "If that girl comes home safe and sound, I'm going to lock her in her room until we are ready to leave for London. And then I'm going to lock her in her room until I need her to come with us to whatever function I choose to attend. And, furthermore, no more of this dilly-dallying around. She must choose a partner and stay with him."

Hands going to her cheeks, she shook her head, eyes wide with terror. "What am I saying—no, no, Lord, no. I shudder to think who she would take a fancy to. A balloonist, a rake, or a gambler, I'll choose the husband. I will. I want her married off. She has a sizeable dowry. We'll pay him, whoever he may be. Let someone else worry about her whereabouts, deal with whatever outrageous start she's taken into her head, not me. I can't do it anymore. I won't."

Paul took her hands and clasped them within his own. "Calm yourself, Mother. I know exactly where she is. Pamela is at Copeland Manor. She must have been at the gamekeeper's cottage. I suppose Simon caught her there doing whatever it is she's been doing, and he brought her to the Manor instead of allowing her to walk back home in the near dark."

Lady Pomeroy's beautiful eyes flew open then dropped like curtains, and she sank in a limp swoon in his arms. He supported her to her parlor and saw her seated in her favorite chair.

Penny had followed them into the room. "I've ordered some chamomile tea for her."

"Where's Father?" Paul asked. "I need him to call off the manhunt."

"I'm here. The groom told me you'd arrived home," Lord Pomeroy said. He entered the room, collapsed in one of the overstuffed chairs, and stretched his legs out before him. "I don't suppose you know where your sister is? We seemed to have lost her. I'm sure she's fine, she's just lost track of time. Probably trying to barter for something or other for this damned school she's fixated on."

"She's at Copeland, Father," Paul said. He stood back to allow Penny to tuck a shawl around his mother's shoulders. "Pamela's fine," he said. "Simon found her at the cottage, I guess. I really don't know what either of them were doing, but anyway, I presume he brought her to the Manor instead of allowing her to walk home in the dark."

He moved to the fireplace to warm his hands. "Audry had invited me to stay for supper. I was about to send word to you of my plan when Simon and Pamela showed up. And we were both going to stay for supper and send word to you," Paul said.

He turned to face his father. "But then…but…but you see, it's the sow. She's gone into labor, and you know Pamela, she took it into her head that she could be of use. I don't see how, but there you are. You know our Pamela, there was no talking her out of it. I assured Simon we'd send the carriage around for her, give her a ride home."

Lord Pomeroy wiped his hand over his face. "I need a drink, not brandy, something stronger, bourbon, I think," he said. He started to get up. Penny waved him to stay seated and poured a shot of bourbon from the decanter on the sideboard. He took the glass, drank it down, and handed the glass back to her, indicating he would take a refill. "Pour one for your mother," he said. Penny raised her eyebrows, questioning the request. He nodded, and she poured him another shot and one for her mother.

The tea arrived. Penny revived her mother, giving her a gentle shake on the shoulder, and asked if she wanted her bourbon added to her tea.

"Please, and cream, and treacle. Did I hear the word pigs?" the lady asked, her eyes closed against the thought.

Lord Pomeroy sat up in his chair, and took a sip of his bourbon, then set the glass aside on the table next to him. "So, Paul, if Simon Lawrence was gone roaming about and ended up at the gamekeeper's cottage, then he wasn't at Copeland, and you were alone with Miss Lawrence all afternoon in a house with only the servants for a chaperone? Do I have that right?" he asked.

Paul's complexion went bright pink. He sputtered a bit before responding. "Well, technically, yes, that's true."

"And your sister, we shall presume, met Mr. Lawrence at the gamekeeper's cottage and spent the afternoon there alone, unchaperoned, together doing, we do not know what." Lord Pomeroy reared up out of his chair. "I'm going to Copeland Manor."

"I'll go with you," Paul said.

Lord Pomeroy said, in a very authoritative, angry parent tone of voice, "You will stay here. You will tend to your mother. You will apologize to the grooms for sending them on a fool's errand when you go now to see the carriage brought to the door. Maybe take them a bottle of port, a couple of bottles. I don't care," he said and waved his hand over his head.

Rounding on his son, Lord Pomeroy said, "You have announced your intentions to take Miss Lawrence to wife. Your mother and I, although disappointed Miss Lawrence is, shall we say, without peerage or prospect, we are happy for you, but you go too far when you disrespect her, and us, by taking advantage of her lack of familial protection. Do I make myself clear?

"Once we have your sister home and you both have spent some time to reflect, we will talk more about this day's misconduct and misunderstandings."

Chapter Thirty-One

"Where do you want her to be?" Pamela asked. They had entered the sty to the sound of Peg's plaintiff squeals of pain and discomfort. Milo lit two lamps and held them up so they could see. Pamela approached the animal's crib with caution, unsure of what she could do to help the poor thing. Peg, to her surprise, struggled to her feet and approached the rail where Pamela was standing on the other side. Pamela reached over and rubbed the pig's ear. Peg grumbled her greeting.

"Over here, just across the aisle," Simon said. He lit two more lanterns and stood back to allow Pamela to have a look.

Looking over the high gate to the crib, she said, "Clear the floor of the straw."

"What? No. The straw is clean. We just put it down for this very purpose. It will absorb the fluids," Simon said.

"I see. But I think Peg would like a straw-free surface. She's very fastidious. Haven't you noticed? She's removed the straw from where she eats in one corner, and moved the straw to where she sleeps in another corner, and she tries very hard not to soil either space. Shouldn't there be a clear, easy-to-clean surface for the birthing? The straw can stay, just not in the middle of the floor where you or Milo will be cleaning the babies of their afterbirth."

Simon looked to Milo and shrugged his shoulders, silently giving leave to Pamela to open the panel to the birthing crib. He handed her the broom, and she began to sweep the straw to an equal depth on three sides of the crib. She laid the blankets over the straw, which made a nice, padded rim for the expectant mother.

Pamela waved the men aside and opened Peg's current crib, then turned and stepped across the aisle to the high, opened, solid gate to the birthing pen. Amazingly, Peg grunted and followed her to the freshly laid-out stall. The pig flopped down, in none too graceful a fashion, laid her head on the curb of soft straw covered with the wool blankets, and sighed.

****

"Well, I'll be—I've never seen nothin' like that before," said Milo.

"We better get ready," Simon said. He reached into a leather feed bag and removed a wad of old curtains he'd pilfered from the gatehouse refuse pile and laundered in anticipation of this event. "We're going to need these if we don't have the straw to absorb the fluids."

He pointed to Pamela. "You stay up at that end," he said, pointing to Peg's head, "and Milo and I will work this end. Keep her calm if you can. Keep your fingers away from her mouth. A pig bite can be extremely brutal. They can rip and shred flesh and crush bone. Do not underestimate her strength." Pamela nodded with understanding and sat down next to Peg's head and stroked her shoulder in a slow, gentle rhythm.

Once the sow was made comfortable and secure, the birthing process proceeded apace. Peg gave birth to three females, one right after the other. Simon was kept busy cleaning them of their afterbirth and umbilical cords and being sure their breathing passages were clear.

Peg raised her head, panting. She snuffled and nuzzled her children to welcome them. The next four piglets, two males, and two females, arrived, once again, one right after the other.

The last four piglets took a bit longer. Peg was exhausted, breathing labored, and her contractions continued. Pamela tried to give her a drink of water, but the sow refused. Milo massaged the animal's hip in a slow circular motion, and the last four piglets, three males, and a female, entered the world with one last, final squeal of pain and release from their mother.

Pamela, weeping copiously, joyously praised Peg for her bravery and fortitude. "Your children are all healthy and beautiful. We'll get you cleaned up and tuck you in. You need to rest."

Simon placed the pink, squeaking piglets at Peg's belly to allow them to find a teat. He got up off his knees and groaned in agony. He had to take several deep breaths before he could stand up all the way.

Milo had the wheelbarrow handy. Simon tossed the afterbirth wrapped in the soiled curtains in it and turned to find the water bucket where he could wash his hands, and that's when he spied Lord Pomeroy standing in the shadows. The man came into the lantern light and nodded to Simon and to Milo. He cleared his throat, sniffed back his tears and brushed the moisture from his cheeks and nose. "Congratulations. Looks to be a fine litter," he said. Unsmiling, he cleared his throat. "Pamela, it's late. I've come to take you home."

Simon helped her to her feet. "Thank you," she said and brushed the straw from her backside. Simon stood aside and opened the gate to the crib for her.

"Goodnight," she said to him and to Milo.

"We have to stop at the gatehouse to retrieve Chance," Simon heard Pamela say to her father, who had her by the elbow, and was leading her none to gently out of the sty.

Simon didn't hear what her father said in response, but he could imagine it wasn't pleasant.

****

The interior of the coach was dark but the silent fury and disappointment emanating from her father was a palpable thing. Chance, thankfully, fell asleep the moment his head landed on her lap. He took up most of the room on the seat, but she was grateful for his quiet repose. The Tidmore boys, she supposed, had worn him out. She didn't know what she could say to her father in her defense. She had done exactly what she'd set out to do to prove she could be a farmer's wife, helpmate, and still be a lady. Somehow, she had to convince her parents it was what she wanted, what she was meant to be. That life might not be what her parents had hoped for her, but it is what she wanted more than anything.

"Father, I'm sorry if I've caused you to worry," she finally said.

Lips tight, body stiff, he said, "You need to apologize to your mother. She's been very worried." He paused and then asked, "Have you been secretly meeting Simon Lawrence at the gamekeeper's cottage?"

"What? No. I have not."

This was awful. How could he think such a thing? Well, she had to adjust her thinking. It really wasn't all that far out of line, she had propositioned Simon. But how dare her father accuse her of such unseemly conduct. On the other hand, perhaps she had earned his mistrust.

"I don't deserve it, but you have to believe me," she said, having to work very hard to speak despite the hard, cold lump that had formed in her throat. "The thatchers came today to put on a new roof, and I wanted to patch up the fireplace. Jamison showed me how to make the slurry. That's why I was there. I've been cleaning and doing—*things*—to make ready for furniture. I told you what I was doing. I thought I had explained."

Her father still remained silent. It was not a good sign. It was a failing to over-explain things when guilty, but she couldn't help it or stop herself. "Today was the first day Simon had been to the cottage since our ride. He didn't expect to find me there. He had no idea I would be anywhere near the place. He was trying out a new goat cart."

In the dark, she heard her father snort in disbelief.

She shook her head and sighed and said aloud what she should have kept to herself. "No, sadly, rest assured, Father, Simon would never ask me to meet him on the sly. He would never ask any woman to meet him on the sly. He's too noble, too moral. I begged him to meet me at the cottage the day of our ride. I offered myself to him, and he flatly refused me. I begged him, Father, and he refused. He doesn't think he's worthy of my attention, you see. He's a lowly, crippled, his word not mine—farmer, and I'm of the gentry class, far above him in status. That's how he feels. But it's not how I feel. He's the most wonderful, kind, caring, loveable, sweet, honest person I've ever met. And I want him so very badly, it hurts."

The silence yawned between them. Finally, her father said, "I want to talk to you and Paul, but not tonight. You will not go anywhere tomorrow. Stay home and try to soothe your mother's nerves. I've asked Paul to do the same. She's very upset. I kept your whereabouts from her. When you didn't return home this afternoon and went missing, I had to tell her I knew where you'd gone and what you were doing. She's not very happy with me right now. We all must do better. So, think about what you are doing and why. Stay home and think, Pamela.

"And may I suggest you change your clothes and clean yourself up before you see your mother this evening. You smell of pig sty. I don't know where you found those garments you are wearing, but they are atrocious. Do not expect any of our servants to launder them for you."

Pamela opened her mouth to tell him she'd traded one of the tenant ladies a pair of her gloves for the apron. And she'd raided the maid's pantry and found the skirt, and of course, she had Paul's old jumper. Then, she reminded herself to stop over-explaining when guilty.

"No," her father said, "don't tell me how you've come by your garments," he said as if reading her mind. "I'm too tired and hungry. I really don't want to hear it tonight. I had a long hike in the dark, over hill and dale, looking for you, along with a half-dozen grooms. You see, we had no idea what had happened to you. You had simply disappeared. Until Paul came home, we thought you were lost or abducted."

Pamela's stomach growled. Suddenly, she, too, was very hungry. It was time, past time she found her own life. Tonight was a prime example of why. She didn't need to be mothered or disciplined like a child. Of course, her parents would continue to be part of her life, and she would appreciate their advice and experience. She intended her life to include more than Pomeroy Chase, more meaning than continuing a bloodline. She would leave that up to Paul and Audry. Yes, Audry, she would make them proud, and also bring new life, new blood into this family. And Penny, darling Penny. Pamela wondered what her little sister's future would hold. Lord knows, as her big sister, she'd done everything she could to demonstrate what not to do.

Chapter Thirty-Two

"I'm really not very hungry. Seems I just had breakfast," Audry said and sighed.

Simon pulled out a chair for her. Mrs. Dorsey had reported that Audry had eaten very little of her breakfast, and she'd spent her morning moping in her room. Simon had been up since dawn seeing to Peg and her new family.

"You had breakfast nearly five hours ago," he said. "Have some lunch. A groom from the Chase handed this to Michael at the Gatehouse. It's for you," he said and pulled up a chair for himself and handed her a small slip of folded paper.

Audry's blue eyes, as well as her whole demeanor, brightened as she read her missive. A wistful smile on her lips, head tilted to the side, she tucked the note under her plate. "Paul won't be visiting today. He will see me tomorrow at church. He says he'll save me a chair in the Chancel choir."

Leaning forward, palms going to the table she said, "I know what you're going to say."

"Good, then I don't need to say it," he said, and spread his napkin over his lap and helped himself to the chicken and dumplings from the pot on the table. "One day away from Paul Pomeroy will give you both a little time to cool your passions." He slid the pot toward her. "Eat," he said.

She did as ordered and selected one dumpling and some of the creamy chicken sauce. The silence between them grew to an uncomfortable void. Simon couldn't think of anything to say that wouldn't sound like a prudish old maid. He was in no position to be cautioning his sister on the pitfalls to be encountered in the romance department, he could barely control his own love life. He snorted at the thought. He didn't have a love life. His sister had more of a love life than he had.

"How is the new mother getting along with her little ones?" Audry asked.

He set aside his glass of cider and dabbed at the corners of his mouth with his napkin, grateful to have a topic upon which he could expound. And it had nothing to do with either Paul Pomeroy or his sister. "It appears to me Peg is a little overwhelmed. Every time she moves or rolls over, she's got piggies hanging on her teats. I think she finds it a little disconcerting right now. When I left her this morning, she was trying to nap, her body nestled against the straw bolsters Pamela had arranged for her. Her children were tucked up against her belly, squealing and nuzzling. Right now, we must make sure she has plenty to eat. Milo made her a mush of grain and milk, and I added a dribble of molasses. She made that disappear. Can't have her eating too much of that, don't want to give her the scours."

Audry laid her fork down and shook her head. "I'm sorry, it was my fault. I brought up the subject, but please, can we talk of something other than Peg's delicate digestive system?"

Simon laughed and shook his head. Pamela had sent him a note, too, via the groom. She wanted to know all about Peg, how she was doing, whether she was hungry, and was getting any rest from her duties as a mother.

In her note, Pamela said she and Paul were restricted to the Chase today. They were to soothe their mother's nerves. She also said she would see him tomorrow at church and tell him more of the story.

Simon answered her in as brief and impersonal terms as possible. But in his heart of hearts, it was impossible to express in mere words what her missive meant to him. She was thinking of him even when she wasn't with him. And he couldn't stop thinking about her.

To stop from laughing at himself and his tortured heart, he pressed his lips together and patted his chest pocket where he had put Pamela's note. "Yes, sorry," he said.

To sober himself, he shifted in his chair and in his mind, and said, "I think you and I should go up to the nursery and then to the attic and start selecting furnishings for the school. They put a new thatch roof on the gamekeeper's cottage, the broken windows have been replaced, and the fireplace patched. I'll have Michael bring around a wagon, and he can help us load it up with our donations to the cause."

Audry sat up straighter and nodded. "Good idea. There might be a few things I would like to keep. I might have children someday. It would be nice to have something of our mother's to pass along."

"Some things I might want to keep as well, for my own child. I do plan on having a family someday. But I will not consign them to that remote, cold nursery," he said, thinking of the note from Pamela, the note he had placed over his heart.

****

"Please, Penny, you have to help me. I must go to the cottage today. There is so much to do."

Penny, who had stretched out on her back on Pamela's bed, gazed up to the voile canopy and shook her head. "Father has said you must stay home today."

Pamela laced her boots, then gathered up her shawl. She'd bided her time sitting in her mother's parlor for the better part of the morning, stitching a length of lace to an under-slip. Over their luncheon, she'd patiently listened to her mother complain and explain why it was important for either of her girls to go off by themselves, not even here in the country. They must take a groom with them at all times and come tell her where they were going and how long they would be gone.

"I know, I know, but here is my plan," Pamela said and headed for her bedroom door.

Penny groaned and covered her eyes with her hands.

"No, no, now listen to me," Pamela said and gave her little sister a shake to get her off her bed. "The day is fine. It feels like spring, the birds are singing, the sky is mostly blue, and Mother needs to get out of this house. I think we should ask her to go up to the nursery with us to select a few things for the school. There are some slates I know, and the desks, anyway, we'll get her to come along with us. It will be an outing for her this afternoon. I'll need her advice, you see. She won't be able to resist giving advice on things. It's what she does."

"What about Paul?" Penny asked as they left Pamela's room.

"Well, I think he should come along, don't you? We'll need help placing the desks and I don't know, but, we'll make use of him somehow, I'm sure of it. Perhaps you and Paul could ride, and Mother and I will take the pony cart. Yes, I think that would be best. We all should get out of this house and enjoy the day. Breathe some fresh air."

"And what about Father?"

Pamela stopped on the landing, a finger going to her lips. "We'll ask. I would love it if he would come along. We should all go, you know, go as a family," she said and started down the stairs.

Chapter Thirty-Three

It didn't take all that much persuasion to convince her mother she needed to get out and take in some fresh air. They'd gleaned the nursery of a half dozen slates, two boxes of very old chalk, three small desks, three child-sized chairs, and some wooden puzzles. Penny, Paul, and their father rode down to the gamekeeper's cottage on horseback. Loaded with treasures they'd found for the proposed tenant school, Pamela, reins in hand, and her mother beside her, rode in the small pony cart used by the kitchen staff.

The very first thing Lady Pomeroy said at first sight of the cottage was she didn't remember it to be so small. "It's been years since I've been here. We used to ride this way all the time. I don't ride much anymore. I should, you know, I really should. How many children do you think will attend?" she asked Pamela as they approached.

"I don't really know. I thought possibly Mr. Ward would have an idea, or the Vicar Bodine. Do you, or Father, know how many of our tenants have children of school age?"

"That is an interesting question," said the lady. "I am ashamed to say that I could not even guess."

Lord Pomeroy helped his lady alight from the cart and took her arm. "They did a good job on the thatching," he said, scanning the exterior of the dwelling.

"But I don't see how you're going to get more than

a dozen children in here," he said upon entering the cottage. "There's only this one room, and it's small. I don't remember it being so cramped. Might it be possible to extend the back wall? Shouldn't be too difficult. The whitewash on the walls helps to make it seem more spacious." He gave Pamela a penetrating look and narrowed his eyes. "Hmmm, a bit messy. Whoever painted that wall probably got some on their hands and face. Look, got some on the stones on the floor as well."

Guilty, Pamela looked away. She'd rolled up her paint-splattered apron, skirt, and jumper and stuffed them in the refuse barrel late last night after everyone had gone to bed. She hoped none of the staff would find them and try to resurrect them.

"Yes, but it's still very dark with so few windows," Lady Pomeroy said. "Paint isn't going to help, I shouldn't think." Interested, she stood for a few moments to take in the construction and layout of the interior of the cottage. "Where would you put the teacher's desk? He should have a desk, I should think. And that fireplace, it's wonderful, but it might pose a hazard to the children. It should have a grate of some sort."

Pamela was impressed. These points her parents were pointing out were very relevant and interesting questions. She wished now she'd thought to bring pen and paper to write these things down. She hoped she could remember all that was said.

Paul brought in the three desks from the pony cart and set them down in the middle of the room. Penny entered with the baskets, with the slates and the chalk. Then they all heard the wagon pull up in front of the cottage. "Now, who can that be?" Pamela said and went to the opened door. She put her hand to her mouth and giggled.

Looking over her shoulder, her father asked, "Did you plan this?"

"No, Father, I did not," she said and stepped outside to greet Simon and Audry. Another wagon pulled up behind the Copeland wagon. The driver of that wagon tipped his hat and said he'd been sent over with a few things from Fairfield and asked where they wanted him to put them.

Pamela, with Simon laughing and joking, eagerly helped the Fairfield groom unload his interesting, exciting cargo of one scratched and marred adult-sized desk, two straight-back chairs, three baskets of books that looked to be mathematics, geography, and history books, some scrolled maps and navigation charts, and more slates and chalk.

Between the two of them, Simon and Pamela managed to unload the Fairfield wagon and send the driver on his way in short order. Breathless, pleased with themselves, they turned to each other and hugged. Simon kissed her forehead, and she kissed his cheek. When they turned around, they found they had an audience.

Simon dropped his arms and quickly stepped away from her to unload his own wagon. Pamela rushed around her father, ducked her head, and went back inside the cottage. Paul and Penny ducked their heads too and proceeded to give their attention to helping Simon and Audry.

Silent, a scowl on his face, her father nodded to her mother. Lady Pomeroy followed Pamela. Her expressive brows furrowed over her warm brown eyes, her lower lip held between her upper teeth. "Oh, dear, I do see the problem now," Lady Pomeroy said and put her arm around her. "I didn't quite understand. I'm sorry. Your father, I think, tried to explain to me, but I didn't see how it could possibly be. You've always enjoyed London, or so I thought. You've practically made it an art form to dance and flit from one beau to another. You love the balls, the costumes and plays, I thought. I never would have imagined you would ever want to give up the rush and bustle of the season in London. I thought you would find one particular beau in time, all in good time, who, like you, would live the hedonistic lifestyle London offered."

Her mother pressed her lips together, shook her head, and sighed a heavy sigh. "Well, you've found that one particular beau all right, but he wasn't in London."

Pamela turned in her mother's arms and began to weep. "I know he's not what you want me to have, but I love him so. I love everything about him. He won't have me. Did Father tell you that? Simon refuses to even consider me as his wife."

"Ah, we'll see," her mother said. "You know your Aunt June, my sister, doesn't come to London very often. She, we all thought, would surely settle for nothing less than to marry a duke or some titled gentleman and live a life of affluence and frivolity in London for all her days. Instead, she fell in love with a man who raises horses. He's a marquis, but he rarely comes to London, and all he can ever talk about is horses. She loves him dearly. Don't miss London, the lovely gowns, the balls, the theater at all, she says. I shall never understand it.

"It's not like your Mr. Lawrence is without land or prospect. He may not have a title, but if he is what you want, what makes you happy, then I want that for you too. I liked how he handled Lord Abernathy. He put him in his place rather nicely, I thought."

"Really, Mother? I won't be going to London with you. Do you understand that? I will stay here. I might come later for a short stay. But I have to stay close."

Lady Pomeroy stretched her arms out the better to look into her eyes. "The school will keep you here. Is that why you've taken this on?"

Pamela shook her head. "No. Well, I don't think so. I want to do this for the tenants. But yes, it will keep me here. For a while, at least, until it opens, and the students come. After that, I suppose I will take on a more organizational role."

****

He'd lost his head. Simon wanted to kick himself. The woman had a really peculiar effect on his brain, well not just his brain, there were other parts of him as well that misbehaved. He'd held her in his arms in front of her parents, her brother, her sister, and his sister. They'd surely seen it, then—*he didn't know what to call it*—the magnetic pull Pamela had on him, and he on her. They couldn't help it, it wasn't possible to deny the attraction, the need, the perfect pairing they presented.

Simon didn't think he would ever forget the look on Lady Pomeroy's face. She appeared positively dumbstruck, mouth agape, eyes wide, hands held tight to her breast. What could he say? No, what should he say?

Nothing, he decided, he would do nothing, pretend it never happened. Silent, head down, he continued to unload the wagon and place furniture inside the cottage.

"Let's try the adult desk over here," Lady Pomeroy said. "I think it should go near this window at the front of the room. If we put it in the corner and place the children out this way toward the back of the cottage, I think we can give everyone more room. Younger children up front and the older children toward the back, I think, would work."

"We can hang the charts and maps on this wall. We must find a bookcase, maybe more than one," Pamela said. "Not today, but when we are ready for the children. I'll, of course, ask Mr. Ward what he wants. But I like the desk there in the corner by the window. The children can see the teacher, and the teacher can see all the children from there."

Chapter Thirty-Four

Simon had never thought of it before, but attending Sunday services was about more than observing the Sabbath, it was a venue where neighbors meet to share events, advice, and do business. Word had spread that Peg had delivered her litter. As soon as the service was over, he sold two of his male piglets to two local squires. He explained that he'd promised Lord Pomeroy the first pick of the males and females. All of the litter would be held until weaned, of course. He also had made appointments for Boris, his boar, to service three sows.

Yesterday, after the church service, he'd only had a few moments of conversation with Pamela. Lord and Lady Pomeroy had kept a sharp eye on their children before, during, and after the service.

"They thought I'd been abducted," Pamela told him as they stood with other members of the congregation outside the church. "Father wanted to know if I had been meeting you on the sly at the gamekeeper's cottage."

At that point, Simon had thought he might explode. "What did you say to that?" he asked, holding his breath, afraid of her answer.

"I told him it would never happen. You would never ask me, or any woman, to meet you on the sly for any reason."

Simon, a bit lightheaded, let his breath go and said more to himself than to her, "Thank you very much.

Good to know I won't have to flee the country. It's what I expected after yesterday. I really expected your father or Paul to take me around the back of the cottage and give me a good thrashing. And I would not have blamed them."

Paul and Audry had their heads together. Simon had to strain his ears, but he'd overheard most of their conversation. "I won't be able to visit you this afternoon," Paul said. "I've been conscripted to help prepare for our soiree tomorrow evening. I will be counting the minutes until I can see you again."

Audry smiled and nodded. "Simon is keeping a close eye on me, too," she said and nodded to Lady and Lord Pomeroy, who were watching them while talking to Squire Miller and his wife. "I understand. I, too, shall be counting the minutes. Save me a dance," she said and moved off to join Penny, who was conversing with a group of young ladies from the village.

The remainder of their Sunday was spent quietly at home, Audry reading and Simon going over the ledgers. He hadn't received any cash so far, but if his calculations were right, the Manor would soon be above water, out of debt thanks to Peg, the new lambs, and calves. There wouldn't be any extra funds, but at least they would be able to pay all of their bills. Audry could have more gowns, and he could possibly stop worrying.

***

After a rather restless night's sleep, this morning he sat in his library counting sheep, his mind drifting off now and then as to how he was to endure the evening's entertainments at the Chase. He envisioned he would stand around like an awkward piece of useless decoration and try to blend in with the wallpaper.

He was overwhelmed with all that was happening now. Audry and Paul? Paul should be allowed to marry Audry and take her with him to London. Paul would protect her, of course he would, Simon knew that, and yet he hesitated to release his sister into another man's care.

And what should he do about Pamela? They couldn't go on as they were now. Of course, it would be easier if she would go away, go to London. He had to believe her. She wasn't going to leave.

He told himself he should go to Lord Pomeroy and confess his love for his daughter. Lay his life out before him and plead with her father to allow him to marry her. That would be the right thing to do. It would also be the most humiliating thing he could possibly think of doing. Her father would most certainly reject his plea. But at least he and Pamela would have their answer. It could never be, never.

"Excuse me, Master Simon," said Suzie from the library door. "There is a Mr. Ledbetter here to see you."

"Ledbetter? Here? To see me? Send him in, Suzie. Send him in."

Mr. Percival Ledbetter was a squat, round-faced, bespectacled gentleman of a mature age with a receding hairline. Considering the man was a lawyer, he had a jolly way about him that appealed to Simon. Their communications were always precise, with an undertone of personal care. In short, Simon liked the man. He trusted him. "Please, come in, Mr. Ledbetter."

Before Suzie could close the door, he called to her, "Bring us some tea."

"Or, would you, perhaps, like something stronger?" he asked his guest. "Mrs. Dorsey makes a very good nog.

And she's generous with the rum."

"Tea would do nicely," Mr. Ledbetter said.

"And scones, please, Suzie," Simon said.

"Right away, sir," Suzie said and closed the door behind her.

"Please have a seat," Simon said. "Good of you to stop by. Are you on your way through? If I recall, you said you have a sister in Huntingdonshire. Are you visiting?"

Mr. Ledbetter made himself comfortable in the overstuffed chair nearest Simon's desk and set his satchel down next to his feet. He unbuttoned his suit coat and took a couple of deep breaths. "Yes, I do have a sister in Huntingdonshire. I'll be staying with her."

"I've been going over the budgets," Simon said and closed the ledger he had on his desk, suddenly ashamed of his bookkeeping style. Mr. Ledbetter's presence today, of all days, made him extremely anxious. It was bad news. He could feel it in his bones. If he kept talking, he could delay the axe that was sure to fall.

"I think I can see some light breaking through the mound of debt. The sow I told you about had her litter, and I've sold most of them, even though they are only a day old and aren't weaned. Also, the boar is going to help us. The lambs are showing up at a fast and furious rate, and I'm finding it difficult to keep up with the count."

His guest smiled and nodded. Simon took a breath and moved the ledger aside. "I must thank you once again for your diligence on behalf of my grandfather. You kept looking, and you found me and my sister. We are very fortunate, and we know it. We've found our home. We've met our neighbors. As a matter of fact, we are invited to attend a soiree this evening at Pomeroy

Chase. I attended Eton with Paul Pomeroy, the son of Lord Pomeroy. At that time, I had no idea the Chase was so close to Copeland or anything about my grandfather. Paul and my sister Audry are courting, and there is more than a hint of a marriage between them in the very near future."

Suzie knocked on the door. Simon bade her to enter. She came in and set the tea tray down on his desk. "Would you like me to pour?" she asked.

"No, thank you, Suzie," Simon said. She bobbed and backed out of the room.

The time had come, and Simon could delay no longer. Mr. Ledbetter moved forward in his chair, a move that said he had something to say, and he wanted to say it now.

"Before we have tea," Mr. Ledbetter said, "let us do what I came here to do." He bent down, opened his satchel, and rifled through what looked to be at least a hundred pages of documents, receipts, and invoices. "I'm not simply passing through. I've traveled here today with a purpose. I've come specifically to see you, my Lord Simon Lawrence," he said, and got up from his chair and laid the pile of papers on Simon's desk.

'Lord Simon Lawrence,' the title percolated in Simon's brain for several seconds before he comprehended the implication. "I have a title? Sir Simon-Loyd Copeland's title?"

Mr. Ledbetter plopped back down in his chair and squirmed, eyes fairly glittering with excitement. "No, and that's why I chose to make this call. You see, I couldn't possibly explain all that has been revealed during this most fascinating journey I've been on. I couldn't possibly explain, in a single written communication, what I have unearthed through my research."

Mr. Ledbetter hoisted himself out of the chair again, tapped the stack of papers he'd laid before Simon, and leaned over them. "Because Sir Simon-Loyd Copeland had no male issue, the title, his knighthood, stopped there."

Pretending to follow, baffled, Simon nodded because that was how he had understood the issue.

Mr. Ledbetter kept tapping the papers, eyes bugging out of his head, snapping with excitement. "You and your sister have inherited the Baronetcy of the third Baron Adonius-George-Wyatt Lawrence of Luckhandry, Northumberland, which makes you the fourth Baron Adonius-George-Wyatt-Simon Lawrence of Luckhandry and your sister a Baroness because the baronetcy was also bestowed on the female issues of the clan, which makes her Cathrine-Helene-Rosemund-Audry Lawrence of Luckhandry."

Out of breath and a bit sweaty, Mr. Ledbetter collapsed back into his chair and dabbed his brows with his kerchief.

Simon sat silent, his brain working to correlate this news into reality.

"There's a castle," Mr. Ledbetter said. "Your last remaining relative, your father's brother, I believe you will find his name there, is George. He currently resides in Luckhandry Castle, Northumberland. He has his own title, so there is no competition there. Although, because he has no issue, a bachelor, there is a good chance you will also inherit his title as well.

"I understand the castle overlooks the Channel. It was built as a fortress to protect us from the Spaniards,

Moors, or some such invaders. Your uncle lost track of your father and you and Audry when the Plantation was destroyed. He has restored the plantation, by the way. He had no idea you had survived and returned to England. And he never would have if I hadn't discovered his name among your father's documents. I looked for birth records, you see. And that led me to titles and baronetcies." He stopped to catch his breath. "I took the liberty to correspond with him to let him know you and your sister were here at Copeland Manor."

The man dabbed at his sweating brow. "I hope I haven't overreached my authority by doing so?"

Simon got up from his desk and poured himself and Mr. Ledbetter a snifter of brandy. He handed the glass to the man, took a good-sized swallow from his snifter, and sat back down. "Once again, I thank you for your diligence. It was a lucky day when I walked into your offices and filed an application for employment."

Mr. Ledbetter bounced back up out of his chair. "Wait, dear boy, there's more, so much more." Once again, he tapped the stack of papers on the desk.

Chapter Thirty-Five

Daylight starting to fade, Simon wrote Mr. Ledbetter, as a finder's fee, a very generous check. He saw the man at the door, wished him a safe journey, retired to his library, and sat down to write a missive to be delivered to Lord Pomeroy.

"What have you been doing in here?" Audry asked. She was wearing a beautiful frock of peach and cream brocade. The low decolletage barely covered her white breasts, but she had artfully disguised her exposed flesh by inserting a delicate, cream-colored lace fichu in the bodice. She looked so incredibly beautiful, her hair in a rich coil on top of her head and cascading down in a curly wave over one shoulder; Simon nearly forgot what he was doing or why.

"You need to get ready," she said. "We leave in less than an hour. It's nearly six o'clock. I had a bite to eat in my room. I thought you were in your room, too. Who was that man? You were in here all afternoon with the door closed."

"Suzie brought us some bread, cheese, and smoked meat. Mr. Ledbetter, the lawyer, do you remember him from London? We had a bite and a scone or two. I'm not the least bit hungry. I was making a few notes," he said and folded the piece of paper upon which he'd been writing into a tight square.

"I'll go get ready. Be with you in less than an hour.

Don't worry. I'll be ready to go shortly. Is Michael in the kitchen with the Dorsey's? I want to talk to him about, ah..about transportation for the evening," he said, keeping his eyes averted, head down.

Audry nodded. "Yes, I think he is, and the children and Suzie."

Simon gave her a kiss on the cheek and left her standing in the doorway to his library. "You are beautiful. You look positively delicious. Paul Pomeroy doesn't stand a chance. Go, put your feet up in the drawing room. You're going to be on them all evening long. Better rest up while you may," he said and laughed all the way across the entry hall and down the narrow hall to the kitchen.

He found Michael in the kitchen and motioned for him to follow him outside to the back stoop. "This," he said, handing Michael the small square of paper, "is a note for Lord Pomeroy. I want you to deliver it right away—*now*—to Pomeroy Chase. If you can, try not to let anyone know you're there. Send a groom inside with the note—maybe? You know some of them, I'm sure. Find one you can trust. Once his lordship reads the note, he'll understand why we must keep this note and its contents a secret for the time being. I'm not expecting a reply. So once this is delivered, you may return home."

"I'll see if I can find Jamison. He'll know how to manage it," Michael said.

"Good, very good, yes, that would be best. Off you go, then. I need this done before we arrive and before too many other guests arrive."

****

Pamela stood in the receiving line with her mother, father, Paul, and Penny. The Vicar Bodine, his wife, their son, and daughter arrived first. Mrs. Springer took their wraps and ushered them into the formal drawing room. The furniture had been rearranged and moved to the side, allowing a large area for dancing and games. Card tables had been set up in an alcove to the side of the big windows that led out to a patio and the gardens. The patio was alight with torches, and benches could be seen from the window for those who became overheated. A refreshment table had been laid out in the antechamber of the big room, tables overflowing with punch, cakes, sweetmeats, and an assortment of savory biscuits decorated with cheese, vegetables, and sliced smoked sausage, plates, cups, dinnerware, and napkins. A small ensemble of musicians had set up a platform in one corner of the room. They had yet to take up their instruments and sat waiting for their cue to begin.

Pamela pasted a smile on her lips and nodded to Lord Fairfield and his lovely bride, but her ears strained to hear what her mother was saying to her father. A gloved hand up to shield her lips, Lady Pomeroy asked her husband, "What is Jamison doing? Why has he come inside? He nodded. Did you see him? He nodded to you. Why? What did he say to Mrs. Springer? He should be outside assisting our guests."

Pamela welcomed the Davis family, ears working like funnels. "Nothing to concern yourself with, my dear. Probably someone dropped a glove or something, and he brought the item inside to give to Mrs. Springer as he should," her father said. "I'm going to see to the Vicar and his family," her father said. He gave Lady Pomeroy a bus on her cheek. "Would you mind? I think someone should be in the drawing room now our guests have started to arrive."

"Yes," Lady Pomeroy said, "yes, you are right. Thank you, dear."

Her father made it to the drawing room door, his back to Pamela. Mrs. Springer made a slight detour, also putting her back to the receiving line, she dipped her father a slight curtsey. Her hand out, she begged his pardon, turned around, and came forward to receive the coats and wraps from their guests. Pamela wondered about her strange maneuver.

Her father hesitated, his back to her and the arriving guests. He appeared to be thinking about something and turned back to look over his shoulder at her and their guests. He smiled and nodded, tucked something into his cumberbund watch-fob pocket, and entered the drawing room with a cunning twinkle in his eye.

****

"Help me," Simon said. It was dark inside the old coach. He thought he could manage to get his gloves on, but the fingers of his mutilated hand weren't cooperating. His work gloves were more roomy. These were skin-tight.

"Well, hold still," Audry said. "Can you stop tugging for a moment? Let me get the glove straightened out. Then I'll try it again. Hold your hand out, close your eyes, and relax, please."

He did as she requested, not to obey, but because he needed to slow down his heart. He could feel it beating way too fast and too hard, and the throbbing pounded at his temples.

Questions and doubt plagued him. *Had Lord Pomeroy received his note? How would he know?* He had asked him to give no hint of what he had in mind to do. Pamela, especially, must not suspect.

"I think we should ask the Pomeroy's for supper this week. Reciprocate. I was thinking, day after tomorrow," he said, eyes closed, taking deep breaths, concentrating on slowing his heart to a moderate pace.

"That is a wonderful idea. Would you like me to ask them, or should you?" Audry said and tapped his wrist. "There, I believe your hand is now encased in your gloves. I'm proud of you, you look smashing in your dark suitcoat and breeches. The wine satin cravat, gold brocade waistcoat, and white collar points are perfect. Very handsome. Will you dance?"

"I'm considering it," he said or rather grumbled. "I, possibly, could manage a sedate reel or two, but not a waltz. I would probably fall over and take the unfortunate lady with me to the floor. As I recall, that's what happened during dance elocution at Eton—hence the wrestling. Don't suppose that would be considered de rigueur at Lady Pomeroy's soiree."

"I hope there aren't too many people," Audry said. "Paul said there would be around twenty or so. And maybe of those, a half dozen will want to partner for dancing. He promised me he would take me outside onto the patio for a breath of fresh air ever so often."

"I'm glad to be wearing gloves," Simon said, expressing his thoughts aloud. "Maybe this damned hand won't frighten the ladies too badly when I take them onto the floor," he said, tugging at the highly starched collar of his shirt points.

"Ah, well, here we are," he said as the coach turned up the drive to Pomeroy Chase. "We both must remember to enjoy ourselves. This is not torture, this is not punishment, this is meant to be enjoyed."

“Yes, enjoyed,” Audry said, with very little conviction in her tone of voice.

Chapter Thirty-Six

Simon and Audry weren't the last guests to arrive, but Pamela had begun to worry Simon had decided not to come at all. When she saw the old Copeland carriage roll up to the entrance, she let out a sigh of relief when Simon assisted his sister to alight. Paul instantly stepped out of the receiving line and helped Audry divest of her black sealskin cape and hand it off to Mrs. Springer.

Audry did appear spectacularly beautiful this evening, a bit flushed, eyes bright and blue as the deepest ocean. Pamela was at a loss for words and simply hugged the girl. Simon, standing behind his sister, fairly beamed with pride as Lady Pomeroy did likewise. Penny latched onto Audry, Paul took up her other side, and they kept her in the receiving line with them until the last guest was shown into the drawing room.

To the side, Lord Pomeroy welcomed Simon with a handshake, which Pamela thought a bit unusual. Normally, her father simply bowed to his guests. But, as Paul and Audry were as good as promised to each other, Pamela put the gesture out of her mind. Her father offered the usual words of welcome and ushered Simon into the drawing room where the other guests had gathered.

Simon had met most of them at church, so Pamela didn't worry that he would feel a stranger to those gathered. She introduced him to the Smith-Mortons.

They were newly arrived from Scotland and did not attend the same church as Simon and the Pomeroy's.

Reginald Smith-Morton, Lord and Lady Smith-Morton's eldest son, had been one of Pamela's more attentive admirers. She hoped to discourage his pursuit this evening. If asked, she would inform one and all that she had no intention of seeing another season in London. She had work to do right here at home. She hoped that would quash any expectations her previous suitors might hold.

****

Simon had to work very hard not to stare. All the ladies, of course, were garbed in their finest evening gowns, but Pamela, his Pamela, put them all to shame. She was a goddess in gold satin. The gown clung to her every curve, simple in design, lacking decoration of any kind except for a single row of diamante at the hem. She wore very little jewelry, save for a crystal and gold star pendant at her throat and crystal star ear dangles that caught the light and flickered when she moved her head. Her beautiful hair was on fire, capturing the light of the chandeliers and candles. A ribbon of diamante interwoven through her coiffed locks formed a halo around her head. The effect was mesmerizing.

He cautioned himself to get hold of his libido, he had to find time and space to read the note Lord Pomeroy had passed to him with his handshake. The man was as wily as Pamela had said.

He barely had time to say more to Pamela than she looked beautiful before the music started. Three men crowded around her, pushing him out of the way and vying for her attention. Refusing to cave to his impulse to pound their prepossessing faces in, Simon caught the nod from Lord Pomeroy. He watched the man leave the room, forgetting all about the note, and followed him. Outside, sconces lit up the entrance to the Chase, but beyond that light, it was full-on dark. Simon trailed his lordship across the drive to the far side of the fountain, well out of sight.

"Sorry, My Lord, I didn't get a chance to read your note," Simon said.

"Well, from your cryptic missive, I presume your man of business gave you good news. And you are now in a better position to ask for Pamela's hand, and you seek my permission. What I don't understand is why the subterfuge?"

"If she found out I now had a title, land, and a modest pot of coin, I wouldn't put it past your daughter to abduct me tonight and haul me to Scotland, where we would be married over the anvil. She hasn't exactly been subtle about making her wishes known. I've been doing my best to discourage her and get her to see that I will never be more than a modestly successful farmer. But now my prospects have changed, I'd like an opportunity to do this properly. I will still be a farmer, you and she must understand, I won't change that. I enjoy being a farmer."

Lord Pomeroy tsk, tsked, and tipped his head to the side. "I do understand, she can be very forceful. She gets it from her mother. Are you sure this is how you want to handle this?" he asked.

"She proposed to me. She propositioned me," Simon said. "She did not make it easy to refuse her. She lives to orchestrate. This may be my one and only opportunity to do something my way. I wish for you, Lady Pomeroy, Paul, and Penny to join Audry and me at the Manor for supper the day after tomorrow, and I will strive to do this right. But I need to know tonight if you will give us your blessing. I won't go any further if you have reservations. And if you do, I completely understand. We've known each other for only a couple of weeks. And the same goes for Paul and my sister. This is all happening very fast. Maybe too fast. But I don't want to wait, and Pamela, well, she is, pardon me for saying so, she is chomping at the bit to get hitched."

"Yes. I see. I'm going to need details," Lord John said. "And I'm sure my wife will want details, a lot of details. I presume you will present them at this supper."

"Yes, I have documents. We will go over them after our meal, that is if you will give me your permission to apply my address."

Lord Pomeroy put a hand on his shoulder. "Good, very good. You don't know how very pleased I am this is going to come about. I firmly believe you two will do very well together. You know my Pamela, she can drive one insane with her maneuverings, missions, and machinations. But if you're aware and willing to take her on, then who am I to stand in your way? She is a special young woman. I've given her as much leeway as I dare, maybe too much. I know you will provide what she has been looking for all this time. I know it."

"I've applied for a special license," Simon said in rather a rush, almost a dare. "I sent the application with Mr. Ledbetter this afternoon. Also, I've asked him to find us a house in London that we can rent for a few weeks. As soon as Pamela has this school set up, we'll come to town. I hope that is all right. I want us to be wed as soon as possible."

"Yes, yes, I agree. What of Paul and Audry?"

"I think they should have a wedding in their church and all the trimmings, don't you? The bands will have to be read. Is there time before you leave for London?"

"Oh, I believe there is plenty of time. We won't leave for the season until mid-March. Should have the knot firmly tied by then. This is splendid. Lady Alice will be right in her element. Stand back. She'll have everybody hopping to her tune. Count on it."

Giving a worried glance toward the house, Lord Pomeroy said, "We better get back in there, or we'll be missed."

"I'll go first," Simon said. "If I get caught, I'll say I needed a breath of air or something. Maybe Milo—yes, Milo, he needed something. I know Pamela's watching me. And you, she's watching you too, you know. She eavesdrops all the time."

Lord Pomeroy simply nodded and tipped his head. "I know another way in. I'll go around to the patio," he said and set off for the side of the house.

Simon entered the house and made it to the drawing-room door without notice, but the second he stepped into the room, Pamela came up beside him. "You've been outside," she said.

He laughed. "Yes, yes, I have. I received a note from Milo. He asked me to step outside for a moment." Simon tapped the small piece of paper in his waistcoat pocket. "He wanted to let me know he could be found at the stables with Jamison and the others. I cautioned him not to drink too much cider."

"I've saved room for you on my dance card."

"You'll be sorry," he said with a smile.

"Never," she said. "The next cotillion."

He nodded. She smiled and greeted her next partner,

a rather dashing, although pockmark-faced young man of the dandy set. Simon thought his name was Horton or Morton. The man had some very interesting and dramatic moves on the dance floor, none of which had anything to do with the music, unfortunately. After watching him for a while, Simon didn't feel so bad. Surely, he could do better than that.

****

So, she wasn't the only one who over-explained when caught out. Simon had just told her a fib. *Now, why would he do that?* Pamela asked herself. She happened to catch sight of her father entering the patio door. He looked a bit sheepish. What was he doing out on the patio?

Her current partner, Reginald, liked to improvise steps. The trick was to ignore him, keep your feet out of his way, and hope the music would end before one tripped.

Pamela smiled as she and Reginald passed Penny and her partner, the good-looking Duncan Davis. Audry was being chatted up by the Vicar's son. She appeared slightly uncomfortable, rather stiff and wide-eyed, but doing well. Paul had Jenna Carmody by the hand and was leading her through the steps, but he had positioned himself and his partner right beside Audry and her partner, so Audry was never out of his sight. He kept looking over his shoulder and his partner's head to do so. In short, he appeared ridiculous, and Jenna did not look well pleased.

One more promenade down the center, and the performance ended. Cheeks flushed and rather lovely gray eyes shining, his lips a little too close for comfort, Reginald congratulated them both on their dancing abilities. "We make the perfect pair. You compliment me beautifully. Come, my dear, we'll adjourn to the patio, and I shall procure us a refreshment."

"Thank you. That is very kind of you," Pamela said. "But I've promised the cotillion to Mr. Lawrence."

"Ah, yes, the colonial," he said with a sneer. "I've heard he raises pigs."

"Yes, isn't he beautiful, and so are his pigs," she said and left the fop standing there with his mouth agape like a fish out of water.

She thought she would have to hunt Simon down, but far from it. He met her before she could leave the floor. "Would you care for a refreshment before the next set? I believe it is my dance," he said and handed her a small cup of punch. "Are you sure you want to partner with me? I don't have good balance with this hip of mine, and it's been years since I've been on a dance floor. And by my observations, you've just suffered a very strenuous reel with Mr. Horton—Morton, whatever his name."

She looked down at her cup of lovely punch and giggled. "He is a bit of a prancer-dancer, but he's harmless. Thank you for the refreshment," she said. After taking a few restorative sips, she set her cup on the serving tray next to the wall. "I'm ready if you are," she said as the musicians struck up the sounding cord for the next set.

Paul and Audry were in front of them going down the line, which made it easier for Simon to mimic the changes. His hip was screaming, and he was grateful for the skin-tight gloves—his hands were sweating, he was certain.

"Now," Pamela said, as they parted. Ladies back,

gentlemen bow. “Tell me what you and my father are up to.”

“Ah,” he said. One step forward, take the lady's hand and march. “I’ve invited your family for supper. I thought we should reciprocate.”

“And you had to leave the room to do that?”

He chuckled, took her hand, and arched. “We also discussed farm animals.”

“Of course you did,” she said and curtsied.

Chapter Thirty-Seven

"I've gathered all of you here," Simon said, looking around the kitchen, "because I thought you should be the first to hear of our good fortune." He looked to Audry as he spoke. She blinked, delicate brows knit together, questioning.

Michael stood behind Suzie. His big hands resting on his wife's shoulders, he appeared braced for bad news. Audry with the toddler Dennis on her lap, Jeremy, between Suzie and Mrs. Dorsey, sat at the kitchen table. Milo stood in the doorway to the back stoop, arms folded across his chest.

"As you were advised, we've invited the Pomeroy's from the Chase to dine with us this evening. They've been very welcoming to Audry and me. This is new to us, a formal gathering, or as formal as we will probably ever get, because I'm not really accustomed to socializing.

"Ellen, you know more of how to conduct this sort of thing than I do. But I was thinking, or rather hoping, Audry and I and our guests could gather in the dining room before we dine now that there is a conversational area in the room. The dining room is a warm and inviting space perfect for an intimate gathering." Simon gave a nod to Michael. "Thank you, Michael, it is very nice and a much better use of the large space. We must decide what we want to call that space. It doesn't feel right to keep referring to it as the dining room. Perhaps the family sitting room or dining parlor. I don't know, but think about it."

Simon had kept silent all day yesterday, keeping the changes in their fortune to himself, going over the accounts, setting up a new ledger, and getting everything straight in his own mind. Pamela, Penny, Paul, and Lord John had paid a call in the afternoon to inspect the litter of pigs. They had enjoyed tea and scones together. Pamela, it was obvious, was suspicious. He supposed it was his demeanor. He knew he felt lighter, less weighted down. It probably showed on his face and his bearing.

This morning was more or less a practice run of what he intended to say this evening. He cleared his throat and leaned back against the kitchen sideboard behind him, hands braced at his side on the counter ledge. "My grandfather, whom I never met, but I've deduced from these surroundings and comments made that he was a sour, lonely man. I can only imagine that he was a terrible husband and father, but he was a courageous investor. And due to his uncanny betting ability to invest in the shipping and mining trade, the Manor is now solvent." His audience, in chorus, emitted a gasp of delight and surprise.

Simon held up a hand to put a halt to his sister's questions. He was sure she had many.

He shook his head. "I won't go into detail, but you all will be receiving a raise in pay and a bit extra shortly. I would recommend that you, Milo, as our land steward, and you, Michael, as our houseman, carpenter, head groom, and man of all trades, put your heads together and determine what you need to make life better for you as far as your duties are concerned. Once you've listed your needs, bring them to me, and I will review them.

"Ellen, as our anchor, our head of all things household, please feel free to enlist whatever assistance you and Suzie need to make your lives easier and less burdensome. We owe you, Ellen, a great deal, you and Milo. Again, allow me to review before you make your changes. I expect changes, so don't be timid. Let's make the Manor an example of efficiency, comfort, and success.

"Oh, and one more thing," he said, having to work very hard to maintain a straight face, "You may now address me as My Lord and Audry as My Lady."

The kitchen erupted in a resounding cheer. Simon tried to explain, over the din of questions and congratulations, that no, they hadn't inherited Sir Simon-Loyd's title but titles on his father's side of the family.

In the end, it really didn't matter to any of them. Mrs. Dorsey was in tears. She couldn't stop weeping and dabbing her eyes with her apron. Milo kept pumping his arm, his good arm, until Simon thought it might fall off. Jeremy, taking laps around and around the kitchen table, added to the chaos. Dennis started laughing, then ended up wailing, probably frightened by all the clamor and cheering. Audry relinquished the child into his mother's arms, and, with tears in her eyes, she wrapped her arms around him, laid her head upon his chest, and wept.

****

Audry followed him up the stairs. "You've been outside since lunch. I want to talk to you before our guests arrive," she said.

"Yes, I thought you might. Therefore, I stayed outside."

"You knew about this for two days, and you didn't

think to say anything. Mr. Ledbetter, he came here on purpose to give you this information, and you didn't think to include me."

He stopped at the top of the stairs and waited for her to reach the hall. "I wanted to organize in my mind how best to proceed," he said.

"Proceed? With what?"

"This evening, I'm going to try to explain how we got here. I think we should, as the Pomeroy family and our family will be combined soon."

"Combined? Soon?"

"Yes, you and Paul, you will be wed within a few months. The bands will have to be read, but that should only take a month."

"You are no longer withholding your permission?"

"I've never been against the union, Audry. I simply wanted you to slow down and get to know each other a little better before you promised to spend the rest of your life with someone you barely knew. But now, you will go to your groom with a proper dowry and a title, and while you wait for the bands to be read, you will have time to become better acquainted with each other. I am very happy for you and Paul. I look forward to becoming an uncle very soon. I have one request: please keep what I have disclosed quiet for a few more hours. I wish to announce our good fortune in my own way."

"And what way would that be, dear brother?"

He reached his bedroom door. "You shall have to wait to see," he said and entered his room and closed the door on his sister.

****

Michael, dressed in a black suit coat and tails, black breeches, a red waistcoat, a white shirt, and high points on his collar, answered the door and ushered their guests inside. Suzie, in her black dress, white apron, and cap, took hats, capes, and coats and hung them up very carefully in the small closet beneath the stairwell. Michael bowed to their guest and indicated they should follow him across the entryway and down a short, sconce-lit hallway to the entrance to the now-so-named dining parlor where Simon and Audry awaited their arrival.

"Thank you, Michael," Simon said. He smiled to himself. The rather dazed look on Lady Pomeroy's face was priceless. Michael did appear to be a very impressive butler. Simon could see Mrs. Dorsey's hand in his performance, as well as Suzie's. He couldn't wait to see what his *staff* had laid out for their meal. He hadn't asked. He wasn't worried. He knew they would go all out to impress.

Before the hearth, an occasional table had been laid with a bottle of brandy and seven petite goblets on a silver tray, as he had requested. "I know it is customary to wait until after the meal for the aperitif, but this is a special evening, and I think it requires a libation and a toast," he said and poured brandy into the glasses.

Audry, nodding and offering the weakest of smiles, passed the drinks around to their guests. Paul accepted his glass and sat down on the wide arm of Audry's chair, his manner possessive and slightly defensive.

Confused, glancing around the room, Lady Pomorey looked down at the contents of her glass. She had taken the overstuffed chair near the hearth. Her husband made himself comfortable in a large wingback chair next to her, his expression inscrutable as always. Penny chose the overstuffed ottoman near the occasional table and eyed the libation with hungry eyes. Pamela ended up in the straight-backed chair that faced the hearth, Simon, and the serving table. She held her glass as if prepared to toss the contents in his face if he uttered a wrong word.

Simon held his glass up to make his toast. "I welcome you as our first supper guests since our arrival at Copeland Manor." His guests obliged, toasted in return, and took a tentative sip of their drinks.

He licked his lips, savored the sweet libation, and cleared his throat. "On his first visit, Lord Pomeroy very eloquently and sincerely made us feel welcome. And because of his kind nature, I shared with him a bit of our history. I asked him, at the time, to keep what I had imparted to himself. But I feel that tonight, I would like to share a bit of my, and Audry's, history as an explanation of our past behavior.

"It will be two years, come April, that Audry and I lost our parents to a very cruel and barbaric death." He gave his company a brief account but quickly moved on, refusing to dwell on the topic. It would only bring forth nightmares and distress, and this was an evening for celebration, not a wake. "Because of all that had happened, Audry and I made the decision to return to England. I had applied for the position of law clerk, and little did I realize it was the very law firm our grandfather had employed to search for his daughter and his heirs.

"Once discovered and confirmed we were the heirs of Sir Simon-Loyd Copeland, my sister and I took refuge here at the Manor. We found friendly and fertile ground upon which to rebuild our lives, never expecting we would find more, so much more."

He paused, took a breath, and turned to Pamela and then to Lady Pomeroy. "I have recently learned that our grandfather made several wise investments, and Copeland Manor is free of debt. I do not inherit my grandfather's title nor his knighthood."

He came around the table and got down on one knee before Pamela. He winced, removed the glass from her hand, and took her hand in his. "I have, however, inherited my father's title of Baron of Lawrence Luckhandry, Northumberland."

Simon shifted his gaze from Pamela's warm eyes and looked to his sister. "Audry has inherited her title of Baroness of Lawrence Luckhandry, Northumberland, as well," he said, with a nod to Paul.

Once again addressing his full attention to Pamela, he brought her hand up to his lips. "I have approached your father for permission to make this proposal," he said. "He has given his consent and best wishes. I want you to understand that I don't intend to change my ways. I will always be a farmer. A farmer with a title is all I will ever be. I don't want to waste time. I've sent my man of business to London for a special license. I expect to hear from him by the end of the week. I've also asked him to find us a house to rent in London for a few weeks during the coming season. I had thought, for our honeymoon, we should travel to Northumberland and visit Luckhandry Castle. I have an uncle who lives there. I believe he would welcome a visit from us. Perhaps we could go as a family," he said, his gaze traveling from Lord and Lady Pomeroy to Penny, then to Paul and Audry.

He kissed her fingers. "If this displeases you, then speak now," he said. "I will have your answer before we sit down to share our meal. I will accept your answer and respect your decision."

****

It was hard to decide. Part of her wanted to pop up out of her chair and dance around the room. The other part of her wanted to slap Simon Lawrence's handsome face. His eyes were lit up like blue lightning. His lips were twitching to hold back his smile. Oh, he was enjoying this. "Hmmm," Pamela said and tapped her cheek with her finger, feigning consideration. The occupants in the room had gone very still. "Hmmm, a farmer Baron? Well, yes, I suppose that will do," she said, took his face in her hands, and planted a very long and thorough kiss on his smiling lips.

"Get up off your knees," she whispered when their lips parted.

Simon came to his feet, holding her hand in his. "One more thing I wish to say. Paul, your father and I agree you and Audry must speak to Vicar Bodine about the reading of the bands. If your intention is to take Audry to London for the season, you will have to move forward with a wedding day. Lady Pomeroy, I leave the planning of the event in your very capable hands. Please send all the bills to me.

"Now, if I am not mistaken, I smell rack of lamb, roast potatoes, crusty bread, and more just beyond that partition, and I am suddenly very hungry."

A word about the author…

Born in Burlington, Iowa, the youngest of six children, all of us spaced three to four years apart, which meant that I had an older brother who was twenty when I was born. Moved with my parents, and an older sister, to Oregon when I was ten years old. Grew up in the Willamette Valley, attended a vocational school, clerk stenographer course, which was enlightening but not useful. Married highschool sweetheart. Had two children.

I've worn many hats: store clerk, meat wrapper, kite factory production line, pumped gas, then I discovered water exercise because of debilitating arthritis and became an instructor. I enjoyed that for eighteen satisfying years. I still do water exercise for my own enjoyment and wellbeing but no longer instruct. I began writing my own stories about the time my husband went on swing shift. I was a big fan of the Georgian period, Georgette Heyer being my favorite author. Back then you had to type the manuscript on paper and send it off through the post. Came close to being published a couple of times. Then the years passed and I started to write Oregon historical fiction. I create characters who become my family. I'm home when I tell their stories, I laugh, I cry, I fume and fuss, I cheer for them, and I'm proud to be near them.

We've moved a lot, lived in: California, Idaho, Washington, Oregon Coast, Central Oregon, but we always return to the Willamette Valley. Every time we've moved we roam and learn the history and the past around us, including the geographical past, as well as discovering the impact of the human occupants. Those details I strive to add to my stories. I want the reader to see, smell, be immersed in the time and place, and join the community in which my characters live. I write stories I love to read.

Thank you for purchasing
this publication of The Wild Rose Press, Inc.

For questions or more information
contact us at
info@thewildrosepress.com.

The Wild Rose Press, Inc.
www.thewildrosepress.com

www.ingramcontent.com/pod-product-compliance
Lightning Source LLC
Chambersburg PA
CBHW052023020726
47501CB00004B/1209

* 9 7 8 1 5 0 9 2 6 1 9 7 0 *